GADSDEN COUNTY PUBLIC LIBRARY

"Thorne, what are you doing? We are not going to do this."

"I'm not doing anything; just driving myself crazy." He had pushed aside her hair and begun kissing her behind the ear. Natalie liked what he was doing, and involuntarily leaned back against him.

His erection strained against his faded jeans as her body moved against his. Natale was surprised by the size of him and her body's quick response.

Thorne kissed her face and her neck, at the same time gliding his hands over her body. He cupped her breasts and squeezed her nipples lightly until they were erect. He slid one hand under her shirt while using the other to span her belly, hips, and thighs.

"God, Natalie, you feel good."

Natalie was beyond words. Her food forgotten, she moaned between his kisses and ran her hands through his hair.

Thorne was beside himself, minutes from just ripping off her clothes. His hands moved frantically, gripping her hips to hold her snug against him.

"Natalie, um, I had better stop."

But flexing his fingers, he unbuttoned and then unzipped her jeans. Natalie turned her face up and began nibbling on his lips. Thorne moved fast into the kiss. Their tongues worked in tandem, sparking flames through their bodies.

With one hand, he massaged her neck while pushing the other hand down her jeans and into her panties until

GADSDEN COUNTY
PUBLIC
LIBRARY
732 Pat Thomas Hwy. Quincy, FL 36351

W9-AOV-749

he covered her. He felt her shiver when his fingers played with the soft nest hiding her sweetness. He moved his hand from her throat and lifted her bra; he could weigh her in his palm.

She moaned when Thorne spread apart the lips that closed over her intimacy and dove into her softness.

"Natalie . . . Natalie . . ." he whispered into her ear.

"Aunt Natalie, we're home!" Tracy called out as soon as she opened the front door.

Natalie and Thorne froze for a split second. By the time Tracey and Lindsey, followed by their father, reached the kitchen, Natalie was once again washing the vegetables, and Thorne was sitting very uncomfortably at the table.

STOLEN MEMORIES

MICHELE SUDLER

Genesis Press, Inc.

INDIGO

An imprint of Genesis Press, Inc.
Publishing Company

Genesis Press, Inc.
P.O. Box 101
Columbus, MS 39703

All rights reserved. Except for use in any review, the reproduction or utilization of this work in whole or in part in any form by any electronic, mechanical, or other means, not known or hereafter invented, including xerography, photocopying, and recording, or in any information storage or retrieval system, is forbidden without written permission of the publisher, Genesis Press, Inc. For information write Genesis Press, Inc., P.O. Box 101, Columbus, MS. 39703

All characters in this book have no existence outside the imagination of the author and have no relation whatsoever to anyone bearing the same name or names. They are not even distantly inspired by any individual known or unknown to the author and all incidents are pure invention.

Copyright © 2008 by Michele Sudler

ISBN: 13 DIGIT : 978-1-58571-270-0
ISBN: 10 DIGIT : 1-58571-270-1
Manufactured in the United States of America

First Edition

Visit us at www.genesis-press.com
or call at 1-888-Indigo-1-4-0

DEDICATION

When you have someone who cheers you on
Gives you their honest opinion
For your own benefit
With your own best interest at heart
Regardless of how you may feel
It's special.

I'm lucky enough to have a family member
Who has been with me since day 90
(I'm exactly three months older)
We've grown up together
Been through a lot together
And even when we didn't agree
We had each other's back.

And this is her book (as she calls it)
So to my 1st cousin
Yvonne "Bubbles" Henry-Whaley
Smyrna, DE

ACKNOWLEDGMENTS

As always, I would like to thank my family for the support that has been given to me from the very first day that I sat down at my computer and began writing the first novel. Most times, the network of support that surrounds you is what keeps you moving forward. I have to thank my small network for all of the love they've shown me and apologize for my absences. To Daddy (Larry Brokenbrough); Mom (Vondra Brokenbrough); and Aunt Bea (Brenda Henry).

I've seen the loves of my life as they grow into beautiful young women and a handsome young man. I am blessed. Gregory, 16; Tanisha, 17; Takira, 15; and Kanika, 10. Thanks for laughing with me all the time. I love you all so very much.

My girls have been with me for over 30 and 25 years. So, when you find people who have your back that long, you know they're more than just friends. They're your sisters. Through thick and thin, good and bad, they have held me down. These are the ones you cut up with, act crazy with, and hold secrets with. It's a good feeling, and I'm glad to have them in my life. Cecilia and Cindy, I wouldn't be me without ya'll.

During the day, I am surrounded by a group of people who support me and back me up to the fullest.

I've never seen a group of people who work so well together. No drama, no conflicts, no problems. They make the day go by fast and peacefully. That gives me time to think up storylines! To Donna "DJ" Jones, Rose "Momma" Valere, Maribel Cardona, Kim "Banks" Williams, Robert "Wall Street" Blake, Michelle La Londriz-Perry, Elaine Salazar, and Vonette Williams.

These guys keep me grounded, even though its arguments all the way around, you gotta love 'em. My brothers, Butch and Jay Sudler. My boys, Marvin Thomas, Keith Dupre', Clarence Perkins, Marvin Brittingham, Byron Lewis, Rickey Harris. I'm proud of and lovin' all ya'll. Keep your heads up and get your hustles on. Thanks for the long talks and giving it to me straight.

There are a lot of people who help me in various ways. I want to take this time to let two of them know that they are appreciated. I don't know if I said it before, but I gotta say it now.

To Cortez Brokenbrough for the excellent job you did on my flyers. Boy, you are truly a wiz with a computer. Everybody loved them.

To Doris Funnye Innis for doing a seriously thorough run-through on this book and *One of These Days*. Thank you so much for your hard work.

CHAPTER 1

Sitting perfectly still in the family pew of the old Presbyterian church was a tough challenge. Restless eyes roamed over to the large stained-glass windows, then up to the high ceiling with its depictions of many celestial beings. He listened as the choir sang one of many congregational hymns with the solemnity befitting the occasion.

His attention was repeatedly drawn to the massive cross at the front of the church, with its carefully crafted edges and magnificent stones. Thorne seemed willing to look at anything except the ivory-and-silver casket holding center stage at the front of the century-old church. It seemed to double in size every time his eyes returned to it.

He sat between his sister and brother and held their hands, striving to be the strong one. In reality, he was drawing strength, support and love from them, although he was the oldest.

Patricia Abigail Connor Philips was being remembered, eulogized by a parade of relatives and friends. The church overflowed with grieving people, old and young, whose lives this wonderful woman had touched.

Still somewhat in denial, Thorne was dealing with the death of his grandmother as best he could. It was hard for him to accept that she was gone. He'd had to deal with death only once before—when his father and step-mother, his siblings' mother, died some twenty-five years ago. He had been a kid then, only 10 years old, still expecting his dad to walk through the door at any moment. A full year had passed before he realized this would not happen.

Although he had seen his father regularly after he remarried, Thorne had continued to live with his grand-parents in Miss Abby's family's great mansion, one of many passed down through the generations, the fruits of very old money.

Abby Philips had been the only mother Thorne had ever known. She had raised him from birth. His birth had taken his mother away from him. When he was old enough to understand this, the knowledge led to a guilt that he had successfully pushed back into the far recesses of his brain.

Now at thirty-six, he was dealing with a new and more frightening emotion. Grief. It made him uneasy, and his mood darkened as the service stretched out.

He occasionally looked at his grandfather, Matthew Philips Sr., sitting prim and proper in the pew on the other side of the center aisle, not a hint of emotion on his face. Hate seemed the only way to describe the feelings between him and this man. Old Matthew, as he was called, barely tolerated Thorne, and Thorne couldn't stand him at all.

His sister, Theresa, was the only one of the three sib-lings who still tried to be polite to the old man. She felt it was her duty to try to maintain some semblance of family.

Thorne and his brother, Michael, didn't agree with anything the old man believed in or said. It had been a blessing from God when his grandmother took control of the family's contracting business out of Old Matthew's hand and gave it to her grandchildren.

Old Matthew had been running the company into the ground. Employees were quitting daily, unable to tolerate his crude and unfair business tactics and management style. Subcontractors refused to work with him, and even the zoning and parking offices dreaded the sight of him. There had been numerous civil-rights violations filed against the company.

However, since Thorne and his siblings took control, business and employees had more than tripled, another branch had opened in Texas, and another area of business launched with Theresa's home interior designs.

These companies, along with the other businesses under the Connor Corporation's umbrella, had made their grandmother one of the most successful and richest women in the world. Miss Abby solely owned the Connor Corporation.

To this day, Thorne could not understand how a lovely, gentle flower of a woman like his grandmother could have been married to a racist, backwater, country field rat like his grandfather. The marriage hadn't been a success, that he knew. To his knowledge, they had never shared a bedroom. His father had been the only offspring of a woman with much love to give, a love that she lavished on her three grandchildren.

3

She taught them to appreciate life, not to take advantage of it. And, they learned the importance of helping and respecting others.

In Louisiana, everything moved slower than in other parts of the country. Other kids called servants and other help by their first names, but Thorne, Michael, and Theresa were taught to use Mr. and Mrs. regularly and with respect. Much to Old Matthew's disapproval, Miss Abby wouldn't have it any other way.

They were taught that all people were equal regardless of color, class, or financial worth. People were to be respected unconditionally until that respect was lost due to someone's own actions. Even then that person was to be justly treated, not according to race or class. Miss Abby was a determinedly fair woman, and she imbued them with a strong sense of fair play.

Thorne had somehow managed to get through most of the service by letting his mind revisit the past. But the hardest part of the ceremony was yet to come—saying goodbye to his beloved grandmother.

He and his siblings filed slowly by Miss Abby's open casket and looked down at her. In a pearly white dress with a high collar and flowing well below her knees, she was a vision of peace and serenity. Thorne thought she actually looked happy. *Happy to die?* It seemed inconceivable to him. She was a powerful woman, and though she lay sleeping, her chin still appeared to be tilted slightly upward as if daring anyone to defy her.

With Theresa's help, her pearly white head wrap, her stockings, and her shoes had all been selected by her the month before she passed away. And, as always, her taste was impeccable.

Thorne caressed his sister's arm, trying to help her through the sobs that wrecked her small frame. Michael, who usually had no problem detaching himself from emotions, was also having trouble staying steady. Thorne barely noticed the tears that freely flowed down his own cheeks. He was thankful his grandmother was finally in Heaven's bliss. That made him feel better, if only a small measure.

They returned to their seats as Old Matthew, with the help of his nurse, made his own way to the casket. He was old, but Thorne knew the pitiful man still had a few years of fight left. Old Matthew didn't look seventy-six years old at all. His body was hard and straight, with a little muscle still visible to the eye. Smoking had made his lungs weak, but the nurse was probably not really necessary. From her age and looks, Thorne suspected she was just one of the fringe benefits that came with old age and money.

Old Matthew viewed his wife's body without feeling, but was careful to stay near the casket long enough for appearance's sake. Making his way back to his seat, he looked at his grandchildren. None of them had ever liked him, and he had never liked any of them. *Especially that oldest boy*, he muttered under his breath. Watching Thorne grow had been a sore spot for him. The betrayal of his own son was so apparent whenever Thorne was near him. It was the only time he could remember being hurt, not because his son had defied him, but because he

5

had no control over the situation and it embarrassed him publicly. He had become estranged from his only son, and this estrangement eventually included Thorne himself.

Thorne looked up into the steel-gray eyes that so mirrored his own, and the face that would be his own face in forty more years looked back at him. He looked exactly like the old man, and both resented that fact every single day of their lives. Thorne had been told that his almond skin tone came from his mother, but that he got his father's strong looks. These, unfortunately, came from his father's father, who got them from his own father.

He was the darkest of the three men, looking as if he had a perpetual tan. His eyebrows and eyelashes were as jet black as his thick hair, which he kept cut above his ears. It was more wavy than straight. His face was rugged, with sharp corners and angles. He wore a thin mustache of fine hair, which he kept cut close and perfectly shaped. Fine hair also grew out of the cleft in his chin, but it did not connect with his mustache. His brother often teased him about not being able to grow a full goatee.

Thorne and Michael strongly resembled each other, except where Thorne was dark, Michael was surprisingly light. He resembled an archangel—a golden child born with just a hint of malice under his skin. He was blond and had green eyes, which he inherited from his mother.

Only an inch shorter than Thorne's six feet, two inch frame, Michael was lean and rangy, Thorne thick and muscular. The thin frame fooled a lot of people; underneath, he was muscularly toned. His shoulders weren't as broad as Thorne's, but they were strong and sturdy.

Thorne smiled when he thought of the fights he and Michael used to get into growing up. Thorne always won, but Michael was definitely a good fighter. Many a time he had suffered a bloody or broken nose, or at least a black eye, compliments of his younger sibling. His brother was tough, no doubt about it, and he had played a major part in that. Besides the male servants, Thorne was the only male figure Michael had who was constant in his life.

Thorne watched him from across the library in his grandparents' home, and pride shone brightly in his eyes. The double-breasted Armani business suit and shoes went a long way in covering the rough kid he had grown up with. He thought "business" was a word that described Michael perfectly. He was all business, had a strong head for numbers and had helped the company make some sound financial decisions over the years.

Theresa was passing him a scotch and water when he turned his attention from Michael to her.

"Hey, love, how are you holding up?" he asked, pecking her on her forehead.

"Thorne, I'm fine," she said, smiling back at him, but he could see the worry beginning to mar her usually cheerful features. "I just want this to be over so I can go home to my son and get some peace and quiet. I miss him so much when I'm away for long periods of time."

He put an arm around her shoulder and pulled her close. "Well, it will be over soon. Here comes Howard now."

Thorne had always felt strongly protective of Theresa. She was tough as nails—just as tough as he and Michael were, if not tougher—but she had a more trusting heart than they. She had made mistakes because of it, causing her more pain than she was willing to admit.

—

"Good morning, everyone, glad you could make it here. For those of you who don't know me, my name is Howard Connor. I was Patricia's lawyer, as well as her cousin. We have gathered here today for the reading of her will." Howard looked around the room, making check marks on a sheet of paper as if he were taking attendance, and continued. "I see that everyone is present. Let's all be seated so that we may begin."

They all took their seats in folding chairs that had been set up by the housekeepers earlier that day. Howard moved to the front of the room and stood behind a large podium and arranged his papers. Once the room was quiet, he began reading.

"'I, Patricia Abigail Connor Philips, being of sound mind, do hereby bequeath the sum of my earthly possessions as follows:

"'To my most faithful servants, Lizzy and Donovan Chandler, first of all, thank you for your many years of friendship and trust. Lizzy, you made my days go faster and my life worth living. Donovan, you kept my flowers blooming even after my heart had already begun to wilt. Though it may be too little too late, I leave you five hundred thousand dollars to live the rest of your days easy. Don't report to work anymore. I know you have meager expenses; let social services handle them. Howard has been directed to help you with any difficulties. I also thank you, Lizzy, for looking after my babies, especially when you had babies of your own at home. Now, I will return your gift with gratitude and take care of your babies. I leave fifteen thousand dollars in trust funds to each of your seven grandchildren to be used toward their college education. Those who choose not to attend college will have to wait until the age of twenty-five to obtain these funds. Those who choose to attend will receive an additional ten thousand dollars cash to help with other expenses.'"

Lizzy and Donovan hugged each other, wiping their tears, surprised and grateful for their gift. And that was how it began. Miss Abby had left small and large sums of money to various friends, servants, and organizations, before ending with her family. Howard continued reading in a clear, precise manner, oftentimes trying to express Miss Abby's tone as best he could remember, pausing for emphasis and jokes.

"'To my great-grandchild, Michael Thorne Philips, whose mother is Theresa Marie Philips, I leave one hundred thousand dollars in college funds to be put in trust and allowed to mature until he embarks on college life. Also, he is to receive a trust of two million, five hundred thousand dollars upon his twenty-fifth birthday. Theresa, no need to tell you to take care of that boy of ours. Make sure he knows that he lit up my dark existence.'

"'Now, to my grandchildren, I leave the entire remaining possessions of my family's vast empire. The

Connor Corporation holds not only Connor Contractors, Inc., but also three oil fields in the South, a chain of twelve hotels, and a cruise line. Michael, I trust you can handle all that, my boy. My wish is for Thorne to keep his pride and joy, Connor Contractors, Theresa to oversee the hotel chain, and Michael to oversee the cruise line and oil fields. But home base will be as always the Connor Headquarters Building in downtown New Orleans. You three work well together. I have no doubt of your success. You have a staff of highly qualified people, so travel should be minimal. Listen to me, still trying to run things. I love you all, my own little angels, that the Lord saw fit for me to raise.'

"'Also, I leave each of you two hundred twenty-five million dollars and a mansion. Thorne shall have Gladewinds. It always reminded me of you, my dear, strong and solid through any storm. Remain that way, please.'

"'Michael, my businessman, shall have Oaktrees— bending but never backing from your strong opinions. And, to my little lady, Theresa, Rosegate, delicate and gentle, with thorns at the ready for those who bring harm to her family.'

"'You three stay strong in your love and support of one another. During your time left on earth, you will all need each other at some point, be there for each other. You are all you have right now.'

"'Oh, Old Matthew, didn't mean to leave you out. Not because of our great love or passion for one another, but because of the fact that you helped to give me the one great possession of my life, my son, Matthew Jr., I will allow you to remain here at Southend for the rest of your days. You will be taken care of with funds already placed in an account for your welfare. At the time of your passing, Southend will be shared equally amongst the children. This home, along with the other family homes in California, New York, Texas, Florida, St. Thomas, England, and Paris will remain family estates for the enjoyment of Thorne, Michael, Theresa, and their children and their children's children, and so forth. I trust you kids will take care of these family estates as well as yourselves. Remember your lessons and prosper.'"

For a long time nobody moved as waves of shock and amazement swept through the library like a tsunami. Thorne stared at Howard as if he were crazy. Michael's mouth was still hanging open just a little. Silent tears fell down Theresa's cheeks. Miss Abby was well off being an heiress and formidable businesswoman, but nobody expected her generosity was so enormous.

Old Matthew was the only one in the room visibly upset by the reading. He narrowed his eyes at Thorne and marched from the room, followed by his friend and lawyer, Peter Bergett.

Champagne was brought into the room, and Howard went around the room congratulating everyone and making small talk. By the time he reached Michael, Thorne, and Theresa, they were in a huddle.

"Well, I want to congratulate you," Howard said.

"I don't know if that's the right word, Howard," Michael said, speaking for the three. Although they were thankful for their inheritance, it couldn't take the place of the woman who left it to them.

"Let's think of it like this. I congratulate you on earning the respect and love of one of the most beautiful women I've ever had the pleasure to call family and friend."

Thorne raised his glass, as did his siblings. "Well, now, I can drink to that," he declared.

CHAPTER 2

Natalie awoke Monday morning lazily stretching in bed. She didn't want to get up. But that was her life's story—doing what needed to be done, not what she wanted to do. The beginning of the week was always the same for her: painfully, dreadfully hard.

She shook her sluggishness off and pulled herself out of bed and into a standing stretch, glancing back at her bed. Ken and Barbie were still sound asleep on her extra pillow, having been tucked in the night before by her nieces. She almost envied them.

She heard her nieces downstairs complaining about the long day of school ahead and smiled. After two months of having her brother and his kids living with her, Natalie had become very comfortable with their weekly morning routine.

"Aunt Natalie, you look awful," her niece blurted when she finally made her way into the kitchen.

"Thank you, baby," Natalie responded, dragging herself to the stove to pour her first cup of coffee. Her niece Tracey was ten and in the early stages of being aware of her femininity.

Not wanting to offend her favorite auntie, Tracey backtracked. "I didn't mean that. I meant you look like you had a rough night. Were you out late? Do you want me to draw your bath?"

"No, baby, I'll do it myself. And, yes, I did have a rough night. I didn't get to bed until real late. Then, I couldn't get to sleep."

Her brother, Stephen, came into the room carrying two backpacks and two lunch boxes. "Umm . . . sis, fix yourself. Your hair is all over the place." He kissed her forehead. "Do you have work to do today?"

"No, actually, I have an appointment with the guy you referred. He agreed to meet me at the house so he can take a walk-through and work up an estimate. I'm going to try to get to the hospital before that."

"Well, don't push it. Find some time to relax today," he suggested. "Okay, girls, five minutes 'til bus time." Stephen had to remind them every minute to have them outside on time.

Natalie smiled as she watched her family scurry out the front door. Her over-protective brother was in the middle of a semi-nasty divorce. He had caught his wife in his bed with another man and had immediately taken his kids and left. They had been staying with her ever since, and she was happy to have them. He would probably end up buying one of her houses and settling down to raise his girls alone. A lot of men were doing that nowadays.

Natalie sank back in the tub of hot coconut-scented water and let the aches and pains flow from her tired body. The night before had been a nightmare. She put her head back on the bath pillow, shut her eyes, and relived one of the most emotionally draining nights of her life.

First, she had been notified by the hospital that her good friend Amanda Henry had been admitted after a car accident. When she arrived at Amanda's room, she wasn't prepared to see her friend barely conscious and scared to death. Amanda wouldn't let the doctors give her anything for the pain because she didn't want to doze off before she talked to Natalie.

"Amanda, you have to take something. You're hurting too much." Natalie took her hand, trying to offer what comfort she could.

"I will, but I need to talk to you first, Natalie." Amanda lay back against the pillows, almost delirious with pain, but she willed herself to continue and to make sense. "Listen, I thank the Lord for your friendship. Not every young woman would take to an old hag like me."

An old hag, indeed, Natalie thought. Amanda was the head of the African-American History Department at a local university. No small accomplishment for a woman who had barely made it out of high school, and then had to go back to school and practically start from scratch.

"I need to tell someone this before I pass on to my Maker. Lord, please forgive me."

Natalie began to smooth Amanda's medium-length cornrows. She knew it wasn't helping Amanda any under the circumstances, but she needed something to do. In emergency situations Natalie was, for all practical purposes, fairly useless. Instead of thinking of ways to relieve the stress, she usually added to it with a bunch of 'I don't knows' and 'What should I dos'. But this time, she concentrated on holding herself together.

"Amanda, relax, calm down. Everything is going to be all right," she whispered in Amanda's ear, basically really trying to convince herself. Natalie began massaging her friend's smooth high-yellow cheeks and shoulder. Afraid Amanda's pain may be increasing, Natalie stopped after a few quick rubs. She really didn't know what to do to help her.

Her friend was very light-skinned, and her skin had started to turn red in the spots where Natalie had briefly massaged her. She could see that Amanda was getting weaker, and she began to panic as she listened to her story.

"Listen, almost forty years ago, I was in love with a man, a white man. We knew we couldn't let anyone know that we were in love, so we snuck around together with the help of some friends. When we found out that I was pregnant, he pledged his undying love to me and asked me to marry him. He convinced me that we could deal with the harsh realities of those times. I believed and loved him so much that I agreed to marry him. We had a beautiful baby boy together." Tears fell unchecked down Amanda's cheeks, but she struggled to keep her focus.

"Eventually, the hardships and the struggles got to be too much for me. I wasn't strong enough. I didn't want my son and his father to endure those kinds of things just because I wanted to be with this man. And believe me . . . I did love him with all my heart."

Natalie pulled out a tissue and began to wipe her face.

"Oh, God, please forgive me." Amanda screamed out and clutched Natalie's hand, guilt causing her to choke on some of her words. "When . . . when our son was two, I left my husband and my son because I couldn't take the pressures and ridicule that he suffered at the hands of his father and other members of his privileged circle. They had never seen my son, but he was just as white as they were physically. I thought that he would have a better chance if his black mother wasn't around." She tightened her grip on Natalie's hand.

"All these years I've been trying to find him. For years, I couldn't even get past the front door of my husband's family's house to ask questions about my son. I was trying desperately to reach my husband's mother. She was a good woman and never objected to our marriage, but she knew and told us that it would be hard."

"Well, she died last month before I had a chance to contact her. When I went to his grandfather a couple of weeks ago, I was told that he, my son, had died shortly after I left, but I can't believe that. His father would have contacted me. Then the old man told me that my son and his father died together. I found information on my Matthew's death, but not on my son's. And Matthew died almost nine years after I left. He had remarried and had two more children. So his father was lying. I know my son's not dead. I can feel it." She turned serious eyes on Natalie. "Natalie, before I pass on, I need to see my son again. I can't leave this world without him knowing the truth. Please, I beg of you, find him for me. Find him."

Of course she would find him. That was Natalie's natural response. "Of course, I will find him." The words fell so easily from her mouth because she knew that was the only way to give her friend some peace.

But, how in the world was she supposed to do that? Once again, she had allowed her heart, not her brain, to deal with a situation. That was a bad habit that she had intended to work on.

Now, amid the bath bubbles in the tub, Natalie was at a loss as to where to begin to look for this long-lost son of Amanda's. But today she couldn't afford to think of anything except the contractor she was to meet at the site of her newly purchased home.

Stephen had recommended him, and because he was her brother, she figured she would give this man a chance. He had the reputation of being a good man with a stable of loyal employees and a low, very low, turnover rate.

Natalie sank deeper into the water and let her remaining time slip away.

She raced through town trying to make it to her new house in record time. A stop at the hospital had put her behind schedule, but she was only ten minutes late. Surely, he would wait ten minutes. She would have called him, but she had left his business card on her desk at home.

Pulling onto the right street, she was relieved when she spotted a man in her front yard climbing into a new cherry-red pick-up truck. She skillfully pulled into the driveway, blocking his exit.

Slamming on his brakes to avoid a collision, Thorne uttered a few choice curse words and jumped out of his truck. It was bad enough that she was late, but she had almost rammed the bumper of his truck. It wouldn't have caused much damage, but that wasn't the point.

Thorne marched over to her as she struggled to get out of her new Honda Civic, determined to give her a nice piece of his mind. He saw her tipping toward the ground, and even though he was mad, the gentleman in him made him dive to catch her.

Natalie hadn't been paying any attention to her seat belt, distracted by the sight of this tall, thick man storming towards her with fire in his eyes. She was instantly intrigued.

The old T-shirt and faded blue jeans hugged his body. She noticed that his muscles bulged and moved in seeming rhythm with her heartbeat. He was handsome, extremely handsome. Even his dirty work boots looked good on him. Before she knew what was happening, Natalie was falling, and she couldn't catch herself.

Thorne only had time to put his body between Natalie and the ground. His only thought was to at least cushion her fall. His hands automatically went around her waist. She landed across his chest and stomach, forcing the wind from him. When the dust cleared, that was the position they were in as cars passed and neighbors strolled down the street of the suddenly busy residential area.

Thorne was surprised to feel the electric shock that shot through him. It was a strange feeling, an unusual feeling, and when he finally recognized it as a strong attraction to this woman in his arms, it became an unwanted feeling. If it had been only a sexual thing, he could have dealt with it. But this was more than that, and he knew it. He didn't get electric charges from simple sexual attraction.

Thorne tried to push her off him, but she couldn't move because her feet were tangled up. The more she struggled with the seat belt, the more he had to struggle with himself.

Natalie already knew that she was attracted to him. Hell, only a fool wouldn't be. But being this close in such an intimate position wrecked havoc on both her learned and innate common sense. She was trying to stand and apologize at the same time. Neither was working. Her mouth rebelled and refused to work, and she couldn't get her feet untied.

Thorne laid his head back on the ground and sucked in his breath, trying to be strong; she continued to wiggle against him. The sweet scent of her perfume drifted into his nostrils, putting him into a near-trance until he could take no more.

Finally, he raised his head and yelled, "Lady, will you please keep still?" He tried to shift away from her, because he could feel himself reacting to her movements.

"I'm . . . I'm sorry, I'm trying to get up," Natalie said. Irritated by the harshness of his tone, she tried to pull one foot loose and inadvertently rubbed against him again.

"Please," Thorne grabbed hold of her hips to keep her still, "lady, have some mercy on me, okay?"

Natalie finally caught on to what he was saying and went very still. "I'm sorry," she replied, embarrassment on her face. She lifted her head and felt his breath on her cheek and neck. She could have stayed like that all day; she wanted to. After momentarily losing herself in the luxury of the hardness of his body, Natalie willed herself to focus on her predicament.

"Yeah, well, I'm not going to say that you need to be sorry. But unless you want things to really get embarrassing, let me get this seat belt off your leg. And whatever you do, please, please keep still." His earlier anger forgotten, Thorne reached behind Natalie and pulled the belt from around her feet.

It was funny to her. When she looked up and saw the annoyance on his face, she started to laugh. Just imagine what people must be thinking of them tangled in a seat belt and wrestling on the ground at ten o'clock in the morning—ten-fifteen, to be exact.

Once they were both safely on their feet, Natalie was still laughing. He wasn't. Something inside told him that this was no laughing matter.

"I'm sorry about that, and I'm sorry for being late," she said, briskly beating the dirt off her pink silk blouse and tan trousers.

Bent over, he was also brushing himself off, thus affording a better view of his biceps and triceps. He turned from side to side, as if posing for a photo shoot, and she played the avid photographer, if only in her mind.

"I told you not to be sorry for that, but as for being late—" he stopped short; his blood was beginning to boil again. "Lady, let me explain something to you. My time is very valuable," he said, looking at his watch. "Now, we have managed to waste twenty minutes of this consultation. That twenty minutes puts me behind for the rest of the day."

Natalie looked up at him and was startled by his intense gray eyes. Words died on her lips, and her mind briefly shut down.

"Ma'am, my name is Thorne Philips. I believe we had an appointment this morning."

"Uh . . . uh . . . yes, yes we did. Please, come inside."

Thorne sized her up as he followed her into the house. She was very attractive. Not overly beautiful, but nice, very nice. Her hair was cut short with curls on top and slicked down at the back. It appeared naturally curly, but with all the chemicals out there nowadays he couldn't really tell from what. He had noticed earlier that she was just a little heavy on top, a definite plus in his mind. Her waist was small, her hips wide and firm. He liked that in a woman—wide hips. The trousers stretched nicely over her round bottom. Her skin was a smooth caramel-rose, and Thorne wondered what it would taste like. His eyes dropped to her backside again—just as she turned around to ask him a question.

Natalie looked at him, her eyes both amused and curious. He hadn't heard a word she had said; he was just looking at her. A warm feeling shot through her body, and she smiled playfully.

"So, Mr. Philips," Natalie began, "do you see anything that you can work with?"

Thorne had never been shy with the ladies. He knew the difference between a snide remark and a flirtatious one. Granted, this was the first time he had ever had this strong an attraction so quickly after meeting someone, but she had already caught him looking at her, so there was no point trying to hide it.

"If we're thinking about the same thing, Ms. Davidson, yes, I think I do." He wanted to take it a little further, but this was their first meeting, and he was supposed to be doing business with the lady.

Natalie decided to let the statement remain open. But when Thorne donned that smile of his, her heart did a slow flip.

"Mr. Philips . . ."

"Thorne."

"Thorne, we are talking about the house, right?" There was a knock at the door, but she ignored it, waiting for an answer to her question.

"Ms. Davidson?"

"Natalie."

"Natalie, someone is at your door." *Hell no, he wasn't talking about the damn house.*

"Seems you were saved by the bell, Thorne." She smiled and went to answer her door, the smile fading when she saw who was standing on the other side.

"Or you were," Thorne said under his breath, walking further into the house.

"Hi, babe. I know I'm a little early, but I had some free time and decided to meet you here instead of at the coffee house." He was poised to kiss her, but Natalie turned her head at the last minute.

"Nicholas, this is a surprise," she said, quickly recovering. "I thought we weren't going to meet until much later." *At five o'clock,* she thought, already suspecting what this was all about.

"Yes, well, I ran into your brother, and he told me you would be here so I decided to stop by." He breezed past her and strolled into the house.

Nicholas was just there to be nosy, of that Natalie was fairly certain. He wanted to see if this new contractor would be a problem for him. Her old contractor quit after Nicholas accused him of trying to make a move on her. And he did it in front of the man's wife.

But Nicholas didn't know that he was the problem. She had dated Nicholas off and on for the past year or so, but the relationship was going nowhere. She actually saw him more as a friend or a relative than as a boyfriend, which is what he called himself.

At first, she thought he was attractive. He was slim and tall, and he dressed well. Dark-honey skin with well-groomed facial hair complimented his other physical attributes. His law practice was very successful, and they did have some great conversations.

Watching him walk over to Thorne, she now wondered what in the world she had ever seen in him. For some reason it was Thorne, with his dark hair and that soft cleft in his chin, who made her blood pressure rise. It surprised her because her romantic interest had never crossed racial lines. There was definitely interest here, at the least a strong attraction. Because she sensed the attraction was mutual, all her thoughts were focused on him. She barely saw Nicholas.

"Thorne Philips, is that you?" Nicholas smiled, extending his hand. "I can't believe it. It's been ages, man."

"Nicholas," Thorne said, taking his hand. "Yes, it has been a while. I don't think I've seen you in at least three years."

"Sorry to hear about your grandmother," Nicholas offered. "She was a wonderful woman."

"Indeed. Thank you." Natalie joined them, and Thorne cautiously asked, "You know, um, Ms. Davidson, here?"

She tried to edge away, but Nicholas pulled her closer. "Yes, we've been seeing each other for about a year now." He tried to kiss her cheek, but she moved away to pick up her clipboard.

Thorne noticed the little byplay.

"You two gentlemen know each other?" she asked, affirming the obvious.

"Yes, Thorne and I grew up together, so to speak. My grandmother worked for his grandmother. We used to play together as youngsters."

"Oh, and you didn't keep in touch?"

Nicholas laughed. "Well, we don't exactly move in the same circles, babe. Thorne is the head of the Philips

Corporation. A multimillionaire rarely has time to deal with us regular folk."

"Multimillionaire?" Natalie asked. Of course she had heard of the Connor Corporation. The contracting company she had hired was one of their businesses, but she hardly expected the president of the company to be working for her. "Wait a minute. I didn't hire a multimillionaire; I hired a general contractor."

"Actually, I *am* a contractor," Thorne said, trying to downplay his role at the corporation. He hated being labeled a multimillionaire, and if he happened upon someone who didn't know who he was, he kept the fact hidden as long as possible. People tended to treat you differently when they knew what you were worth. "My brother, Michael, runs the business for the most part. So do you have a list of the things you want me to run estimates on? We can go room by room. That would be fastest. I don't want to keep you from your date."

He was trying to be smart. She could tell by the twinkle in the corners of those gray eyes.

"Sure. Nicholas, have a seat in the living room. This shouldn't take long." She could have been talking to the door; when Natalie moved, Nicholas moved. She heard a snicker from Thorne and shoved the clipboard into his stomach as hard as she could.

CHAPTER 3

After finally getting rid of Nicholas, Natalie retreated to the sanctuary that was her home and called her sister Tamya, who she figured was probably in the back office of the restaurant she co-owned with her twin, Tamia. She couldn't wait to vent to someone—to release the anger she had been holding in since Nicholas showed up at her house.

She was so tired of him, but she was supposedly his girlfriend. It had taken her a while to figure out that he meant *girlfriend,* not *girl friend.* She didn't know when he first began using the term, but she hadn't exactly stopped him when he started referring to her that way. Many times over the last year, she wished she had.

Never had she uttered the word *boyfriend,* but again, she never stopped the presumption when it presented itself. So, to her regret, she had become Nicholas's girl-friend as far as his family and hers were concerned.

"Noah's Ark. Tamya speaking." Her liquid-smooth voice came over the line cheerfully, expecting a customer to be on the other end.

"Hey, girl, it's Natalie. What's up?" Natalie's voice wasn't as cheerful. She wasn't in the mood for happy.

"Nothing. Just trying to get some of this paperwork under control. If I could get that wild-behind sister of yours under control, this would be a lot easier."

"Where is she?"

"Who the hell knows? I've been here for an hour now. I guess she'll be here sooner or later. Anyway, how was your day?"

"Oh, Lord. Let's see. I got up this morning, went and visited Amanda, was late for a meeting with the contractor. Oww . . . by the way, he is so gorgeous. Girl, you got to see this guy."

"What does he look like?" Even though she was in a committed relationship, Tamya was always willing to listen to one of her sisters talk about any man in their acquaintance.

"White guy, about six feet three, muscles—"

"Whoa . . . white guy . . . you?"

"Yeah, Tamya, a white guy. His name is Thorne Philips."

"Thorne Philips? That name sounds real familiar, but I don't know from where."

"You've probably seen him on a magazine cover or something."

Tamya laughed. "What is he, a model or something?"

"No, but he could be. He's part of the Connor Corporation downtown, one of the owners. Two boys, one girl, right? I don't know if he's the oldest or youngest brother."

"Oh, yeah. They were looking into the restaurant at one time."

"You're kidding."

"I think it was the sister that Tamia talked to not too long after we opened. Someone from their company had come in and tasted one of Tamia's dishes."

"Well, why—" The question was on the tip of her tongue, but Tamya interrupted her defensively.

"We were just getting started, and this was our baby. There was no way we were going to sell it."

"I understand that. You know that damn Nicholas came to the house." Natalie quickly changed the subject when she remembered why she had called her sister in the first place.

"I thought you were meeting him later."

"So did I. He ran into Stephen downtown somewhere and asked him where I was. He just wouldn't leave us alone."

"Of course not. Nicholas isn't stupid. He knows he doesn't have you the way he wants, and he's having a real hard time facing that fact."

"Well, he needs to get a grip. You should have seen him following us around the house. I couldn't even turn around without bumping into him. It became embarrassing. He was right on top of us— like he was the police or something."

"What did Thorne have to say about that?"

"He just laughed at me."

"At you?" Tamya listened to Natalie talking comfortably about this man, almost as if she had known him for a while.

"Yeah, I can't explain it, but it was like we had a quick kind of understanding happening. Five minutes after meeting, we had argued, laughed, joked, and been sarcastic with each other."

"Sounds kind of interesting. That could have been a whole relationship right there."

"That's what I know. Crazy, ain't it? I shouldn't even be thinking like this really. I'm probably crazy for even thinking about him. He wouldn't be interested in me."

"Whoa . . . now, you know I'm not hearing that." Tamya almost didn't believe she was having this conversation with her sister, the smart one, the one whose confidence level was so high that she didn't need a self-help book for anything. Natalie was the one they all went to for help and advice. "Why are you selling yourself short like that? You got just as much to offer a smart man as the next girl."

"I know, but . . ."

"This must be serious. I've never heard you doubt yourself before. Not like this. Any other time, you're the one trying to keep us afloat."

"I don't know; it just seems like a long shot."

"Girl, you better go for it. Look, I gotta get off this phone. I'll talk to you later. Miss Thing just walked in. I got to get her working before she thinks up an excuse. Love ya."

"Love ya, too."

Natalie sat on the cushiony sofa trying to convince herself that wanting this man was all right. She wouldn't make the first move for fear of embarrassing herself, but she would definitely keep the possibility open and see if he was feeling any sparks.

At six the next morning, Thorne Philips was leaving his luxurious penthouse atop the Philips Building. It was one of three penthouses taking up the three highest floors. The other two belonged to his siblings. They all had their own place to stay when meetings ran late or started early and for when charity and business functions required their presence.

Thorne turned the key to begin his descent, and his mind once again involuntarily traveled to the caramel-skinned, voluptuous woman he had met the day before. Last evening, his mind had taken similar trips several times. It irritated him to no end that she was occupying what little free time he had.

The sudden vibration that signaled the elevator's arrival at the next floor ended his reverie. He straightened himself as the door opened and his brother got on.

"Hey, man," Thorne hailed Michael. "It's a little early for you, isn't it?"

Michael made no effort to hide his sour mood. Usually, he tried hard to appear calm and unflappable, but since it was just Thorne, he relaxed, allowing his normal persona to surface.

"Didn't feel like staying in bed." His answer was short and not forthcoming. The elevator continued its steady descent.

"Want to talk about it?"

"Nah, just some girl trouble."

"Anybody I know?"

Michael shook his head. Actually, this Asian beauty wasn't someone he himself knew all that well. She was a flight attendant for their airline. It was a privately owned company, comprising of only twenty-five luxury jets, with thirty pilots and sixty-five flight attendants. The jets were used mostly for business purposes, but occasionally family members used them to hit this or that vacation spot. Unfortunately, neither he nor his siblings had taken vacations lately.

Yaw Dig Na had been his attendant on many business trips, always overly friendly, always showing open interest. Although he was flattered, Michael was used to forward women. He had been getting that kind of attention since he turned sixteen. He tried to practice restraint, because even though she looked good as hell and he was interested, she was an employee. And that was a no-no.

However, on this trip, his business acumen kicked in a little slower than usual—right before her knees hit the floor. Unfortunately, the front zipper of his Versace double-breasted business suit was already down and her left hand was inside his pants wrapped tightly around his swollen manhood when Danielle, the other flight attendant, walked through drawn curtains into the lounge area of the plane. He was furious, more at himself than at her, to be caught in such a position. Not with Yaw Dig Na on her knees about to please him, but with an employee. That was very stupid of him.

Now he found himself between a rock and a hard place. Was he going to give them nice hefty raises or fire them? The latter was not an option. There really was no reason to fire them; they hadn't done anything wrong. If he fired them, he could be sued for sexual harassment. It was two against one. Should he tell his brother and let him help work it out? No, Thorne would read him the riot act, but only after laughing and making jokes at his expense for half the day. After that he would never be able to live down the mistake. It wasn't like him to do something so stupid.

The bell rang, alerting its passengers that the elevator door was about to open. Thorne glanced at Michael with concern. Usually, his brother was able to talk to him about anything going on in his love life. This must be a biggie. He decided to let it go and wait for Michael to come to him. It never took longer than a day or two.

The brothers walked side by side, both having a similar spring to their stride that spelled determination and confidence. They were on the fifteenth floor, where the executive offices were located. They moved through a wide lobby decorated in mauve and tan and filled with plants and trees, complete with a large lounge/waiting area, two bottled-water machines, a reception desk usually manned by two employees, public phones, and a touch-screen directory with listings for all of their employees in each department of each business under each corporate umbrella.

They walked down the hall leading to their offices. The other hall led to a library, restrooms, and conference rooms. Each of three offices went in a different direction like a fork in the road. Michael's was to the left, Thorne's in the middle, and Theresa's on the right.

Instead of going to his own office, Thorne followed Michael to his.

There was so much on his mind, Michael had forgotten Thorne was with him.

At Michael's questioning glance, Thorne opened with the subject on his mind. "Michael, have you ever met someone that you felt an instant attraction to?"

"Unfortunately, all the time. It's brought me more trouble than I care to mention."

"No, I mean a real attraction. Not sexual . . . well, sexual, too, but . . ."

"You mean a love at first sight sort of thing?"

Thorne wasn't going anywhere near that question. Was Michael crazy? There wasn't any such thing as love at first sight. This was a bad idea.

"Never mind," Thorne said, turning to leave the room. Michael was obviously in a really foul mood if he was using the "L" word.

"Wait a minute, big brother. Did you meet somebody?"

"Yeah, I did." He still wasn't sure if he wanted to talk to Michael right now.

"And?" Michael put his own problems aside momentarily as he listened to his brother's.

"Well, it's the owner of the house I appraised yesterday. She buys houses, renovates them, then sells them. I'm hoping to take her on as a permanent client."

"And? What happened?"

"I don't know . . ." He was honestly confused. "I just think that we got along really well for it to be our first time meeting."

"So, what are you going to do?"

"I don't know. I don't think that I should try to pursue her because she'll be a client. You know that's kinda like mixing business with pleasure."

Michael's mistake came back to haunt him once again, but he quickly pushed it away. "No, Thorne . . . I really don't think so. I think it's different. Hell, if we committed to not having relationships with everyone we conducted business with, we would have to put half the women in this country in the 'don't touch' column."

"True. This woman is nice, too, man. She's not tall, not overly beautiful like Alicia and other snobby debutantes we know. I don't know. She is pretty and has a nice body, but that's not what I'm attracted to. She's witty, with a smart mouth on her. She's quick-minded."

"You know all of this from one meeting."

"Man, you got to meet her. Nice smooth brown skin. Fat behind, wide hips."

"Oh . . . that's what got you, isn't it? The hips. You were probably a goner the first time you looked down and saw them." He laughed, knowing his brother's weakness.

Unlike himself, Thorne had always loved women full-figured. He said that Michael's dates usually looked as if they were still developing. Although they both dated many women, when they chose steady companions, they each had specific preferences.

"So what should I do about it?" Thorne asked his brother.

"Not, what should you do, but what are you going to do? Call the girl and ask her out on a date."

"No . . . I don't think that would be a good idea," Thorne disagreed.

"Why not?"

"I just don't think it would be a good idea."

"Then why the hell did you ask me? You're not going to do what I say, anyway." The edge in his voice was because of the frustration with his own problem, not Thorne's.

"Just forget about it. When is Theresa coming back into town?"

Theresa lived in Texas with her son, Michael. She moved there two years earlier when Michael's biological father had suddenly been released from jail. Although he hadn't seen his son since birth, the prospect of his son's inheritance was enough to spark his interest in his off-spring.

"She'll be back next week. Did she tell you that she was thinking about paying Ryan off and having him sign custody papers?"

"Why would she do that when she already has full custody of Michael?"

"She wants Ryan to sign over any and all parental rights he might have. Howard has been looking into it for her."

"Well, then, I know she won't have a problem. I don't see why she left, anyway. Theresa has always been a fighter. There was no need for her to run to Texas."

"I think she liked the time away from here, but hates the traveling back and forth. And Michael is doing great at that private school she found for him."

"Ryan hasn't popped up there, has he?"

"No, but I'm sure he's looking for her. Some lawyer came here looking for her a while back. Her secretary informed him that he would have to contact Howard. I don't know what happened after that."

"All right, Michael. I guess I'll get started on some paperwork. I'll stop by later."

In his office, Thorne kept the curtains open so that he could view the city below. He didn't want to sit back and relax. Natalie was still on his mind, and he planned to get her off it before lunchtime.

As if to punish himself, Thorne dove into the pile of papers on his large mahogany desk instead of going into the field to help his crew out on a new building project. Being onsite with his employees was what he liked most. All the paperwork, business calls, and meetings were necessary, but not his favorite part of the business.

After an hour, Natalie finally stayed at the back of his mind. He was working steadily, happy with what he had done. He was about to take a lunch break when his secretary buzzed him.

"Mr. Philips, there is a Natalie Davidson on the line for you."

Dumbfounded, it took him a second to respond. "Um . . . okay, I'll take it."

"Hello, Mr. Philips."

"Thorne."

"This is Natalie Davidson. I was wondering if you had a chance to look over the um . . . prices." She was lying through her teeth; he had just looked at the house yesterday. She knew he wouldn't have the estimates done, but what other reason could she give him? She couldn't say, "I just called to hear your voice."

"Ms. Davidson . . ."

"Natalie."

"Natalie, I don't work that fast." Thorne could feel his heartbeat quickening as she talked to him. Damn, he didn't like where this was taking him. Not right now.

They fell silent for half a minute, neither knowing quite what to say and apparently stuck in a tunnel of deep thought.

"Natalie . . . I'll call you tomorrow with the price estimates.

"Okay . . . thank you very much."

Natalie then heard the dial tone's steady drone. *That didn't go well,* she thought. She wasn't even sure why she called. She had no reason other than hearing his voice. She wanted to see him again, but she wasn't going to ask him out. Regretting making the call, Natalie sat back down at her computer and continued her search for new homes.

Thorne's mood darkened as he returned the phone to its base. Now he had to try to erase her from his memory all over again.

CHAPTER 4

"This is Ms. Davidson," Natalie said, grabbing the phone from her brother. She was out of breath, having just run into the house after visiting Amanda.

"This is Thorne Philips. I have the estimate for the repairs to your house." Her eyes told Stephen to get lost, and he reluctantly left the kitchen.

"Oh, that's great, Mr. Philips," she replied nervously.

"Thorne," he corrected.

"Thorne."

"Would you like to meet somewhere so that we can go over the figures?" Thorne was desperate to see her again; he couldn't get his mind off her all night.

"Sure, Thorne. Where would you like to meet?" she asked, trying to sound matter of fact. *Of course, she would meet him—anywhere, anytime. Who wouldn't?*

"It's dinnertime, so why don't we make it a business dinner at the Old Sage Room?"

The ensuing silence was brief but seemed endless. He was slightly nervous and couldn't believe that he was actually doing this—trying to hit on an attractive lady and using a business dinner as a cover wasn't usually his style.

"Hello?" he said after long seconds had passed.

"I'm here." Natalie whispered, licking her lips and tasting blood. She had bitten her lip to stop herself from screaming as she danced around the room. Trying not to sound overanxious, she asked jokingly, "Thorne, are you asking me out on a date?"

"No, I just invited you to a business dinner. It will be a business meeting with dinner," he continued, sticking with his story.

"You sound as though you're trying to convince yourself rather than me," she said archly.

"Look, are you coming or not?" he asked, slightly agitated. This was exasperating; he just wanted an answer from her.

"Yes, I'll be there. What time?"

"Can you be there in two hours?"

"Sounds great. See ya."

Her dancing had drawn her brother back into the room, and he watched her until she hung up the phone.

"That wasn't Nicholas," he said, leaning against the doorway.

"I know." She tried to walk past him, but he blocked her path. "Excuse me. I have to get ready."

"Ready for what? Who was that?" he demanded.

"A business associate."

"A business associate had you jumping around the kitchen like a damn fool? A business associate has you this excited by a phone call?"

"I wasn't jumping around the room."

Stephen crossed his arms over his chest, his raised eyebrows forming a question. "Does Nicholas know about this business associate?"

"Why should he know about my business?"

"Natalie, don't try to be cute with me."

"I'm not being cute. I'm being a grown woman who doesn't have to answer to anybody about her business." She expelled a long breath, deciding it was best to tell him everything and get the sermon over and done with. "For your information, it was Thorne Philips."

"Thorne Philips?" Stephen looked at her puzzled.

"Yes, the contractor you recommended. He wants to meet and discuss the estimates for renovating the new house."

Instead of responding right away, Stephen launched into a mini-review of his sisters' accomplishments.

"I don't think I've ever told you how proud I am of you and the girls." He walked around her and leaned against the refrigerator. "Mom and Dad would have been proud, too. You owning all those houses and building your own little real-estate empire. And the girls owning and operating their own restaurant. You three turned out to be strong women."

"Thanks, bro," she replied, reaching up and giving him a peck on the cheek. "But you didn't do too shabby yourself. You have two great kids and you're a world-renowned, highly respected sculptor. And don't forget, Mom and Dad did get to see you make it big. They were very proud of you."

"Yeah, I really miss them, though."

"Me, too," Natalie smiled. "But enough of that. I got a meeting." She pranced by him, but was stopped by the tight grip of his hand around her arm. Stephen spun her around.

"Natalie, I know who you're going out with. I can't believe you were jumping all around the kitchen like that over Thorne Philips. What's going on?" he asked, smelling trouble.

"Nothing's going on," she angrily replied, pulling her arm free.

"You can't be serious about going on a date with him," Stephen insisted.

"I never said it was a date." Her temper rose. "And why not?!" Natalie demanded loudly.

"Because he's—"

"Don't you dare say it's because he's white. Don't you dare say it!" she warned.

"Forget it! Dammit, just forget it." He stormed off to the far corner of the kitchen. A neutral corner.

"Stephen, just because you had a bad experience with a white woman doesn't make all whites bad. You just picked a bad one." Natalie tried to reason with her brother, who was suddenly fifteen years back in time and reliving his first nightmarish relationship.

Sabrina had been a young intern at one of the major art houses in New York when Stephen was just being discovered. At twenty-four, Stephen was still naive about the faster pace of living in the North. Even though he was from New Orleans, most of his free time had been spent locked up in the attic at home, which had been made into a studio for him.

They began a secret and torrid affair. He was in it for the thrill of something new and different. It was his first interracial relationship, and Sabrina was very daring and highly sexed. She didn't care what they did or where they did it, and she was turned on by the possibility of getting caught. Which was great for him—until they really did get caught.

Her father, a prominent attorney, came home from work and found them in the walk-in closet of his bedroom lying across his tie cabinet. That's when Stephen found out that Sabrina was actually only seventeen years old. Before he got out of the front door, he was facing all kinds of jail time from rape allegations leveled by none other than Sabrina herself. Having been through the same thing at least twice before, her father had the charges dropped.

Years later, Sabrina found the nerve to track him down to apologize, but the damage had already been done. The resentment never went away. The only thing that made him feel better about the whole situation was the fact that the twins confronted her in a nightclub once when they visited him in New York. They never touched her, simply scared her to death with words.

"Yeah, tell me about it," Stephen suddenly replied.

"Well, that was a long time ago," he said, shaking off the past. "And it seems I pick bad women period—black and white."

"Well, Thorne seems to be a nice man."

"Yeah, I guess. But are you sure? You know he's worth a lot of money, even though he doesn't act like it. Neither do his brother and sister from what I'm told. But can you imagine having all that money? Sometimes that can lead to trouble."

"When I met him a couple of days ago, I would never have guessed it if Nicholas hadn't brought it up. He just seems like an ordinary guy."

"So who's going to call the twins and cancel our weekly family night?"

"Nobody. I'll meet you all at the restaurant after dinner. We've been talking too long. I gotta get dressed; I only got an hour and a half."

"Okay." He kissed her forehead as she passed him on her way upstairs.

Natalie ran up the steps two at a time, excited about her evening. It only took her about forty-five minutes to decide what to wear, which gave her a half-hour to dress and fifteen minutes to make it to the restaurant. She was still twenty minutes late.

Thorne sat at the table with a frown etched into his handsome face. He checked his watch for the third time since arriving at the Old Sage Room. His patience was slowly wearing thin. *Damn her.* He should have known.

The restaurant wasn't very crowded. It never was. That's what he liked about the place. The atmosphere could be conducive to romance or to business. Tonight he wanted both, though he wasn't sure why.

Everyone he saw since coming into the building wanted to talk business. But he was used to this sort of thing. It came with the territory.

Many of the women patrons were boldly flirtatious. He was used to that, too. He knew some of them, the majority of whom were very married. His highly exaggerated reputation as a bachelor and playboy had moved rapidly through elite circles thanks to a couple of very satisfied debutantes he had gotten to know over the years. All it really took was one good date for your reputation to grow. He had many.

Of course, Thorne knew that his wealth didn't hurt him any. Neither he nor his brother was particularly attracted to socialites, but a man could only be a man, and nothing more. His time was too limited to search for any serious companions. Because of this, he often ended up dating the daughters of his business acquaintances.

He sat on the thick cushions of the cozy banquette at the back of the restaurant, leisurely sipping a beer. How, he wondered, had he gotten himself into such a state in two short days? Natalie Davidson had moved right into his brain and made herself at home.

During the day, it had taken an extra effort to keep her image away so that he could concentrate on work, especially when he was on a work site with one of his crews. The work they did could sometimes be dangerous, and constant vigilance was absolutely necessary. With a woman on the brain, caution could be thrown to the wind. He had reminded his men of this numerous times over the years.

In the past two nights he had tossed and turned in his king-size mahogany sleigh bed either willing his dreams of her away or lusting after her. It was enough to drive a lesser man insane; good thing he was not a lesser man. Still, he didn't think he liked the way his feelings for this one woman were moving.

Natalie moved through the restaurant, gracefully following the maitre'd. He was going to be mad at her tardiness. She figured that time was something he'd been brought up to regard as precious. She allowed that if she were helping to run a multimillion-dollar conglomerate, time would be precious to her, too. But he would get over it when he saw the results of her extra effort. He might have been a little confused about their instant attraction to each another, but she wasn't.

Natalie had never been one to waste too much time worrying. She might let doubt rule her for a moment or two, but then she would regroup and keep moving forward. Life was short, and she was going to live it. She did what she wanted as long as she didn't intentionally hurt anyone else. That the man she was currently attracted to was white surprised her, but it didn't stop her from wanting to move forward and open herself to new experiences.

If only her brother could be a little more optimistic about life, he would be so much more at peace. Carrying past baggage as he did only made it harder for him to find his true soulmate—or for her to find him.

One dark eyebrow arched extremely high, Thorne watched her slow approach to the table. He had to admit she looked delectable. He absently licked his top lip. *Now, where in the hell did that come from?* To appear nonchalant, he lifted his beer to his lips, but over the brim of the bottle, his eyes stayed on her. He noticed other men were looking, too.

She wore a long cream-colored column dress with thin shoulder straps. A cream, tan, and dark-brown belt hung loosely around her waist. The material seemed to slide down her body and move with her. A thin choke necklace made of wood and matching her belt was tied around her neck, and she wore small-heeled brown slip-ons. Her toes were painted a dark red; he liked painted toes.

As she neared the banquette, he stood, thanking the Lord that his suit jacket was cut big to accommodate his shoulder width and that it hung loose on him. The stirring in his loin area both surprised and irritated him. He wasn't some high-school teen about to get his first piece of tail. Hell, he didn't act like this when he was about to get some for the first time.

What in the world was happening to him? He was Thorne Philips, dammit—a very successful businessman and known as a lady's man, a playboy, and a very fulfilling lover.

"Late again, I see, Ms. Davidson." He did not try to hide his irritation.

Natalie just smiled and sat down. "No 'Good evening' or 'Well, don't you look lovely'?" she asked.

"I reserve those for ladies who don't waste my time," Thorne replied snappily.

"What's got you all uptight, Mr. Philips?" She figured she might as well get right to the problem.

"Thorne," he said, still irritated. *She looked too damn good.*

"Well, if you call me Ms. Davidson, I have to call you Mr. Philips."

"Fine. Call me whatever you want to."

"Okay," she said, putting her hands on the table. She didn't have to put up with his shit. "You obviously don't want to be bothered this evening, so I'll just be going." Natalie slid across the seat and was about to rise when his hand covered hers. Neither of them moved for a second as an electric charge passed between them. She stopped moving and tried to breathe normally.

Thorne kept his hand on hers. "Did you feel that?" He asked, already knowing the answer, but needing to hear it. "Natalie, did you feel it?" he asked again, looking her in the eyes.

"Um . . . yes, I felt something," she answered, suddenly unsure of herself.

"Yeah, well, that is what's got me all uptight," he said.

Natalie looked at him almost indignantly. She tried to pull her hand away, but he only tightened his grip.

"Don't look at me like that. I said it has me uptight. I didn't say that I didn't like it. Mind you, I don't want to like it, but the truth is that I do." He leaned back and waited for her reply.

"And that makes you uptight?" She looked around the room and lowered her voice. "Thorne, I have to ask you straight upfront: Is it because I'm a black woman that you don't like it?"

"That would make it easier for you to deal with if that were the reason, wouldn't it? I see that little head of yours working, ready to throw stones and march for the cause." He tilted his head to the side. "No, that's hardly the case here. I grew up respecting people of all races. You're only a darker shade in the rainbow of life to me. That's how my grandmother taught us to see things. My siblings are a lighter shade in the rainbow than I am."

"That's a nice way of seeing things. Most people can't get past skin color. So, what's the problem?"

"I have a couple of problems. First, I don't want to be attracted to anyone. I like being unattached and free. And second, I don't think I like you that much."

"Oh," she laughed, "is that all?"

"Yeah, that's about the gist of it. So, you know my problem. This attraction doesn't seem to want to go away. Are you going to be able to handle it and still give me your business?"

"I haven't hired you yet. Are you afraid you may become a bit too attached to me?"

"I'm afraid of getting too attached to anyone. Besides, you still have your Nicholas, right?"

"He's still around," she answered hesitantly, not sure if she should explain their current status.

"See, that's another problem that I have with this situation." He began making little designs on the back of her hand.

"Oh, that you know each other?" She liked what he was doing to her hand. The steady rhythm of his fingers was intoxicating.

"No, that I don't share my women."

"Your women? Exactly how many women do you have?" Her attitude was beginning to surface, and he saw it.

"Calm down. I don't have any women, but when I do, I don't share." He laced his fingers through hers and rubbed the inside of her wrist with his thumb. His eyes stayed on hers, and she could feel the heat from his hand spreading throughout her body.

When the waiter approached the table, her eyes sent a silent challenge. Thorne smiled and kept his fingers interlocked with hers.

"Evening, madam, Monsieur Philips. Would you like to order?" the friendly waiter asked, oblivious to the quiet tug-of-war underway.

"Yes, we would, Brian," Thorne answered, watching her face drop. "How are April and the kids?"

"Fine, sir. Thank you for asking. Youngest will be starting school this year."

"Really? Well, let me know what school next time I come in; better yet, call my secretary tomorrow and leave me a message. Maybe someone could donate some computers and such to the little tykes." Thorne reached into the inside pocket of his jacket and pulled out a business card.

"Splendid, sir. Thank you. That would be splendid," the waiter said gratefully.

"I would like you to meet a new friend of mine. This is Natalie Davidson. Natalie, this here is Brian Plummet. He's the best waiter in town." Brian and Natalie laughed and shook hands. He took their orders and left them to return their attention to each other.

"You are a surprise," she finally said.

"Why do you say that?" he asked, not sure he understood. "I'm not like any of the other millionaires you know?"

"True, not that I know many. But none of them would take the time to get to know a waiter's name, let alone ask about his family. Nor would they care about school supplies or be sitting here holding my hands in a very posh restaurant at dinnertime."

"You're funny," he laughed. "I saw that hint of a challenge in your eyes when Brian was walking over. You thought I was going to pull my hand away like some scared kid caught with his hand in the cookie jar."

"I-I just wanted to see what you would do," she confessed. They both laughed.

"Well, now you know. Natalie, I'm not the kind of person to care what people think. At the risk of sounding conceited or arrogant, I have enough money not to have to worry about the opinions of people who aren't close to me. Right now, my brother and sister are the only people whose opinions I do hold dear."

"Okay, okay. I'll behave. But you have to admit a lot of people aren't going to like it if we do decide to start seeing one another occasionally."

"I do admit that. But I make people mad everyday. Somehow I manage to live on."

51

"Would your family mind?" she asked.

"No. I told you we don't care about stuff like that. My brother would probably ask me to introduce him to one of your friends, honestly."

"Oh, he's a lot like you, is he?"

"No, not really. Michael's more business, but when he plays, he plays hard."

"And you?"

"I always play hard."

He had on an easy smile, and her heart began to beat overtime as he gave her one of those slow smiles that took forever to fully show.

"And your sister?"

"She's business and play and very protective of us boys. Theresa's like our mother hen. She has a son named Michael Thorne from a previous relationship that went bad. I guess she couldn't think of anything else. He's seven and already a whiz with numbers and stuff. Takes after my brother, Michael, a lot. She's tough. I guess even a financially stable single parent has to be."

Their food arrived, and they ate while Natalie told him about her little family. The twins, Tamia and Tamya, were gorgeous and co-owners of a restaurant/bar. Then there was Stephen, her overprotective brother, who did know about the date and was expecting her to show up at the restaurant at a decent hour.

"That's it? I see you have a small family, too. Good, fewer people for me to get to know."

"Well, I do have one other family member. She's like an extension, but the whole family has embraced her.

Her name is Amanda. She's in the hospital right now, a car accident."

"Nothing serious, I hope."

"No, I don't think so, but she's older. They're still checking her for internal injuries, and she's been in and out of consciousness. She's a history professor at the university."

"Really? That's interesting."

"I was one of her students a lifetime ago. That's when the friendship was formed, and it's been going strong ever since. She asked me to do her a favor the last time I visited her, but I don't think I can do it."

"Oh, what is it? Maybe I can help."

"Thanks, no. It's kind of personal. I'll have to get her permission to bring you in." Natalie played with the napkin her drink rested on. She wanted to talk to him about it, if only to help her sort out the details of the whole chaotic business.

"No, problem. I understand." He wouldn't push.

The evening sailed by as they went over the estimates and material that would be needed to begin work on her house. Natalie listened as Thorne methodically went over the quotes. He seemed efficient, honest, and more than capable to do the job and anything else she needed. She wished she had known about him when she started her business of buying and selling homes.

Over the years, she had built up a sizeable little nest egg from doing basically nothing. Even though she had a degree in history and had taught high school for a couple of years, she had found that it really wasn't her forte.

When her parents died, she and her siblings were left with the family home. One by one they moved out, and the house got to be too big for her alone so she bought a smaller house with her savings and rented out the big house. The extra money was good and came in handy, so she bought another house and sold the smaller one. Then she used that money and bought two more houses that had been seized from drug dealers. Those two came very cheap, but were in excellent condition, so she was able to rent them at a higher rate and buy a couple of fixer-uppers.

Over the past ten or twelve years, Natalie had bought and sold over thirty-five homes. She also kept ownership of at least ten to keep rented. Once she got the hang of it, learned the market's rules and regulations, she found that she liked managing her own real estate, making money, and working only when she pleased.

Natalie knew she was lucky to be able to do as she liked. Many women she knew were tied to jobs they hated or men they didn't want just to survive for themselves or their children.

Again, she focused on Thorne and wondered if he was something else that would please her. They were talking about their respective businesses over coffee when Natalie realized how late it was getting.

"Oh, my goodness, look at the time. I really have to go."

"I'm sorry. The overprotective brother thing, right?"

"Yeah, something like that. On Wednesdays, we all meet at the restaurant to enjoy each other and talk about the ups and downs of the week."

"Oh, that's a good idea. Families should meet weekly. Ours is usually over a boardroom table or a conference call."

"Could you ask someone to hail me a cab?" she asked, gathering her purse and papers.

"Nonsense. Let me take care of this bill, and I'll drop you off myself."

"Are you sure?"

He just gave her a stupid look. "Are you afraid?"

"Of course not."

"Well, I'll take you then." Thorne paid the bill and left a huge tip. As they walked out, he would pause briefly to speak to people he knew. That did not surprise her; he was a personable guy. But she was surprised he never let go of her hand. Their fingers were hooked together, and when he felt her tense and try to pull away, he held on tighter.

CHAPTER 5

They were quiet on the ride to the restaurant. Natalie was still in something of a daze. Finally, unable to keep it to herself, she said, "I can't believe you did that. Are you crazy?"

"I guess I might be," he replied easily.

"You gave them something to gossip about for weeks."

"Nah, not really. Juicier news will be along soon enough."

"I don't think so."

"You were scared?" he asked.

"Not for me, for you," she declared.

"Well, I can take care of myself. Listen, if we are really going to think about doing this, seeing each other, than we have to be on the same side. Our side."

"I know . . . I know. But you have to understand that this is new for me." She gave him a sideward glance. "Have you—"

"Yes, I have," Thorne quickly interjected before she could finish the question.

"See. Well, I haven't." She should have known. He obviously had a lot more experience than she had in some areas.

"There is no difference in the people you're dating. It's the people who see you dating who have the problem.

And just to clear the air on the subject, I have dated a lot of women across racial lines. Actually, most times it wasn't even what you could call dating." He caught that look again. "Oh, please, don't tell me you've been deeply involved with every man you've ever slept with."

"I guess I haven't slept with that many men."

"Well, I'm not going to complain about hearing you say that. If it makes you feel any better, I'll go get tested and everything. I do take care of myself, you know, above all else."

"I'm sure you do, but we'll both get tested anyway. You can't be too sure nowadays."

"Fine, but I can't believe you're actually going to make me get tested," Thorne said incredulously.

"It was your idea." When they pulled in front of Noah's Ark, Thorne was still miffed, but Natalie was amused. He opened the passenger-side door to his 2004 Dodge Durango and helped her out. Then he pulled her next to him alongside the car. He just stood there looking at her, his hand on her waist.

"What?"

"Nothing," he replied, shifting his gaze from her to the ground and then back to her.

"Well, what do you want?" she asked.

"Are you going to tell Nicholas to back off tomorrow?"

"Yes," she said, looking up into his gray gaze. That wouldn't be hard. She had wanted to do that for a while, anyway. Now she had a reason. "Yes, but I'm not going to tell him about you, though, because I don't want to add to his insecurities. But I will tell him that it is over. It's actually been over for a long time now. We're more friends than anything, but I don't think he wants to see it that way. I'm talking to him only because it's time to make him understand how I feel."

Thorne stepped a little closer. She could smell the strong blend of his soap and aftershave. The scent made her feel warm and safe. As his arms enwrapped her, Natalie rested her head on his chest and let her earlier hesitations slip away.

"Tell him tomorrow, Nat. I'm not going to share you."

She lifted her head. "So you've—" She was silenced when his lips brushed hers. Natalie waited for more, but he lifted his head shook it from side to side. "What was that?" she asked, smiling.

"I told you; I'm not going to share you. I shouldn't have done that."

"You're kidding me, right?" She put her arms around him, refusing to let him go when he tried to pull away. She tightened her hold.

"Natalie, let me go."

"No. If you want to leave, you have to do better than that," she countered playfully.

"No, those are Nicholas's lips." He struggled lightly against her arms, enjoying this little playacting.

"No, these are Natalie's lips—always have been and always will be."

Thorne let out a long, deep breath signaling surrender. "Okay, one kiss. Tomorrow you had better tell

Nicholas or there's going to be a lot of hell going on. Promise you'll talk to him."

"What, you don't trust me? On second thought, it's not as if we're actually making a relationship out of this. We're just going to be getting to know each other better."

"But if you go with Nicholas, how can I get to know you at all? You need to be single."

"Why should I end my friendship with him? I don't have any guarantee that we'll be together," she teased, smiling all the while.

"With the kind of currents we have been sending one another, you'd be a fool not to talk to him."

"A fool?" Natalie asked, taking offense at his choice of words. She had decided to talk to Nicholas, but it seemed Mr. Thorne had a little conceit after all. "A fool?"

"I'm just saying you felt it, too. You know that kind of connection doesn't happen often. You want to explore it just as much as I do."

"You think so?"

"Just promise. It's important."

"I promise," she said, lifting her head to his mouth. Once again, he lightly brushed her top lip. He kissed the corner of her mouth.

Thorne thought that he would stop after that, but her fingers spread across his back under his coat, and she let her tongue run over his bottom lip. Before he could grasp what was happening, he had her against the car. His kisses, which had started soft and light, became hard and urgent. The resulting electricity caused the hair at the back of his neck to stand on end.

"Open to me," he whisper, pushing his hand into the soft curls of her hair and pulling her head back.

Natalie did as she was told and held on. The force of first waves of pleasure took her by surprise. A moan escaped her throat and became Thorne's undoing.

He tasted the sweetness in the deep recesses of her mouth. He felt the heat from her hands as she ran them over his back and hips. His own hands were burning from their journey down the side of her body to her bottom. Everything he gave her, she gave back. She brought her hands up to play in his hair and pulled him deeper into the kiss.

"Nat, I've . . . got to . . . go."

"Okay . . . soon . . . okay."

But neither was trying very hard to separate.

"Nat," Thorne said, finally breaking off the kiss, "I didn't mean to ravish you right here on a public street like that." His chin was resting on the top of her head. "We have to stop." Then he did what he had wanted to do all night. He leaned down and kissed her bare shoulder. "Please make sure you talk to Nicholas tomorrow. I think if you don't, he'll be dead by Friday." They both laughed. "Now, go on inside to your family."

"You're not going to meet them? They know we're together. They might get the wrong idea." *Damn*, she thought, *I'm practically begging*.

Thorne smiled, grinding his hips into hers. "If they meet me like this, they will get the wrong idea."

"Oh," Natalie said, surprised.

Thorne stepped back, instantly sorry for his crude action.

"I didn't say move," she whispered, pulling him closer.

"Okay . . . okay. Let me calm down some. You should fix your hair and lipstick. Oh, damn, I guess I have it on me." He pulled out a handkerchief and wiped his lips, then hers.

This was not the first time Thorne had been at the restaurant; he and his family had eaten there once. He could remembered his sister had suggested offering the owners space in several of their hotels. It was not his area of immediate concern, so he wasn't sure if it had actually happened.

He also remembered that the owner was indeed beautiful. He didn't know at the time that she had a twin. Michael had even said that he would like to have a date with the owner once he saw her.

The atmosphere in the restaurant was comfortable and cozy, with the large number of plants surrounding the foyer and greeting area giving it a down-home feeling. On either side of the spacious foyer was a short hallway leading to each of the two dining areas. Directly in front of them was the raised bar, which was surrounded by gray sheer curtains on both sides that separated it from the dining rooms. In the dining areas, dimly lit sconces and red planters littered the walls. The bar included two large screen televisions, high tables, and a small fire pit surrounded by a circular sofa. The gray carpet of the dining rooms matched the stone floor of the bar area. Thorne felt that he could cuddle with his sweetheart or watch a ball game on the big screen with his friends at the same time. He really liked it.

Natalie knew it was her turn to put up or shut up. As she moved through the foyer, she glimpsed a grin on Thorne's face. He couldn't wait to see what she would do. Neither could she.

The restaurant had a cross section of patrons, so she knew he wouldn't be the only white person there. She had known most of these people for years. They would probably be curious for half a minute and then would find something else of interest.

Wait a minute. Why was she stressing herself out like this? She didn't really care what these people thought of her or what she was doing. She was going to enjoy herself, period. How big a fool would she be if she let anyone rain on her parade, especially after the kiss he had just given her? She could still feel the heat.

Natalie took a deep breath, squared her shoulders and continued through to the back of the restaurant. Thorne followed. He had planned to walk a few steps behind her to let her set the tone. But she turned around, smiled at him, and then took his hand and led him through to the bar.

A few of heads, both black and white, turned. He assumed it was just curiosity, or maybe some of these people still knew her as Nicholas's girlfriend.

Thorne saw Stephen's brows come together in a very straight line as they approached the bar. He was fairly easy to point out as he looked just like his sisters. And he was the only one in the room who seemed to be waiting for an excuse to jump him. *This one could be a problem.* Natalie must have seen, too, because she held his hand a little tighter.

"You're late, as usual."

"Good evening to you, too, Stephen," Natalie said, leaning over and kissing her brother's cheek. "This is my new friend, Thorne Philips. Thorne, my brother, Stephen."

After a noticeable pause, Stephen extended his hand and Thorne eagerly accepted. "Friend, huh? Seemed to be a little more than that by the way you're dragging him through here."

"Well, I sure hope it will be. But for now, we're just friends. Actually, I'm about to be an employee," Thorne explained.

"Oh, so you will be working on the house?" Stephen asked.

"Yes, as of Monday morning."

"Thorne, Stephen was the one who recommended your company to me," Natalie happily added.

"Then I guess I need to thank you twice—for the business and for making it possible for me to meet your sister." He could have sworn he saw a frown cross Stephen's face, but it was gone in a flash. Maybe he had just imagined it. It would probably be best to just change the subject. "So what is it you do for a living, Stephen? Oh, wait a minute . . . Stephen Davidson. You're the sculptor?"

"That would be me," Stephen replied.

"I have a few of your pieces."

"You do?"

That got his attention. Since his separation, Stephen's work had suffered terribly. He needed all the encouragement he could get from whomever was willing to give it to him.

Thorne was ready.

"Yeah, I picked up my last two in New York about three years ago. My sister and brother also have a few pieces."

"Well, I knew that there were some located in the Connor Corporation Building, but I wasn't aware that you kept some as personal pieces, also. And, I don't mean to offend you, but my work primarily depicts African-Americans," Stephen stated hesitantly.

"So you have to be African-American to appreciate good art?" Thorne asked. "That sounds a little like reverse bias to me."

"No, I'm not saying that. I just didn't think you would get the meaning of some. A lot of them deal with slavery and racism. Some do have biblical themes, but those are also depicted as blacks."

"Yeah, I know. My brother must have every angel you've ever done. But don't tell him I said anything; he would only deny it. My sister has a few of sculptures of mothers with children. I guess she misses hers more than we thought. I particularly like the slavery themes. Those showing the struggle and strong will of a man to prevail even under the worst of circumstances are my favorites. Teaches me that my problems are minor compared to some."

Stephen was speechless. He was totally amazed that this man was someone he had characterized and prejudged as unsuitable for his sister.

"I think that I owe you an apology and a beer, Thorne."

"I'll take the beer. No need to apologize for being an older brother, though. I have the same problem." Thorne had released Natalie's hand sometime during the conversation and was now sitting next to Stephen.

Feeling like a third wheel, Natalie decided to go in search of her sisters. She found them in their office, pouring over the paperwork.

"Hello, ladies."

"Thank heavens," Tamia said, tossing her pen onto the desk. "She made me promise to do paperwork until you showed up."

"Well, at least I got an hour out of you," Tamya replied. She was younger by three minutes, but she was the most responsible and reliable of the two.

Natalie often wondered why Tamya hadn't chosen a profession like doctor or lawyer. She could have easily succeeded at either, given her determination and intelligence. But she became a bartender and was very successful at it. While in New York, she had worked and trained at one of those bars where the bartenders juggled bottles expertly and created all kinds of crazy drinks. On crowded nights, she sometimes still put on a show. She had even taught some of her most loyal bartenders a few tricks.

Tamia was a world-class chef. You never would guess it by looking at her. She had trained in Paris and London but had started out in New York, too. She was good, really good, but her attention span beyond cooking was very fickle. She was wild and carefree and had a temper to match.

Natalie lavished praise on her sisters as they put their work away. "You girls are doing such a wonderful job with this place. It must be one of the top ten restaurants in the city."

As identical twins, the girls had grown up with the usual expectations that they dress exactly alike, have the exact same hairstyle, and have the exact same toys. Except for the different colors they used as identifiers, it was impossible for most people to tell them apart.

As they got older, their parents decided to add name charms to the mix. Luckily, it was a fad at the time. All three girls sported earrings, necklaces, and bracelets showing their names. They also had name belts and stacks of spray-painted tees, sweats, and jeans.

After their late-teens rebellious years, during which Tamia decided to cut her hair and dye it blond and Tamya decided to wear hers long and jet-black, they began to settle down and accept the fact that being twins wasn't a bad thing. So, they sat down and made plans to open a restaurant and make it a success.

As Natalie looked at her two girls, still looking very much alike with their tall, slim figures, each wearing her hair long and straight—Tamia's parted down the middle; Tamya's on the right side. Their designer eyeglasses were the same, except Tamya's frames were brown while Tamia's were a flaming red.

"Actually, right now we are at number thirteen, but next year we'll be much higher." Tamya walked around the desk dressed in black trousers and a white blouse. It was mandatory that all employees wear white tops, black bottoms, and black shoes.

"I know you will. Listen, before we go out front, I have to tell you something. I brought someone here with me," Natalie said a little apprehensively.

"Yeah, we already know. Mr. Thorne Philips," Tamya replied nonchalantly. "It really isn't that big of a deal."

"I've seen pictures of him," Tamia said, eager to talk about anything that would give her a break from paperwork. "Is he really that good-looking?"

Natalie smiled. "No, he's better looking. And he has these smoky-gray eyes that pull you right in and—" She stopped when she saw her sister's intent stares. "What?"

"Oh, nothing." Tamya said, glancing at Tamia.

Tamia spoke up. "Someone around here seems to be taken with a certain white gentleman."

Suddenly defensive, Natalie asked, "Is that a problem with you two—that he's white?"

"Girl, please, don't be ridiculous," Tamia said, holding up her hand and waving it at Natalie as if she were swatting at a gnat. "A man is a man is a man." She looked at Tamya for agreement, and her sister quickly obliged.

"Well, I wouldn't care if he was red and purple as long as he caused you to look as you do right now," Tamya replied.

"Thanks," Natalie said blushing.

"Hey," Tamia finished, "Are parts of him red and purple?"

"You're nasty, Tamia." Natalie wagged a finger at her sister, laughing. "You are so very nasty. Come on, let's go out front. And get your mind out of the gutter."

"Just wondering," Tamia said.

The rest of the evening was uneventful. Thorne left about an hour after they arrived to get some work done at home. Natalie walked him out to his car and he immediately pulled her into his arms. She thanked him for meeting her family, and he said he thoroughly enjoyed it, adding that Tamia was a handful. She had flirted and joked with him outrageously.

"I think I'll bring Michael with me next time. He would probably enjoy meeting Tamya."

"Oh, trying to hook your brother up?"

"I just think he needs to settle down and start looking for the right woman. No harm in putting one in his face."

"Well, what about you? You're the oldest child. Why haven't you settled down with the right woman?" She pretended to still be joking, but she was dying to know.

His was very still for the briefest moment. "Well, I would say that I think I'm about to, but that would scare you, wouldn't it? Besides, we don't know each other well enough yet. And . . . you still belong to someone else."

That got her dander up. "I belong to myself," she said tightly, pushing his hand away.

"Calm down. You know what I mean. You're still with Nicholas, and until you make your situation with him clear . . . look, I can't think of you as anything but a friend until you do."

They were silent for a minute.

"Tomorrow, Natalie. Do it tomorrow," Thorne insisted.

"Okay," she murmured, more than willing to do what he asked.

"I got to go."

And it was over, her euphoria passing as she watched his car pull away from the curb. She turned and went back into the restaurant.

"I like him, sis," Stephen said as soon as she sat on the chair beside him.

"Yeah, we did, too," the twins concurred.

"Good, because so do I."

Their family night ended with a light dessert and drinks. They all loved these weekly get-togethers, during which they openly shared their ups and downs, their triumphs and setbacks. Their love for each other was deep and uncompromising. And each respected the opinions and ideas of the others. They were the picture of a close-knit family.

CHAPTER 6

Natalie did not want to get up. Shutting her eyes, she burrowed her head into her pillow and willed her dream to come back. But like many other women, Denzel only came around when her eyes were shut.

She had a busy day ahead, so after showering she got it started by calling Nicholas and making an appointment for lunch. That way she could kill two birds with one stone: eating lunch and making sure that Nicholas understood that their relationship was platonic. Or so she thought. Still, she would have to reshuffle her other plans for the day.

Amanda's house needed to be checked, and she needed fresh bedclothes at the hospital. She told Natalie she couldn't stand being ass-out. That was funny coming from a college professor.

Books Amanda needed for a future lecture had to be picked up from a local distributor, and there were some papers from her office at the university that she wanted Natalie to bring her. Natalie figured she would read these once she regained full use of her faculties. For now, she asked for whatever she could think of when she was awake. If she was aware enough to ask for something, Natalie was happy to oblige her. Even if she never looked at the stuff, at least her mind was working. That was a good thing.

After Natalie finished all of that running around, she still had some personal things to attend to: a dentist appointment, bills to pay, clothes to dropoff and pickup from the cleaners, and a 5:00 P.M. hair appointment.

⌁

She was starving by the time she arrived at the café for lunch. Nicholas was already seated and had ordered lunch for both of them. She was so hungry she didn't bother to tell him that she didn't like blue cheese salad dressing, sour cream on her baked potato, or her steak medium-rare. She didn't bother because, one, he would order her the exact same thing if they ever eat there again; and, two, if she ever ate there, it wouldn't be with him. As she took her first bite, she prayed that this meeting would go smoothly.

A full ten minutes of sitting politely at the little round table in the center of the upscale café had passed before she broached what was uppermost on her mind.

"Nicholas, we need to talk about something."

"Sure, babe, I'm listening."

She hated being called 'babe', and he knew it. His use of the word only reinforced her determination to tackle the subject without delay.

"Well, I think, um, that we should date other people. We should stop seeing each other."

Nicholas's fork slipped from his hands and fell onto his plate. "Are you serious?" he asked unbelievingly.

"Yes," Natalie said nervously. "Yes, I would like . . . no . . . I need some time and space."

"And what brought this on, Natalie? Have you been seeing someone else?"

"No, but I think we both need to get out and see other people."

"Why? I've already met the person I plan to spend the rest of my life with." He reached across the table.

That was the wrong move, and before she could stop herself, she blurted out her true feelings, "Well, I haven't."

"What do you mean, you haven't? I love you, Natalie." He was looking at her with those puppydog eyes of his, eyes that at any other time would have her feeling so guilty she would simply give in to his pleas, but not this time. She was determined to stand her ground and get through her declaration without changing her mind.

"I'm sorry, Nicholas, but . . ."

Suddenly, he stood up and threw their lovely little table to the side. It flew just inches past the head of a patron, who happened to be walking by, and landed on its side. Food and drinks landed on the jackets, shirts, dresses, and slacks of the people sitting at the four tables closest to theirs. Nicholas stalked over and stood directly in front of her. She was glued to in her chair, frozen and in shock.

"You're sorry?" he asked in an undertone before exploding. "YOU'RE SORRY?! Natalie, I have given you everything I have to give over the past year, and you can sit here all prim and proper and tell me that you . . . are

. . . sorry. Well, to hell with that and to hell with you, Natalie."

He was screaming at her in front of a café full of people. Luckily, they were strangers, but that didn't make her feel much better. She was so embarrassed that all she could do was sit there and ride it out.

"Nicholas, calm down," she begged, reaching out to him and hoping to rein in his fit of rage.

"Don't tell me to calm down, dammit. For the past year, I have loved you. I was ready to propose to you, but none of that matters, does it? *Does* it?" With all his soul, Nicholas was hoping that she would say that it did matter, that she had changed her mind. He would willingly take her back and forgive her in a heartbeat. She was all he had, and he was losing her.

"Nicholas, I just think—"

"You think? You think? Just forget it. I never thought that I could hate you, but guess what? It's not that hard." His mind was jumping from one thought to the next. She didn't want him. Why? He had money, a nice house, a new car, and a good job. He could have satisfied her sexually if he would let him. Nobody else was complaining. All she had to do was be with him, and he would give up the others. He had been thinking about asking her to marry him, and here she was talking about separating. But she didn't want him. Well, to hell with her.

Crushed and confused, Nicholas's rage grew. She hadn't given him the right answer. He didn't see a hint of remorse in her eyes for her hurtful words. She was unrelentingly serious.

Disgusted, he stormed from the café and left her looking and feeling like a battered wife. She might have found the scene comical if she hadn't been one of the players in it.

Thirty minutes later, Natalie figured that maybe it took a little longer for her prayers to reach Heaven. The staff at the café turned the table upright. Everything had started out well enough.

The staff clearly felt bad for her, but they mistook her shock for hurt and shame. When the mess was cleaned up and she had pulled herself together, the check for lunch appeared on the table in front of her.

The rest of her day went by in a blur. She still couldn't believe what Nicholas had done, but she was running around so much she didn't really have time to think about it. She called Thorne on his cellphone while standing in line at the dry cleaners.

"Philips." Crisp and all business, Thorne waited for a response. *Time, time, time . . .*

"Hello, Thorne," Natalie said after hesitating a second or two.

"Yes." Irritation began to creep into his voice.

"It's me."

"Well, hello, me. How are you?" Cradling the phone on his shoulder, Thorne continued writing on a notepad.

"Fine. Listen, I talked to Nicholas today. You'll never believe how he acted."

"Natalie?" He put down the pad and held the phone in his hand.

She was silent for a minute. *I'll be damned*, she thought. "Yes, Natalie! Who the hell else did you expect it to be?"

He was giggling, actually giggling, laughing at her. That was the final straw. All day long, she had been running around like a chicken with its head cut off for a friend. Then she had to sit helplessly by and listen to another supposed friend vent his anger out on her—all because she wanted to get to know him better. To top it all off, he was now laughing at her.

That did it. It was time for her to step back and have a time-out for herself before she became completely unraveled.

"You know what? I don't even want to know. Just forget it. Just forget the whole damn thing! You can go to hell, Thorne Philips—you and your damn harem of women."

"Nat—" That was all he could get out before the phone went dead. "Damn," he said, stamping his booted foot on the ground. She had actually hung up on him. Now, that was a first. He smiled and wondered how he was going to make it up to her.

Thorne used the back of his hand to wipe his forehead, leaving a streak of dirt across his sweaty brow. Several crewmembers, holding an impromptu meeting, looked up at him. They were at the site of the new recreational center his company was donating to the city.

"Damn," he exclaimed again. She was probably really mad. Maybe he should let her cool off first. No, that wasn't her style. She was likely to stay mad forever, thinking he would forget her. But wasn't about to forget her. Last night had been one of the longest, loneliest, and most sleepless nights of his life, and he didn't plan to have too many more of those.

Thorne didn't even know where she was. His brows drew together in a frown, and his eyes grew darker. Snickering from his crew brought him back to the present, and his mood became even more sullen when he realized he probably had been the butt of a couple of their jokes.

"Meeting adjourned," he announced abruptly, stalking off toward the onsite trailer.

Natalie's last curler was in place and she was about to sit under the dryer when the door to the hair salon opened. She leaned back and tried to relax to release some of the stress and tension she had incurred as a result of her day so far.

Sharmaine, Natalie's stylist and friend, and also owner of the shop, hurried to the front counter, her eyes wide with curiosity.

Natalie didn't hear the oohs and aahs from the other clients. Her eyes were closed, and all she heard was the steady humming of the hair dryer. She did feel the light tap on her shoulder.

"Natalie, dear, something was just delivered here for you."

"What?" She leaned forward, grimacing as the cracked vinyl material of the dryer chair scraped her leg.

Sharmaine reached behind her and turned off the dryer.

"I said something was just delivered here for you." Reacting to her friend's obvious confusion, Sharmaine added, "I'm telling the truth."

Natalie sat up and realized that the room, which was usually abuzz with conversation, had become deadly quiet, and all eyes seemed to be on her. *What now?* She rose from the chair and sat back down with a thump when she saw what everybody else had already seen.

Vases of roses, a lot of vases of roses, were sitting on the table, a chair, and the counter in the small reception area.

"Well, get on up and out there," Sharmaine coaxed. "We're dying to know who sent them. I know that cheap-ass Nicholas didn't." Sharmaine had never cared for him or his slick ways. She knew more about him than she had let on to Natalie.

Natalie already knew who they were from.

"Well, come on," Sharmaine urged, nearly dragging her into the reception area. "I counted them when the delivery guys brought them in; there are twelve dozen."

"Oh," Natalie said, shocked and speechless for the second time that day.

"They're numbered. Here's number one," Sharmaine said, handing her the first card.

Her fingers numb, Natalie read the care:

Please forgive me for my earlier mistake. Believe me, it's not what you think. Now, that you've talked with Nicholas.

She looked up and saw that Sharmaine already had the next card waiting for her.

It simply read, *2008*. Sharmaine continued to hand her card after card, and each had the succeeding year written on it.

2009
2010
2011
2012
2013
2014
2015
2016
2017 and so on.

She took the last card and anxiously read it aloud: *Allow me to take my time showing you how much you have come to mean to me.*

"Wow!" Sharmaine exclaimed, as did several other ladies in the shop.

Natalie's heart was beating so fast she had to sit down.

"Wait, there's no signature," Sharmaine said, turning each card from front to back. "Now, Natalie, girl, I know you are not going to leave us hanging like this."

Natalie didn't even hear her; she was in a daze.

Nobody had ever done anything so romantic for her. Well, nobody she had ever dated would have had the means to afford it. Then she caught herself. The number of flowers or the price didn't really matter. What mattered was the fact that he had taken time out of his busy day to try to brighten hers. Time was so precious to him.

She was in trouble, especially if he had started to feel anywhere near what she was feeling. But they had to slow down. Things were happening way too fast. They had only admitted their attraction to each other the day before, and already he was sending her dozens of flowers. They had shared an intimate moment—*one* intimate moment. And, for him, she had broken up with her boyfriend, albeit that it had not been a real relationship, anyway. What in the world was next?

She didn't have to wait long for an answer. Ten minutes before she was about to walk out of the shop with her hair freshly texturized, a long black limousine pulled up to the curb.

Natalie knew it was Thorne as soon as the ladies in the reception area started chattering about it. Word spread throughout the shop, and everybody waited anxiously to see who would step out of the car. She didn't know what he had planned for the evening, but she wasn't dressed for anything fancy. Natalie looked down at her blue jeans, ran her hand over her North Carolina Tarheels sweatshirt, and nervously tapped the toe of her Timberlands against the base of her swivel chair.

Sharmaine, who had been trying to pull bits and pieces of information out of her ever since the flowers arrived, walked over and sat next to her. "I guess my prayers are about to be answered."

"What makes you think so?" Natalie countered smoothly.

"Well, Miss I Like to Keep Secrets, nobody in this shop has any idea who is about to get out of that car. But here you are all laid back and apparently not the least bit interested. Come on and pay the tab so I can see what's what for myself."

Reluctantly, she let her friend pull her out of the chair and into the reception area to settle her bill.

Sharmaine took her sweet time ringing up the exchange and making out a receipt, something she normally didn't do. With her head bent down, she secretly smiled, thinking she was about to have her question answered. The front door finally opened. Her mouth almost hit the counter when she lifted up her head and saw the most delicious-looking man she had ever seen in her life walk into her shop.

Handsome and gorgeous weren't even good enough adjectives to describe this man. Delicious, maybe. He looked kind of Italian or Greek or something. But who cared? He looked tasty and familiar; she just couldn't remember from where.

The silence was deafening. Every woman in the shop had stopped what she was doing to have a look at him, and they got an eyeful. Natalie stood facing Sharmaine with her back to the door, trying to act as if she didn't know he was there.

"Sharmaine, can I have my receipt?" Natalie asked pointedly. After she had held her hand out for at least thirty seconds, she exclaimed, "Sharmaine!"

It was to no avail. Sharmaine's hand was still as Thorne approached the counter.

Dressed in a navy Armani business suit with a white dress shirt, sky-blue necktie and matching handkerchief, Thorne felt like a cow with six legs. He hadn't enough time to change after a late afternoon meeting. A dozen pairs of eyes were on him, all except for the pair he was seeking. She was doing it on purpose. He could tell by her stance that she knew he was there. He stood patiently for a minute his arms folded in front of him. She never turned.

Well, he could play a few games, too. He had already told her that he played hard. So she had been forewarned. Why hadn't she listened? Now he'd have to let her know with whom she was dealing.

Thorne walked over to Natalie and spun her around to face him. Before she could protest, his lips closed over hers in a passionate kiss that left her breathless. Sharmaine and the other ladies were struck dumb. For added effect, he took small bites at the corners of her mouth and licked her bottom lip before releasing her.

Floored by his powerful kiss, Natalie swayed, leaning heavily against the counter. The kiss affected every part of her being: muscles, nerves, senses. The other ladies were smiling at him.

He smiled back.

"Good evening, ladies. Sorry to intrude on your beauty ritual." He continued charmingly, "I just came to pick up my lady friend." He looked down at Natalie, who had managed to pull herself together. "Are you ready, love?"

Embarrassed beyond belief by his boldness and her reaction to it, she simply allowed him to escort her out.

"Bye, Sharmaine."

"Bye, Natalie. Call me." It sounded like a command. "Um, Natalie, wait. What about all these roses?"

She had been so overwhelmed by his presence, she had forgot all about her flowers. "Oh." She picked up one vase. "I have the notes, so give one to every client, and you and the girls take whatever is left. Is that okay with you?" she asked Thorne. She really wanted to take them all home, but that would be selfish. It was better to share them with the ladies, since they had been so anxious to solve the mystery of the roses.

"Sure, love, however you want it."

Thorne placed a hand on the small of her back and felt her slight shiver. He threw Sharmaine a quick wink and a smile before guiding Natalie out the door. "I have a special surprise for you, love," he whispered in her ear on their way out.

"Oh, yeah? And what is that? And how did you know where I was?"

"You're going to have to wait and see. But I have taken the initiative and decided that we will have stars and entertainment tonight. And don't worry about how I found you. I found you, didn't I?" He helped her into the limousine, sliding in after her.

"Natalie, Natalie, you don't seem to be listening to a single word I'm saying. What's wrong?"

"Oh," Natalie replied, starting slightly. "I'm sorry, Amanda. I was just thinking, that's all. I came by to get some information so I can start the search for your son. Please continue."

But her thoughts kept running back to Thorne. Every few minutes she had to make a conscious effort to keep her train of thought on track. It had been that way all morning.

"That far-off look in your eye tells me that a man is involved. What gives? Are you and Nicholas finally on the right path?" Amanda asked, but knowing full well that Nicholas could not possibly have put that twinkle in Natalie's eye.

"No, it doesn't have anything at all to do with Nicholas. I broke things off with him three days ago." She saw that the news did not surprise Amanda.

She also saw the dark circles and bags around Amanda's eyes. Guilt swept through her.

Amanda was obviously not doing well. The doctor had told Natalie that occasionally she still slipped in and out of consciousness. They were still conducting tests. And here Natalie was sitting by her hospital bed and thinking of Thorne. She hadn't even told Amanda about him. Given Amanda's recently revealed history, she was not too sure she should. But she missed talking with her friend. She finally decided that it was best to talk to Amanda as much as possible while she was conscious and alert.

"Amanda, I met the most wonderful man," Natalie blurted out.

"Do tell," Amanda urged.

"He's white," Natalie went on, pausing for a reaction.

"And?" Amanda asked nonchalantly.

"And he's perfect," Natalie continued happily. "He's attentive and romantic; fun and comical. We just seem to click. I don't know how because we argue so much. But when he holds me, my mind shuts down, and my heart flips and dips."

"Oh, girl, sounds like you got it kind of bad." Amanda was happy for her. She knew that Natalie had been unhappy for a long time.

"Yeah, I'm really trying to take it slow, because this is all new for me, but I like him a lot."

"Well, that's a start. How does he feel about you?"

"I don't know. He likes me, but I think that he might be holding back some, too. Then again, he doesn't seem the type to hold back. He goes after what he wants, and I think he's used to getting it. You would like him, Amanda. He's a take-charge kind of guy. And people listen to him."

"What's his name?" Amanda asked, interested to learn more about the man who had so entranced Natalie.

"He's a multimillionaire," Natalie said. "I would have thought he wouldn't waste time with me, but he's right there. I haven't seen him since Thursday night because he went out of town on business, but guess what he did?" She looked at Amanda, who was smiling brightly. "Thursday, I got mad with him on the phone over something stupid and childish. So I'm at Sharmaine's getting my hair done, and he had twelve dozen roses delivered to me there with the sweetest apology."

"Wow . . . you said twelve dozen?"

"Yes, twelve dozen—one hundred and forty-four roses—red and white and pink ones. Then he picks me up from Sharmaine's in a limo. He came right into the shop, spoke to the girls, gave me the most passionate kiss, and whisked me away."

Natalie's eyes were shining; and there was a lilt in her voice.

"He said that he thought I would like to eat out, and when I told him I wasn't dressed for it in my jeans and sweatshirt, he said that I was being silly. He had on an Armani business suit, so I thought he had somewhere classy in mind. Girl, we pulled up at the park. A picnic table with a basket of food and apple cider had been set up for us. It was the most romantic date I've ever had. We watched a couple of Little League games. Oh, I just had the most perfect time with him." The glow in her cheeks had grown deeper and the shine in her eyes brighter as she recounted her magical evening.

"My goodness, I think I'm in love with him, too," Amanda said, taking Natalie's hand and giving it a little squeeze. "So who is this mysterious millionaire?"

"His name is Thorne Philips. You've probably heard of the family. They own the Connor Corporation."

Amanda's expression froze and her face paled. The hands Natalie held were wet and clammy.

"Are you all right, Amanda? Should I get the doctor? I'll get the doctor." As she started to rise Amanda grabbed her hand.

"Help," she whispered.

Frightened, Natalie began pushing the nurses' button frantically. She was scared to death. What in the world was happening to her friend?

Amanda clutched her chest and groaned, but was unable to utter whatever words she was struggling to get out.

Two hours later, the doctor found Natalie sitting in the drab waiting area alone and worried sick. He told her that Amanda had suffered a slight heart attack, but was resting comfortably. *What was a slight heart attack? Weren't they all serious?*

Natalie couldn't believe it. The accident aside, Amanda had always been in excellent health. She exercised and jogged on a regular basis, ate all the right foods. She had even been trying to get Natalie to take better care of herself. What could have happened to make her have a heart attack?

The question preoccupied her during the twenty-minute drive home from the hospital. Weary and depressed by the whole vexing ordeal, Natalie entered her house ready to put the day to an end.

Tracey and Lindsey were in overdrive. Their mother had just dropped them off after their scheduled weekend visit, and they were full of stories about their mother and her new much younger boyfriend.

For his daughter's sake, Stephen listened to their stories with stoic attention, struggling not to show anything negative towards his estranged wife, but Natalie could tell that it was hard for him. She finally took pity on him, having herself grown tired of hearing about Paula, and asked the girls if she could do their hair for school the next day. This one question did the perfect job of, one, changing the subject and, two, getting them both out of his hair for a minute. She ushered the two pre-teens upstairs, and Stephen started preparing a small Sunday dinner.

"Thanks, sis," he said later, after putting two very restless angels to bed.

"Hey, what am I here for?" Natalie was stretched out on the couch sipping a glass of wine and only half watching the Sunday night movie that was playing on TV. The book she had planned to read lay unopened on the coffee table.

"So what's new with you? Why the long face?" he asked, visibly concerned.

She told him about her visit to the hospital and Amanda's sudden attack.

"Damn, I hope she'll be okay. So, what do you think happened?" He and the twins had whole-heartedly adopted Amanda into their family years ago after Natalie graduated college and began working for her.

The ringing phone caused her to jump. "I don't know, but I think maybe I had better get a move on finding out information about her son. She hadn't gotten around to giving me any names." She picked the phone up. "Hello."

"Hello, love, how are you this evening?"

"Hello yourself. I'm just fine." She looked at Stephen, who winked at her and quickly left the room. "So where are you? Still out of town?"

"No, actually, my sister and I flew back into town this afternoon on one of the company planes. We had a priority meeting with Michael and some of the vice presidents of each branch in the corporation. Twice a year, we pull everyone together and brainstorm. Anyway, enough of that. What are you doing?"

"Nothing. Sitting on the sofa, watching a movie on the TV, sipping a glass of wine. I came back from the hospital a while ago."

"Oh, your friend, um, what was her name?"

"Amanda."

"Right. How is she?"

"Not too well. She had a slight heart attack today right in front of me." Her voice cracked and grew unsteady, sure signs tears were soon to follow. She was losing it.

"Hey, hey, now. Take it easy. She'll be all right." He couldn't stand for a woman to cry. "Are you okay?"

"Yeah, this is just the first time I've had to really think about it."

"Are you alone? Do you want me to come over?"

"No. It's getting late, and we both have to get up early."

"If you're sure that you'll be okay."

"I'm sure."

"Okay. You can expect the crew to be at the house by seven in the morning. I gave the key to the foreman. I usually like to work with the crew. It gives me time to think and exercise, but I have a couple of meetings in the morning. I'll be there sometime in the afternoon, though."

"All right. I think I'm going to sleep in a bit. Since Amanda pulled this little scare on me, I think I'm going to start searching for this long-lost son of hers. It will be hard because I don't have any names, but—"

"How are you going to search for somebody without a name?"

"Well, she had the heart attack before she could tell me his name. I wasn't really listening to her tell me the story because I was daydreaming about—" Natalie stopped. She wasn't going to put herself out there like that.

"About who?" Thorne asked, a laugh clearly at the edge of his voice.

Natalie heard the smugness. A big grin was probably on his face. "About nobody."

"You were daydreaming about me?" he asked as if surprised.

"Did I say you? Actually, I was daydreaming about this tall, dark, and handsome guy that I had a wild one-night stand with last week."

He was silent.

"Thorne . . . Thorne?"

"Natalie, do me a favor." His voice had taken on a very serious tone. "Don't even joke with me about something like that. I'm only human, and a male at that. Jealousy, temper, and rage are all a part of my makeup.

You would have had me tracking every man from here to Texas until I found this one-night stand of yours."

It was Natalie's turn to grin. "Well, Thorne Philips, I would have never guessed that a big, strong man like you would ever fall prey to such feeble emotions."

"You better believe it, Natalie. So now you know and have been forewarned. You're my woman, and I care for you. Like I said, I play hard. That also goes for caring and loving."

Natalie was silent for only a second. "That was very nicely said, Thorne. And it's good to meet a man who's not afraid of expressing himself. But I'm my own woman."

"Oh, I'm not afraid at all. That's just me. But we could argue all day about whose woman you are. Don't let the suit, tie, or money fool you. I'm just a regular old fellow at heart. I was brought up to be just me. That's the best I can give you or anybody else."

"I got a feeling that regular is the last thing you'll ever be."

CHAPTER 7

On Monday, Natalie decided not to ride over to the house until 1:00 P.M. On days like this one she was thankful that she worked for herself. She had gotten a late start that morning, not because she couldn't roll out of bed, but because she and Thorne couldn't seem to tear themselves off the phone last night.

The conversation ranged from their school days to which schools had the best football and basketball teams in the state, from historical sites and landmarks around the state to world news and celebrities.

All the chattering and joking and reluctance to hang up added up to a three-hour phone call.

The search for Amanda's son began very slowly. Natalie had been in the library for two hours before she remembered that Henry was Amanda's second husband's name. The Internet gave her only limited information on an Amanda Henry because she didn't have her social security number. She did remember that Amanda had said she had changed back to her maiden name after her first divorce. After a morning without results in the library, Natalie decided to go by Amanda's office and house.

Amanda's maiden name was Staples. She couldn't believe she had forgotten that. They had often joked about Amanda being part of a singing family but not being able to carry a tune. At the office, she looked through Amanda's files for any clue to a former life. At the house, she found Amanda's social security number on some business papers in her desk drawer, but she didn't find a marriage license or birth certificate.

The day's detective work had left her tired and a bit frustrated. It was hard being Natalie Davidson, P.I. But she decided to stick with her plans for the day and head over to her latest acquisition.

Even after having acquired close to forty houses, every new purchase was still satisfying. She was making a very nice living and helping others at the same time.

As she neared the property, the construction noise reminded Natalie to compose a letter of apology to the surrounding homeowners, especially those mothers sitting at home furious that they can't get their babies to sleep.

She parked up the street and walked toward the house. Just the prospect of seeing Thorne made her anxious. Despite their three-hour phone gabfest she was still eager to hear his voice again.

As Natalie stepped onto her driveway, the beep of a car horn caused her to turn around; her bad morning became a bad afternoon. Nicholas was pulling up to the curb. He had been calling her almost nonstop since the scene at the restaurant. She had stopped answering his calls to her cellphone and had put a block on the home phone for all his phone numbers. *Lord,* please *don't let him cause a scene.*

"Hey, babe," he said, jumping out of his new burgundy Lexus coupe and handing her a bouquet of flowers.

Natalie was irked by the use of 'babe' and by his very presence. "What are those for, Nicholas?" she asked, waving off the gift.

"Call them a peace offering," he answered, catching up with her as she continued walking toward the house.

She looked at him suspiciously. "A peace offering?"

"Yes." He stopped and put a hand on her arm. She stiffened, so he eased his hold but didn't let go. "Now can we forget about that little argument we had at the restaurant the other day?"

"*We* didn't have an argument; *you* did." She pulled away from him. "And stop touching me."

"Now, Natalie, look—"

"No, Nicholas, you look," she said, cutting him off. Turning to face him, and unaware that her voice had risen or that the construction noise had stopped, she continued: "I told you once that I do not wish to be involved with you anymore. I thought that we could remain friends, but now I doubt that even that is possible. This has become borderline harassment."

"Harassment? You've got to be kidding!" Nicholas spat out in disbelief.

"No, I'm not kidding at all."

He grabbed her arm and pulled her close to his face. His teeth clenched and his anger mounting, he hissed, "Just who in the hell do you think you are? You're just some . . ."

"Is there some kind of problem here?" Thorne asked, coming to stand next to Nicholas. Apparently, he had been observing the whole scene unfold.

Only three crewmembers had seen the look on Thorne's face, but it only took three. When he put his clipboard down, so did the foreman, who then walked over with him. Other members of the crew began to gather. In minutes all work had ceased. The unexpected silence caused the workers inside the house to come outside and investigate.

"Mind your own business," Nicholas warned before turning to see who had dared to interrupt his harangue. "Oh, Thorne, I didn't know it was you," he said, looking slightly embarrassed.

"It's me," Thorne replied.

"I'm just having a conversation with Natalie. We seem to be having a minor disagreement. But everything is under control."

"Is that true, Natalie?" Thorne turned and looked at her. He saw that she was mad, very mad.

"No, it's not true," she said, seizing the chance to set Nicholas straight and to make her position known to the world. "Now that I have an audience, I'll repeat myself. Nicholas Dowing, I don't want to have anything else to do with you. You and I are no longer dating each other, if that's what you want to call it. I don't ever want to see you again. Please have a joyous life with whoever will accept your shortcomings."

His eyes flashed fire. She had the nerve to try to embarrass him and degrade his manhood. Blind with fury, Nicholas clenched his fist reflexively and took a step toward her.

Thorne quickly stepped into his path. "Whoa . . . now, Nick, I know you don't think that's a good idea. There are too many of us out here counting on this lady and her employment for us to let you do whatever it is you're thinking."

"Natalie, I want to talk to you in private," Nicholas demanded.

"No, Nicholas. Good-bye." *He must be crazy to think I would actually walk off with him away from my protection, especially after what he just did.* She tried to walk past him, but he grabbed her arm.

"This is not over, Natalie," he growled, applying as much pressure as he could to her arm.

She winced in pain.

"Oh, yes, it is."

Before Nicholas could realize it wasn't Natalie's voice he had heard, Thorne had landed two hard blows to his jaw and eye.

Nicholas stumbled backward, but immediately regained his balance and instinctively raised his fists.

One of the men grabbed Natalie and pulled her away from the fracas. She was now in the midst of about seven or so men itching to see a fight. Her own adrenaline began pumping. This, she thought, was going too far. Scared out of her wits for Thorne, she bolted from the group but was quickly pulled back in.

The two men began to walk around slowly, warily sizing each other up. Meantime, the crew acted as if they were ringside at a boxing match.

"You can take him, boss."

"Watch out, little man; the boss is a beast."

"He looks like the sucker-punch type."

"All right, now, get him, boss."

"Just like old times, huh, Thorne," Nicholas asked, initiating a verbal mano a mano.

"Seems so, Nick," Thorne replied, keeping his eyes on his old playmate.

"Tell me, why were you so quick to come to the lady's aid? It's not like you to butt into other people's business."

"As I said, she pays the bills."

"Well, let's get this on then. Will I have to fight all your friends, too?"

"No, that's not how we do things."

Neither man appeared to hear Natalie's loud protests. But just as they came together, the sound of a siren pierced the air. Natalie jumped at the chance to step between them.

"I can't believe you two," she scolded.

"What?" Thorne asked, hunching his shoulders. "I told you last night how it was."

"Last night?" Nicholas asked, realization finally dawning. "Oh, I see." He turned to Natalie. "Now, I see. You got your hooks into the rich white boy over here. Now poor black me isn't good enough for you."

"Nicholas, I'm not like that, and you know it. You and I have never had a real relationship; you just refused to see it."

"I see it all clearly now. But don't worry, when master here is finished visiting the slave quarters, come see me. I might be willing to take you back."

"You bastard," Natalie said, slapping him as hard as she could across his face. That felt good, but not nearly good enough. She was about to slap him again, but Thorne grabbed her hand.

"Natalie, he's not worth it. Nicholas, just stay away from her."

Nicholas looked into Thorne's steel-gray eyes, the eyes of a man he had furiously hated his whole life. *Who does he think he is, ordering me around? I don't work for him. I'm not one of his servants.* Nicholas had thought that he was over the bitter jealousy and resentment he had grown up harboring for Thorne. They no longer moved in the same circles, hadn't even seen each other in years. But here Thorne was once again taking what was his. First, it was his grandmother's time and love, now Natalie.

Nicholas saw the challenge in Thorne's eyes. He could see that Thorne would have loved to go a few rounds with him. They had each taken his share of bumps and bruises from the other during their younger years.

"We'll see, Thorne, we'll see," he said, still seething. Then he abruptly turned away and walked to his car. A patrol car pulled in front of Natalie's house as he pulled off.

⌒

"Look, Natalie," Thorne said, sitting at the kitchen table in Natalie's house, "I hope you don't think too much about what that asshole said today. Nicholas has always hated me. Even as kids, he was jealous and saw me as the cause of his problems. He went to a great school, has good friends, nice women, a good job, and still he's not happy with his life. Now he's thinking that I've taken you from him, and I guess that I kind of did." He felt a twinge of guilt, but swiftly pushed it away before adding, "Natalie, the race thing isn't an issue here. I want to be with you because of you. I'm not some young boy sniffing out a fine black woman just out of curiosity. You're not the first black woman I've dated."

That earned him a very stern look. "So you've already said. Could you keep that to yourself? I don't want to keep hearing about it."

"Jealousy won't get you anywhere," he teased, handing her a tomato from the shopping bag.

"Shut up, Thorne," she ordered.

"Come here." He tried to grab her, but she ducked out of reach.

"Thorne!" she said, exasperated. He was beginning to make her already tattered nerves worse. Her nieces were meeting Thorne for the first time, and she was feeling a bit anxious.

"Fine, I'll bring them over to you." He put the salad greens and vegetables on the sink and backed her against it.

Natalie turned and began washing the vegetables, but he came up behind her and braced his hands on either side of the counter top, basically trapping her. She ignored him. He edged closer.

"Thorne, what are you doing? We are not going to do this."

"I'm not doing anything; just driving myself crazy." He had pushed aside her hair and had begun kissing her behind the ear. Natalie liked what he was doing, involuntarily leaning back against him.

His erection strained against his faded jeans as her body moved against his. Natalie was surprised by the size of him and her body's response.

Thorne kissed her face and her neck, at the same time gliding his hands over her body. He cupped her breasts and squeezed her nipples lightly until they were erect. He slid one hand under her shirt while using the other hand to span her belly, hips and thighs.

"God, Natalie, you feel good."

Natalie was beyond words. Her food forgotten, she moaned between his kisses and ran her hands through his hair.

Thorne was beside himself, minutes from just ripping off her clothes. His hands moved frantically, gripping her hips to hold her snug against him.

"Natalie, um, I had better stop."

Flexing his fingers, he unbuttoned and then unzipped her jeans. Natalie turned her face up and began nibbling on his lips. Thorne moved fast into the kiss. Their tongues worked in tandem, sparking flames through their bodies.

GADSDEN COUNTY
PUBLIC
LIBRARY
732 Pat Thomas Hwy. Quincy, FL. 32351

With one hand he massaged her neck while pushing the other hand down her jeans and into her panties until he covered her. He felt her shiver when his fingers played with the soft nest hiding her sweetness. He moved his hand from her throat and lifted her bra; he could weigh her in his palm.

She moaned when Thorne spread apart the lips that closed over her intimacy and dove into her softness.

"Natalie . . . Natalie . . ." he whispered in her ear.

"Aunt Natalie, we're home," Tracey called out as soon as she opened the front door.

Natalie and Thorne froze for a split second. By the time Tracey and Lindsey, followed by their father, reached the kitchen, Natalie was once again washing the vegetables, and Thorne was sitting very uncomfortably at the table.

He kept his attention on the children, asking them questions about school and their friends until the frenzied heat of passion released its hold on his body. *Tomorrow,* he promised himself, *tomorrow, we'll go get those damn tests done.*

For the third day that week, Natalie sat at an old, wooden desk in the corner of a small, dusty room in the basement of the state's county building. At the beginning of the week, she had telephoned the vital statistics office and was told the information she needed could not be given over the phone. They also told her that marriage licenses dating back more than twenty years had not been put on the computer, but were still in manual files in the office.

When she arrived at vital statistics, an older woman named Blanche helped direct her to a room filled with bulging crates of old papers.

Natalie was not going to look at every license in every crate, so she figured out a year with which to logically begin her search. Amanda was fifty-eight years old and had been married forty years ago. Natalie decided to start with that year.

She and Blanche pulled out twelve crates for that year. Each crate contained a month's worth of marriage licenses. Natalie found it hard to believe that so many people in this county alone got married per month, but Blanche informed her that the licenses were for the entire state. The records had been sent to this building for storage until they could be put on disks.

It had been rough going for a while. Blanche left after helping her pull out the boxes. Natalie was bored out of her mind and found herself frequently daydreaming about Thorne.

She hadn't seen him since the night he had dinner with her family the week before. He was out of town on business again. They talked nightly, with him always asking if she had gone to the doctor yet. It had become a running joke between them. He would be back in town Saturday, and they planned to have dinner and watch a movie at his house. She didn't even know where his house was.

On day two, Blanche offered to help her look through the pile of marriage certificates. After she learned the reason for Natalie's investigation, she became intrigued and was eager to be a part of the search.

"This is such a good thing you're doing for your friend," the gray-haired, stocky woman said, slowly flipping through the licenses, careful not to damage her perfectly manicured nails.

"I just hope that I can find her son soon." Natalie hated to think of anything worse happening to Amanda, but the reality of the situation was very frightening.

"I just can't stop this strange feeling that I've heard that name before—Amanda Staples. I seem to remember hearing something about her." Blanche stopped flipping the papers for a moment and looked up at the ceiling as if trying to summon a memory. Then she lowered her head, her face still blank. "I just don't know. I want to say that there was some scandal behind it, but back in the day, what wasn't? There was so much gossip going on about this and that."

Natalie listened closely, suspecting that the gossip had to be something racial. Amanda did say that her first husband had been a white man. That would have caused a good bit of gossip back then. "Have you lived here your whole life, Ms. Blanche?"

"Yes, dear. My folks were from here, too. Unfortunately, we came from the poorer side of town. But my parents did the best they could for us. My sister married into a good family. Of course, she had to practically disown my parents and me. I think that I resented her for it, but they were happy for her. She had a good life and never forgot about us. She even put me through college."

"Why did she have to dissociate herself from her family?" Natalie asked.

"Child, back then, times were very different. There was so much prejudice. We were what was called poor white trash. Her husband was wealthy—from old money. His parents didn't really want him to marry her. But they finally accepted her after they made her over, made her debutante material."

"I feel sorry for her."

"I didn't at first because I was younger, and I didn't understand. But then I found out what my sister had put up with just to be with the man she loved. Even though they changed her manners, her speech, and her appearance, they never let her forget where she came from, that she was beneath them. She was the least favorite out of their three daughters-in-law. They never hid that fact."

"So to be with the man she loved, she chose to sacrifice everything?"

"You know what? My sister died of an aneurysm four years ago. I've never seen a man more distraught than her husband at her funeral. Now he visits her gravesite once a week, planting flowers or cleaning up or just sitting next to the tombstone talking to her. So I often ask myself was it such a huge sacrifice?"

As Natalie listened to her new friend, she, too, was mulling that question. "To be loved by a man that much—well, a few ignorant people wouldn't stop me," Blanche continued. "His parents and some other family members might have given her a hard time, but that man loved my sister."

"So a love that great would be worth a small sacrifice?"

"And that was how she saw it. After my sister and I talked things out, we became inseparable. She was my best friend," she confided, her eyes bright with held-back tears. "You know, a lot of people did a lot of crazy things back then for love. Girl, I could tell you some stories."

"I bet you could," Natalie said. The both laughed, and the sadness slipped away.

"But I won't, out of respect," Blanche said, laughing louder. "This is a good thing that you're doing, though. Your friend will be so happy when she finds her son. You know sometimes family is all we got."

"I just hope he wants to be found." Suddenly, a new possibility occurred to Natalie. What if he didn't want to meet his mother? What if he had a bad life and blamed it on her leaving? She was going to have to meet this man first. In her present state, there was no way Amanda would be able to handle rejection and blame.

By the end of the day, Natalie and Blanche had gone through seven boxes without finding Amanda's marriage license. But a camaraderie had been formed. The two women had lunch together and talked mostly about how life used to be and the differences between that world and today's world.

She gave Natalie hope that her search would uncover something useful in the end and that everything eventually would work out for the best. Feeling renewed after the all-day search, Natalie stopped by the hospital on her way home to see Amanda.

The doctor said she was doing better but was heavily medicated, which kept her in a state of drowsiness. He assured her that it was best that she be well rested. Natalie sat on the side of Amanda's bed and watched her sleep for an hour and then headed home. She prayed that she would be able to do what her friend asked of her.

On her third day in the storage room, she was alone and working on the fourth box in the stack. She was expected to speak at a home-ownership seminar at three. It was now one-fifteen. Knowing her problem with punctuality, she decided to stop early. Natalie was reaching for the box's cover when the name on the next sheet caught her eye. Amanda Staples. *Praise the Lord.*

Trying hard to keep her excitement under cover, Natalie picked up the paper and read the names: Amanda Jean Staples and Matthew Charles Philips married September 12, 1965. Matthew. That was the name Amanda had given her in the hospital.

Natalie ran to the old copier in the corner of the room and made five copies of the document. She returned the original to the box and then hurried off to her seminar.

Okay, she thought, walking up the front steps of her house, I'm a step closer. She was going to do this. She was actually going to find Amanda's son. Natalie had the name of Amanda's first husband. All she had to do now was figure out how to find the name of the son. If she had time in the morning, she would have to call Blanche to ask her a few questions about birth certificates.

Stephen and his girls were already home. They had planned to surprise Natalie with a home-cooked meal of pork chops, mashed potatoes and gravy, and green beans. Not wanting to ruin their surprise, she stayed away, waiting for them to call her.

Natalie was in the living room going through the mail when she saw the white envelope. It had no stamp or postmark, just her name on the front of it. Curiosity got the better of her, so she ripped it open along the seal.

If you value your life and the life of your sick friend, you will put a stop to this silly little investigation of yours. You have no idea what may happen to you.

Fear raced through her so fast that her hand went numb and the letter fell to the floor. The message was entirely in block print letters and had no signature.

A scream worked its way up her throat, and once it started, she couldn't stop it. She didn't mean to scare the girls, but hell, she was scared. Stephen was by her side in a split second. While holding her hand he checked for signs of physical distress.

"What is it? Natalie, what is it?" he asked over and over.

She couldn't get her mouth to open, the fear increased when she pointed at the letter. Trying to calm herself, Natalie began walking aimlessly around the room. But when she saw her frightened nieces she forced herself to sit down beside them.

"Come here, girls," she said calmly.

They did as they were told and hugged Natalie as if to protect her from whatever had scared her. Stephen read the letter then went to the phone.

"What are you doing?" Natalie asked.

"I'm calling the police. Do you have any idea who this is from?"

"NO . . . Nobody knows that I'm trying to find Amanda's son. Oh, God, what if someone tries to hurt her? She's always drugged up. I have to go." She started to rise, but he stopped her.

"No, you don't. You're not going anywhere. I'll call the hospital. The cops will know best how to handle this."

A sudden knock at the front door caused everybody to jump. Stephen went to answer it, and was gone for a while.

"Stephen?" Natalie finally choked, thinking the worst. Her imagination had taken control of her.

"I'm coming," he answered. But she heard footsteps coming toward her even when his voice sounded far away.

She was surprised and relieved when Thorne came into the room and rushed to her side.

"Hey, love, are you all right? Stephen just filled me in. Hi, Tracy, Lindsey."

He wrapped his arms around her, which had a calming effect on her frazzled nerves.

Tracy and Lindsey walked over to their father and sat on his lap. He tried to talk them into eating, but they wanted to wait for everyone, especially since Thorne was there. His approval of their cooking was a must.

"Now, Natalie, what exactly are you trying to investigate for your friend, Amanda?" Thorne asked, now sitting beside her on the couch.

"Thorne, I already told you. She asked me to find her long-lost son. When she first tried to find him, the boy's grandfather told her that he and his father had died in a car accident, but she doesn't believe that. After receiving this letter, neither do I."

"Okay, have you found out anything that might be a threat to anyone?" Stephen asked.

"Not really. Oh, Thorne, I wanted to ask you if you knew someone named, um, wait; I have a copy of the marriage license I found today. Here it is. Um, Matthew Charles Philips. I wondered if he was a distant relative or something." She looked up at him when he remained silent. His face showed shock and bafflement. "Thorne?"

"Matthew Charles Philips?"

"Yeah. See?" She handed him the paper. "He's the man Amanda was married to." Thorne looked sick. "Thorne, what is it?"

"That was my father. Matthew Charles Philips was my father."

Natalie's mouth dropped, as did Stephen's. "Are you sure? I mean—"

"Of course I'm sure. I know who my father was. There must be some kind of mistake; my mother was his first wife." Thorne began pacing the room as he read the marriage license a third time. He didn't like the way these tables were turning. "I was young, but I can't remember anyone being in his life before he married Susan, Michael and Theresa's mother."

"Well, there has to be some explanation. Is there anyone you could talk to about it?"

Thorne thought for a minute. "Sure, there are family members who would know. My grandfather, for one, but the chances of him talking to me, let alone telling me anything, are pretty slim. We don't exactly like each other. I wouldn't be surprised if he already knows about all this. It would not be beneath him to put little spies on my brother and sister and me or on our friends. I'll definitely talk to Michael and Theresa in the morning. We could use the research department over at the head office." When Natalie looked at him, he explained: "Well, I now have an interest in your investigation, and I'm going to help you. Besides, won't you need a big strong man next to you, what with this threat business you've gotten yourself into? For some reason, somebody doesn't want you to find this man you're looking for."

The police officers finally left around nine-thirty, telling Natalie that a detective assigned to the case would probably be around the following morning. Natalie, Thorne, and Stephen were all exhausted. Stephen trudged off to bed, while she and Thorne arranged to meet with his family the next morning at the Philips headquarters to talk and strategize their research.

Natalie spent the rest of her night worrying about Thorne. Before leaving, he had assured her that he was fine. If he wasn't, she knew he would have told her. It was good to find a man who wasn't afraid to show or express his true feelings. Still, she worried about him, at the time wondering what kind of mess her friend had gotten her into.

Thorne slept like a log after calling Michael and Theresa, who was still in town. He was tired from the flight and all the meetings. Sitting in a boardroom going over purchases, selling, contracts, and the like took more of a toll on his body and mind than looking at blueprints and erecting buildings.

He told each of them about Natalie and what had happened. They were not surprised he had a new woman in his life, but were thoroughly surprised and, therefore, intrigued by the way he talked about her. Both siblings were more than willing to assemble first thing in the morning to meet her.

CHAPTER 8

Michael Philips stood at the wall of floor-to-ceiling windows in the conference room looking down twelve stories at the busy street below. Thorne studied him as he check the time for the second time since coming into the room. He guessed he should have told them that she would be late, but it didn't matter. His secretary had told him that they had both canceled all of their meetings before noon, as he knew they would for an emergency family meeting.

Michael was his pride and joy. He was so proud of the man that his brother had become. Not just his looks or his attire, which was always impeccable, but his quiet strength and gentle kindness. He was a man of intelligence and good instincts and had a calm, cool demeanor, all qualities that enhanced his natural leadership abilities.

"Thorne, I thought you said eight a.m."

Patience, however, Thorne thought, *was definitely in short supply.* That and his irritation with himself when he was struggling with a problem were almost unbearable.

"That's what time I did say. Just take it easy. You don't have anything to do right now. What's wrong with you, Michael?" He looked at his brother curiously. "Something has you pissed off."

"It's nothing," Michael replied, still undecided about whether to tell his brother that he had made a very huge mistake. He was sure Thorne would find out sooner or later; he always found out. Since childhood, he never could hide anything from Thorne for long.

"Come and have some coffee. Is it one of those stewardess friends of yours?" He smiled, knowing that would get his brother's dander up.

"No, it's not. Please, the last thing I would ever have trouble with is keeping a couple of women satisfied and under control." *Not the stewardesses you're talking about, anyway.* Playing off the comment as best he could, Michael joked with Thorne.

"Michael Andrew Philips, I can't believe I just heard you say that." This came from Theresa, who had finished a phone conversation with her son, who was back in Texas with his nanny. Their bond remained tight even when her work had her traveling back home to Louisiana. She was open with him, and that made him trust her even more.

"You weren't supposed to hear that."

"Well, I did. Now, apologize," she demanded on behalf of all womankind. Her brothers . . . she loved them to death, but they both needed to learn a lesson or two about women. She couldn't wait until they were both tied down and bound to a strong woman. All this womanizing was sickening.

"I'm sorry, Theresa, damn." Michael turned back to the window and continued watching the traffic. He needed to be alone with his thoughts.

"Excuse me. Obviously, you need to spend a little more time attending your church services instead of lying between the legs of those stewardesses you so easily satisfy."

"Now, Theresa, don't start in on him." Thorne intervened from his seat at the conference table, silencing her with a raised hand. "He obviously has some things on his mind. You know how he gets. And I don't need the two of you arguing this early in the morning."

"You're right, Thorne," Michael said, turning on his heel and strolling to the table. "Besides, I think she was about to revert to her filthy-mouth days." They all laughed. "To be honest, I don't think they ever left her."

"You're right about that. I can still get down and nasty with the best of them," Theresa replied, showing off her best pimp-walk around the room. At seventeen, Theresa had been trying to find herself in the projects and numerous housing units of New Orleans. Instead of hanging around with preppie socialite types, Theresa ran with a different crowd, fancying herself a roughneck, a thug. That's how she had met her son's father.

"It's hard to believe, looking at you today, that you were ever out in the streets, hanging with such a rough crowd. I remember Grandma chasing after you once when you snuck back into the house and got caught," Michael laughed.

Thorne's smile slowly brightened until it was identical to Michael's. He couldn't count the number of times he and Michael had gone out hunting for Ryan McGee because he had done one thing or another to their sister.

But no matter how bad things got between them, she wouldn't leave him.

When she was four months pregnant she had gone to their grandmother, beaten up and seething with anger and humiliation. She had caught Ryan in bed with one of her supposed girlfriends.

Theresa laughed. "Yeah, I think I ran around that room for about fifteen minutes. I thought she would tire out before me, but I was wrong. She beat me good behind that one."

When Natalie opened the door to the conference room, she felt a strong sense of longing. She saw Thorne smile and her heart skipped a beat, her pulse pounded. He was so ruggedly handsome.

Please, she prayed, *please just don't let my heart get broken.*

She knew she cared for this man deeply already. They had known each other less than a month, but her heart was reacting to the sight of him, his voice, and his laughter. Natalie acknowledged that she was falling in love with him, and all her nervousness slipped in to grip her. But at the same time, she was thrilled.

Thorne's smile froze when he saw her standing in the doorway watching him. His gaze was riveted on her face, then slowly slid down her whole body. No matter how many times he saw her, he would never get used to it. She had a fresh and gentle beauty that made her look more delicate than she really was.

With a shiver of recollection, he remembered that as a child he liked to sneak into the laundry room whenever they played hide and seek. He would climb into the dryer with the freshly washed towels all around him. He loved to squeeze them and breathe in the fresh scent of the wash. That's what he wanted right at that moment—to hold and squeeze her and breathe in her scents.

Putting his fantasy aside, Thorne rose and went to meet her. She didn't know how to greet him; he could tell by the way she uneasily glanced at his siblings. Thorne crossed the room, taking charge of the situation with quiet assurance.

"Ah, here she is, guys," he said. "Hi." Stopping in front of her, the smile in his eye containing a sensual flame.

"Hi." She returned his smile and stepped into his out-stretched arms.

Thorne took hold of her arms and bent down to kiss her. Pulling her into his embrace, he showered kisses around her ears and along her jaw.

Natalie was lost in the tenderness of his caresses. She had forgotten about Michael and Theresa and eagerly returned his kisses with abandonment. She wrapped her arms around his waist as joy bubbled up inside her.

Michael cleared his throat after a minute of watching this display of affection because, one, he was still mad about the conversation he had the night before with his now ex-girlfriend; and two, jealously was an unwanted emotion.

Slowly, Thorne pulled away. When he released her, she swayed against him still, unable to focus.

Theresa regarded them with amusement as Natalie let out a long breath and Thorne led her to the seat next to his.

"Show off," Michael whispered behind Thorne's back. This only caused Thorne to wink at him and widen his smile. "All right, can we get started now?" With a deliberately slow movement, he turned and faced Natalie, giving her body a rakish gaze. She was beautiful, he thought. His big brother had excellent taste.

Michael especially liked the bronze tone of her skin and the way it seemed to shimmer and shine as she moved. He also liked her teeth. Perfectly straight white teeth were one of his weaknesses. She had a small waist, which flared into agilely round hips and a nice plush, but firm, backside. He did not try to hide his great appreciation. Out of the corner of his eye, he saw one of Thorne's black eyebrows arch in protest. Because he was not about miss an opportunity to irk his brother, Michael took hold of both her hands.

"My goodness; Natalie, is it? I must say you are truly beautiful. My brother barely scratched the surface when he told me you had a pretty face." He held her hand delicately, entrancing her with his compliments. "I am Michael Philips, and I'm definitely at your service. Could I please get you a cup of coffee, or some tea, perhaps?"

"Well, coffee would be nice, thank you." She didn't miss the look Thorne sent Michael's way. "Please forgive me for being late. I know how important your time is."

"Oh, don't even think about it. It was a privilege to wait for someone as beautiful as you."

She blushed. From embarrassment, Michael thought, but Thorne thought it might have been something else. That was all it took for him to send an elbow into Michael's ribcage. She was about to get upset until she heard Theresa's gentle laugh ripple above the play-fighting.

"Don't pay them any attention. Hi," she said, her hand extended for and receiving a firm shake. "I'm Thorne's sister, Theresa. It is nice to meet you." The two women liked each other immediately. When they looked up again, Thorne had Michael in a headlock.

Michael, ever ready to irritate, said mockingly, "Natalie, dear, don't worry about me. I let him do this occasionally to keep the sibling rivalry alive and well in our family."

Her eyes sparkled as she watched the horseplay, and then they settled down to begin the meeting. "It's hard to believe that two corporate bigwigs use the boardroom as a wrestling ring."

Thorne sat next to her with Michael and Theresa across the small table. "Oh, we only do it to release tension," Thorne replied, his eyes wide with good humor.

"I would think that two good-looking men such as yourselves could think of other ways to release tension."

Thorne captured her eyes with his. "Oh, believe me, we think plenty. Have you met Theresa?"

"Yes, while you and your twin there were playing Stone Cold and The Rock."

"Good," Thorne began. "Now let's get started. I already told Michael and Theresa about your investigation and what you have found so far."

Natalie noticed how he had instantly switched to an all-business posture.

"Natalie, if our father was married to your friend, then we have an older brother out there somewhere that we never knew about," Theresa said, shaking her head. "It just doesn't make sense."

"According to this license," Michael added, "your friend was married to our father on September 12, 1962. Well, it must have been a very short marriage, because Thorne was born February 15, 1963. Did you find a divorce decree?"

"No, I didn't look for one. That may as well be the next step. Maybe she was pregnant before they got married. Or they only got married to give the baby a name. You know back then biracial offspring would have been a lot more taboo then they are now. Your father probably thought that he was doing the right thing by marrying her."

"But you said that she left and gave the baby to him, right?" Thorne asked. "I don't believe that he would have married any woman just to give the baby a name. Michael and Theresa didn't know our father that well before he died, but they've heard enough about him to know the kind of man he was."

"We agree with you, Thorne," Theresa commented. "If he married this friend of yours, Amanda, there is no doubt in our minds that he loved her."

"And she told me that they were very much in love," Natalie agreed. "She said she left when her son turned two."

"So I should have noticed another baby running around the house," Thorne muttered uneasily. "Wait, so she left him in 1964?"

"Not necessarily. She said she left him two years after her baby was born. We don't know when the baby was born," Natalie replied, choosing her words carefully.

Theresa picked up the phone during a lull, during which she fought for self-control. "Please transfer me to research. David, hi, this is Theresa. Do me a favor, please. I would like to use the computer in the conference room to do some research. I just need to know the system ID's to enable the use of county, state, and federal databases . . . yes, yes, thank you, David." Looking at the rest of the group, she seemed very pleased with herself. "Okay, troops, let's get to work. Thorne, turn on that printer."

"Oh, boy, Natalie, you've gotten her started." Michael chuckled. "Let me call April and tell her to cancel my appointments for the rest of the day."

"Tell her to have Michele cancel mine also, Michael." Thorne took off his jacket and loosened his tie.

"You might as well tell her to call Kimberly, too," Theresa called out. While Michael was on the phone he also called the cafe to place a lunch order to be brought up later. He had a feeling it was going to be a long day.

Four hours and four pair of bleary eyes later, the group decided to break for lunch. Information was emerging, but at a slower pace than they had expected.

The search for a divorce decree was easy and produced results quickly. They used the two names and the date of the marriage along with their father's social security number that Michael had found in the company's internal records, and the decree appeared onscreen almost immediately and was sent to the printer. It was dated March 20, 1965.

As the search progressed, Thorne became increasingly quiet, his mouth finally twisting into a sour grin. Something was not right with the picture coming forth. Fear of the unknown was snaking up his back, causing his neck hairs to stand on end, and he didn't like the feeling. He sensed that a happy ending was not to be the outcome of their little investigation.

"Thorne, are you sure that was her full name?" Michael asked hesitantly, torn by conflicting emotions. He saw the troubled look on his brother's face. "Maybe it's the wrong name; maybe that's why we can't find a marriage license or death certificate for her."

"Michael, right now, I'm not sure of anything. I know that Grandma and Old Matthew always gave me the same name." He began intoning the words that were embedded in his head from years of reciting them: "My mother's name was Maria Annette Gamio. She was the daughter of Italian-American parents. She married my father, became pregnant with me, and died during my birth. They told me that her parents didn't want anything to do with me because I reminded them too much of her. That's why they never came around."

"Is that all they told you?" Michael asked in an odd but gentle tone.

"Yes. After a while, I guess I stopped asking questions. I had Grandma, and she gave me more than enough love." His voice was husky with emotion.

"Well, Michael and I certainly agree with you there," Theresa said, reaching out and stroking his hand. "Let's see now. The facts are, one, Dad was married to Amanda Staples from 1962 to 1965; two, Thorne was born in 1963; and, three, we don't have any record of a Maria Gamio. Okay, now I think we need to find a birth certificate for any child born to Amanda and Matthew Philips Jr. Agreed?"

Everyone agreed, and after lunch they resumed their search. Natalie stayed close to Thorne. She could tell by the distinct hardening of his eyes that he was becoming agitated by the whole process.

"Thorne, could I talk to you for a moment in private?"

"Sure, Nat." He led her into one of the side offices. "Is something wrong?"

"I just want you to know that I'm very sorry for dragging you and your family into this mess. If I had known that it would go this far, I would have never gotten you involved like this."

"Come here, Natalie." Thorne pulled her into an embrace and kissed her forehead. "I can't honestly tell you that I like the way things are looking right now, but it's certainly not your fault. Anything that we find out is long overdue. Family secrets are never good, and they don't stay secrets for long. But I do thank you for your concern."

"You know what, Thorne Philips?" she asked, keeping her voice light.

"What?"

"I think if I don't watch myself, I could easily fall in love with you and your honest ways."

Thorne's face broke into a wide grin, and his eyes flashed a hint of mischief. "We are still on for dinner and movies later, right?"

"Yes, we are," she answered, pulling his head down until his lips brushed against hers. The kiss had just begun to deepen when Michael opened the door.

"Thorne, man, I think you two should see this if you can keep apart for a second. We found a birth certificate." They returned to the conference room just as the printer began cranking out a document.

"Michael, grab that off the printer for me." Cluing in Thorne and Natalie, she added, "We found a birth certificate for a male child born to Amanda and Dad. Thorne, I don't think you're going to like this."

"What do you mean, Theresa?" Natalie asked, partly eager to know, partly dreading the knowledge.

"Well, according to this birth certificate, and mind you, this doesn't mean anything yet, but according to this," she took the paper from Michael and held it out to them, "their child was born on February 15, 1963."

Thorne was momentarily speechless, grabbing the paper and studying at it. "What? That can't be possible. The name on this birth certificate is for a male child named Matthew Charles Philips III. Who the hell is that?" Thorne was visibly upset, experiencing a gamut of perplexing emotions. He sat down at the table and pressed his open palms to his eyes.

Natalie immediately went to him and began rubbing his back. "Maybe we should stop. It's been a long, hectic day, and we all probably need to take a break." Natalie's suggestion was prompted by her concern for Thorne.

"That sounds good to me, Natalie. I, for one, am tired of this investigation. Theresa and I will cancel our meetings for Monday morning, and we can pick up where we left off. How does that sound?"

"That sounds great, Michael." Theresa agreed, also concerned for Thorne. "I'm leaving for the weekend, but I'll see you guys bright and early on Monday morning."

"Are you leaving for the airport soon, Theresa? I wanted to invite you all to my sisters' bar and restaurant for happy hour."

"Actually, I do need to leave right away. My son is waiting for me, and I miss him terribly."

At age seven, her son had adapted well to the living in Texas. But Theresa still felt a tremendous amount of guilt for having him shuttered away at the exclusive private school. Guilt was what led to her purchase of an apartment nearby so she could be closer to him. She stayed there on weekends so that they could spend as much time together as possible. A company helicopter flew her to the country-side every Friday after work and back Sunday evenings. It was an incredibly tiring and difficult commute, but for her son's safety it was an easy sacrifice to make.

"Well, tell the little man that Uncle Michael said hi and to keep up the good work in school. Oh, and I plan to call him and offer him a temporary position as my assistant during his next school break if he can come home for a while." She nodded absently, and he turned his attention to Natalie. "I, for one, would love to accompany you to happy hour." He bounced cross the room, and placed an arm around her shoulder. "Thorne, will you be joining us?"

If anybody could pull him out of his current stupor, it was Michael. He and his brother knew each other well, sometimes too well. They also loved each other too much to let the other hurt for long.

"You better believe I'll be joining you!" He pushed Michael away from Natalie, putting an arm around her waist possessively, his concerns briefly forgotten. "Do you think I would let you alone with one of my women?"

"One of your women?" Natalie pushed his arm away, studying him coolly.

"No. Now, Natalie, you know I didn't mean it like that." He pulled her back into his embrace. "You know what I meant . . . right?"

"I'll chalk that up to a slip of the tongue, but don't let it happen again." She forced a modicum of dignity into her voice and walked to the door of the conference room. "I'll see you Monday, Theresa, have a safe trip." She called behind her, every curve of her body shouting defiance. She could hear Theresa teasing Thorne as he kissed her good-bye.

"You'll have to stay on your toes with this one, Thorne."

"Don't I know it, but I think that's going to be half the fun." He followed Natalie out of the office and let the bad feelings he had toward the day's finds stay in the room. The weekend was here and he was determined to not allow any worries to ruin his time alone with her.

CHAPTER 9

Happy hour was always busy at Noah's Ark. Young professionals would loosen their ties, take off their double-breasted suit jackets and just relax, perhaps with a game of pool, a cold beer, or a song selected from an old jukebox Natalie had found at a defunct bar she had been considering buying. Singles knew it was a good time to meet and greet friends and to make new acquaintances. Homebound married people used the time as a kind of respite before continuing homeward. With more people out than usual, Friday's happy hour was especially busy.

Michael went up to the bar and Thorne and Natalie sat at one of the few empty tables in the restaurant area. They were eating there so they wouldn't have to rush off to the movies. Michael's eyes had a hint of envy as he watched them, even though he was happy for his brother. They were an attractive couple and seemed to be well suited. Thorne was a good man and long overdue for a good woman. His brother never allowed any of his former female friends to swindle or use him, but it seemed that every woman either of them had been involved with only wanted one thing from them—money.

He was glad for Thorne because Natalie truly seemed to be a very different kind of woman; she was exactly what his brother needed. Thorne would definitely need

Natalie's support if the results of this investigation turned out to be as bad as it appeared to be. Picking up his half-empty glass, he decided to cover up at least part of his own miseries with alcohol.

As if the situation with the stewardess wasn't enough, he had to break off his current involvement. Susan, his most recent disappointment, would be easily dealt with. He had practically convinced himself that he had finally found the right girl. They had a couple of things in common and got along reasonably well. She wasn't the smartest person in the world, but what she lacked in smarts she made up in ambition and hard work, loyally toiling for a reputable brokerage. Their physical relationship wasn't great, but it was coming along. She seemed terribly shy, afraid to let loose and enjoy herself. But he had been working on that. Now he would have to forget about her.

As much as he wanted to settle down and start a family, Michael knew it would have to be with someone who could love him and not his money. He had made a promise to himself, just as he was sure that Thorne had, not to settle for less than he deserved. That was probably why it was taking all three of them so long to marry.

Just the night before he had almost made the biggest mistake in his life and asked Susan to marry him. The ring was still in the bottom drawer of his dresser. Luckily, when he came out of the bathroom after his shower, she hadn't heard him, but he had heard her talking to one of her friends about how she had him and how she was going to be rich and the envy of all her friends. He stayed in the background until she finished her phone conversation, then he told her he had a busy day ahead and a lot of work, so she couldn't stay the night. He took her home, kissed her goodnight, and thanked God for giving him a warning. Michael finished his beer and was about to leave for home when he heard her.

"Excuse me . . . hello. Are you all right?" Her tone was casual, displaying just a touch of concern.

"Oh, I'm sorry. I didn't hear you," Michael said, turning to focus on the body belonging to the voice. He was instantly interested in what he saw. "Can I help you?" His eyes roamed over her body.

"That's what I was just saying to you. Let me get you a refill. You look as if you may need it. She must have been some woman," Tamia said, smiling and wondering the cause of his distress.

"I thought she was, but I was wrong." Shrugging, he smiled back, then glanced over at Natalie and Thorne, who were totally engrossed in each other.

"Nice-looking couple, huh?" Tamia said, curious after seeing the change on his face. After all, that was one way to see how he felt about interracial couples.

Michael's brightened, thinking that the lady must not object to interracial dating. "Yeah, looks like he's one lucky bastard."

"He is? You sound a little envious."

"I guess I am." He extended his hand, amusement flickering in his eyes. "By the way, name's Michael."

"Hi, Michael," Tamia said shaking his hand and leaning against the bar facing him. "So, is she forgotten yet?"

Michael looked at the woman across from him, saw her pencil-thin brow inching up, and weighed his options. "Who?" he replied with a smile, curious to see what would happen next.

"You didn't have any kids with her?" Tamia asked, trying to put all the pieces together.

"No, no kids. I believe you should be married before children start popping into the picture. And I'm very glad I didn't go that far with her."

"You were thinking about it?"

"You sure do ask a lot of questions."

"How else do you expect to find out what you want to know?"

"You seem to want to know a lot." Michael didn't think he was being smart or disrespectful. He was just irritated, and she was trying to get into his business.

"Hey, all you have to do is tell me to mind my own business. I just thought you looked as if you could use an ear, but if you want to be left alone, so be it."

Turning away without waiting for a reply, Tamia walked back to the kitchen, which was really her territory, anyway. She sensed an odd twinge of disappointment. She had stood in the doorway watching him for three or four minutes before she got up the courage to say anything to him at all. He looked familiar, but she couldn't quite put a finger on where she might have seen him. She slowly gazed at him from top to bottom, taking in his features and his impressive style of dress.

That in itself was difficult for her to accept. Men didn't usually put her off-guard. Her heart had been racing the whole time as she systematically memorized each pore on his clear, tanned face. She was caught off-guard by her reaction because it was fast and strong.

Being the adventurer that she was, Tamia had dated white men before, but something told her that this was different. He looked so sad—no, not sad, disappointed, and she felt compelled to try to cheer him up a little.

Now she was sorry she did as she hurried back into the kitchen to prepare salads and desserts for the dinner crowd. She liked him even more since she had heard the husky, deep silkiness of his voice and seen the fullness of his smile. Such were her thoughts as she butchered lettuce, dissected vegetables, and slammed bowls.

Michael was just finishing his second beer when he saw her walk back out to the bar. He had told himself that the only reason he was still there was to apologize to her for his earlier rudeness. She was only trying to cheer him up. He had been sitting at the bar not wanting to disturb the magic that Natalie and Thorne had woven around their table. He waited anxiously until he had her attention.

"Hi, can I get you a refill?" Tamya asked cheerfully as she approached him.

"Sure," Michael said hesitantly. Maybe he was reading the signals wrong or something, but she acted as if this was the first time she had ever seen him. They had talked long enough for her to remember him. *I must have really pissed her off.*

Not only that, but he wasn't as attracted to her as he thought he had been. She was still beautiful, just not as appealing to him. His pulse didn't quicken when he watched her turn and reach for another glass. He didn't feel the blood stir in his loins when he took a brief glance at her hips and backside.

"Listen, I want to apologize for . . ."

"Um, sir, I don't think you need to apologize to me." Tamya immediately knew she wasn't the one he should be talking to.

"Michael."

"Well, Michael . . ."

"Can't anyone even get a word in edgewise with you?" His patience was beginning to slip away from him. He worked hard on keeping that part of himself under control. "I really need to tell you something, okay?"

"Okay, if you insist, but I'm only trying to tell you that . . ."

"Shh . . ." Michael actually put a finger to his mouth and looked at her sternly as if he talking to a child. "Let me finish."

"Okay," Tamya said, laughing to herself. It probably was easier to just let him talk and then tell Tamia about it later.

Michael was about to speak when Thorne and Natalie walked up. "Hey, man, what happened to you? I thought you were coming back over to the table." He placed a hand on Michael's shoulder, giving it a squeeze.

"And mess up the vibes you had going on over there? You know, three is still a crowd."

"Not for family, Michael." Natalie moved over to put a hand on his arm. Michael looked from her to Thorne and smiled.

"Besides, if I had gone over there, I would have had no choice but to try to take you from him, and I wouldn't want to do that. You're actually the best thing that's happened to him in a long time."

"Well, that was a sweet thing to say. I see charm must run in the family. Speaking of family, I see you've met one of mine. Tamya, this is Thorne's brother, Michael. Michael, my sister Tamya."

"Hi, Michael, nice to meet you." She extended her hand, and once again he felt as if he was looking at a total stranger, not someone he had argued with earlier.

"You mean again, right?" he asked. "It's nice to meet you—again."

"No, I mean it's nice to meet you for the first time," she answered honestly.

Now he was really confused. Thorne and Natalie were sharing some private joke behind him, and he turned to see what was so funny. "What?" He didn't hear the steps coming from behind him as Tamia finally joined the group.

"Michael, turn around," Thorne said off-handedly.

He looked at Thorne and hunched his shoulders, but he did what he was told. Michael's mouth fell open when he turned around and saw both women standing behind the bar. He took a step back and bumped into Thorne's shoulder. A frown formed across his forehead as realization began to set in.

"Ha, ha, ha. I'm glad it was so funny. Everybody got a good laugh off Michael. It's been happening all week, no need for you all to be any different."

"Hey, Michael, ease up, man," Thorne scolded, wondering what was really behind his brother this inner turmoil. "It was just a little joke."

"Well, I don't see the humor in it, okay?" He turned to Thorne, releasing a long sigh as his shoulders dropped heavily. "Look, man, I've had a really bad day and last night wasn't any picnic, either. Maybe I should just go home. I don't want my bad mood to mess up your evening. Besides, happy hour is nearly over."

"I'm sorry, Michael," Tamya said, truly apologetic. "But I *was* trying to tell you."

"I know; it's all right. I should have known from your disposition that you weren't that one," he said, gesturing at Tamia.

"And what's that supposed to mean? Let me tell you something," Tamia was on her way around the bar to confront him directly.

He didn't want her anywhere near him. As much as he tried to fight it, his blood was already starting to heat up. The last thing he expected when she rounded the bar was to see her wearing an itsy-bitsy, teeny weenie black miniskirt with sheer black nylons and high-heel pumps. He damn near swallowed his tongue when it rolled back in his mouth. But because his brother was standing next to him intently watching the scene play out, he kept his cool and held himself together.

"I don't know who the hell she was," Tamia immediately started in, reaching her boiling point in no time, "or what she did to you, but don't start blaming whatever she did on me. I was trying very hard to be polite to you, and, to be honest, right now, you're very lucky you're Thorne's brother or you would be out of here with one of my bats sticking out the side of your head."

Michael wasn't listening to her. He saw the swell of her breast underneath the top edge of her white blouse and concentrated on the rise and fall pattern of her breathing as she vented her anger out on him.

"And for all that, you still owe me an apology for being such an asshole earlier," she snapped, finishing her ranting.

"Oh, shut up, would you?" Michael said nonchalantly. He and Thorne had so much in common, Natalie thought. All he had to say was one sentence to get his point across.

But she knew her sister, too. Tamia was the wild one, the one who was always ready for confrontation. This was going to be good. She took a seat on a stool and pulled Thorne over to stand by her. All eyes were fixed on the scene unfolding in front of them.

"Who in the hell do you think you are? I know you didn't just tell me to shut up." She spat her words out contemptuously, her voice rising a notch or two higher. Tamia was about to unleash her fury. Her neck moved in rhythm with her hands and hips as her temper flared.

"Excuse me. Tamia, we are in the middle of running a business. Maybe you and Michael would like to finish your discussion in the office where you can have some privacy and not draw more attention to yourselves," Tamya suggested, hoping to quell the fuss. Tamia usually didn't care where she was when she was on a roll.

"Good idea, Tamya, that way I can let you know what I really think about you, you arrogant, no good . . ."

"Yeah, whatever, save it. Thorne, I'm out of here." Enough is enough. As attracted as he was to her, he didn't have to take this kind of dressing down.

"That's right, run, just like a scared . . ."

Michael had taken enough from this little pain in the ass. He was going to go back in that office and let her have it. This was good; just what he needed was someone to let out all his pent-up anger on. He turned back to her, his green eyes ablaze.

"Lead the way, Ms. Tamia."

As he walked behind her into the room, Michael loosened his necktie and ran his fingers through his hair. But try as he may to stop himself, his eyes had a mind of their own. Every glance down was more painful than the last. Her bottom and legs, her calves and ankles tormented him mercilessly.

"So, what do you think?" Thorne asked Natalie.

"I don't know, but that was funny. Are you ready to start our date?"

"I sure am. What would you like to eat? I know you have the menu memorized."

"I was planning to have one of Tamia's specials, but since she's occupied let's just have a salad."

"Salad? Nat, you know I need more than that. You want my endurance level to be at its peak tonight, right?"

Natalie laughed at him, "Well, when you put it like that, how about oysters, clams, steak and potatoes for you?"

"Better," he said, his laughter reaching to his gray eyes.

It was too late for the movies when Natalie and Thorne left Noah's Ark. They had enjoyed themselves so much it was hard to leave. They decided to go to Thorne's house and watch movies. Thorne left his truck with Michael, who was still sitting at the bar enjoying the evening, and rode with Natalie. They both noticed that Michael and Tamia had remained respectfully calm after they came out of the office, but had kept their distance from each other. Michael was currently socializing with a pretty brunette who was insisting that they had met before.

Natalie was surprised when Thorne pulled into the garage at the front of the corporate headquarters building. "I thought you said we were going to your house."

"We are at my house, well, my penthouse. It's on the top floor of the building. Michael's is on the next floor and Theresa's is on the floor below that one."

"Oh, well, I guess that's convenient."

"It is; my house is in the country. I'll take you there some weekend. It is a nice getaway, but I couldn't take the long daily commute. The house we own in the city is currently occupied by my grandfather, whom no one particularly cares for."

"You mean to tell me that your grandfather is this close to you, and you don't go see him? None of you?"

"That's right, and before you start judging, you need to know all the facts. First of all, he doesn't like any of us, and we don't like him. Not all grandfathers are old fogy-stogies who dote on and spoil their grandkids. My grandfather is a very evil and hateful man. If it weren't for my grandmother, I would have left this city two weeks after I moved in with them. Now she was a kind soul."

"But if she was so kind and married your grandfather, then he must have had some good in him."

"To tell the truth, I don't think they really loved each other at all. They had an arranged marriage. After my father was conceived, I don't think they ever slept in the same bed again. Anyway, that's enough about my family."

He helped her out of the car and led her to the private elevator. Using his key, he opened the steel doors and pushed the button for the top floor. With the elevator door closed, she became sharply aware of his scent. With his sensational eyebrows and lashes, his full luscious lips, and his thin mustache and half goatee, he was easily the best-looking man Natalie had ever seen.

"So, what are we going to do tonight?" she asked, her eyes on those full lips as they turned up one of his slow and easy smiles.

"You have to ask?"

"Well, I would like to know what I'm getting myself into."

"Are you trying to tease me?" he asked, looking at her upturned face. *Beautiful.*

"Of course not. I'm not a tease." Nonetheless, she smiled seductively.

"I sure hope not. Did you bring a change of clothes?"

"I always keep a change of clothes in my trunk."

"Oh . . . why?"

"Because you never know. It's all about being prepared. My mom used to always tell us to be prepared for anything."

"And are you prepared for this?" he inquired, blocking her exit when the door opened. "I'm serious; I don't want you to think that I'm forcing you to move faster than what you are ready for."

"You see me, right? I'm using my own two legs to walk into your penthouse. That means that I'm making this decision on my own. Now come on."

He laughed as she dragged him into his own house.

Natalie paused at the bottom of the two steps leading into his living room, causing him to bump into her. He grabbed her to keep them both from falling.

The room was spacious and airy with white carpeting and a white leather sectional. Accented in gold, it was a beautiful room. There were gold-framed pictures on the walls, gold statues, and gold statuettes on glass end tables with gold trimming. The room was spotless, almost as if it wasn't meant to be used. She began exploring the rest of the penthouse. A short staircase led to the second floor, which had a balcony suspended over the lower room. She could see doors, which she assumed opened to bedrooms.

Natalie moved down the hallway and entered the first room she came to. It appeared to be a library or office.

Judging by the piles of paper spread across the desktop, Thorne obviously spent a lot of time in this room. Two phones, a copier, and a shredder were on the table next to his desk. Shelves crammed with books bracketed a built-in entertainment center across the room. It was a large room and definitely a lived in room.

The next door led to a bathroom. It was welcoming and tastefully painted in peach and mint green. She was tempted to ask him who did his decorating, but she was afraid she wouldn't like the answer.

Thorne followed closely behind as she went from room to room, enjoying her display of genuine interest and pleasure. She finally reached the door at the end of the hall and walked into the warmest room she had seen thus far.

The room had a masculine aura. She could feel Thorne in every corner of the room. It was decorated in black and gold. This was his family room, he explained. He came here most often, he said, to relax or chill with friends. A bar in the far corner was directly behind a black leather sectional sofa. Both sides of the black entertainment center were filled with movies and DVDs. A stereo on the right side had a stand filled with CDs next to it. A Playstation game was on top of the TV, and wires led to the controls, which were on the arm of the sofa.

Another computer was in one corner of the room, and a pool table was set up in another. It was the largest room in the house and the most relaxing. Natalie decided this was where she wanted to be, so she kicked off her shoes, sat on the sofa, and stretched out.

"Can I get you anything to drink?" he asked.

"Um, wine would be nice, I guess. You have a very nice little bachelor pad going on here. And you have good taste in decor." *Okay, so she did want to know.*

"No, my sister has excellent taste in decor. One arm of our corporation is her interior-decorating business. She did this for me as a moving-in present. She also did Michael's."

"Well, it's nice to have a home interior decorator in the family."

"Yeah, it is," he said, bringing the wine over to her and sitting next to her on the sofa. When he sat down, the unbelievably soft cushions of the sofa sunk around him, causing her to slide closer to him. He put his arm across the back of the sofa so that she slid into his body.

"I'm sorry. Your sofa is really smooth."

"Don't be sorry." He put his hand on her hip when she tried to slide away from him. "And don't move." Thorne reached for the remote control and turned on the stereo. Smooth jazz sounds floated from the mounted wall speakers and enveloped the room. "So what movie do you want to watch?"

"You mean to tell me you've seen all these movies before?"

"Actually, I have seen only a dozen or so, but I like to keep up with the times, so I buy them with the intention of watching them. I just never seem to find the time."

"Well, let's watch a comedy, something that will keep us awake. I'm so tired, and it's late."

"We don't have to watch a movie. If you prefer, we could just take a shower and head for bed. There's a TV and VCR up in my room."

"That sounds like a plan."

As Natalie followed him back down the hall and up the stairs to the upper level, she became very nervous. She watched his back muscles strain at his shirt as he walked up the stairs and knew she was definitely heading in the right direction, but apprehension began to get to her.

What if he wasn't satisfied with her? Was she willing to risk their good friendship? How would things be in the morning? Would he still want to see her? Endless questions flew through her mind before she took a hold of herself and forced such questions into the furthermost recesses of her brain.

She told herself to calm down and enjoy this new experience. If he had been a black man, she wouldn't be so unsure. That was her problem, she decided. She was starting to see Thorne as a white man, which was something new to her, instead of as Thorne, a man she liked and enjoyed. And that's exactly what he was—a man, no more and no less.

"Natalie, are you sure?" Thorne asked when he reached the top of the stairs. "I have an extra room; perhaps you'd rather stay in there?"

"Yes, I'm sure, Thorne," Natalie said, laughing to cover her uncertainty. "Am I giving off vibes or something?"

"No, but maybe I'm just as nervous as you are. I don't want us to have any regrets tomorrow morning, that's all. I mean, I know I won't, but I really want you to be sure.

I know this is a first for you, and you might be a little nervous."

She looked at him. It was kind of weird how he had mentioned the exact same thing that had been running through her mind. It was nice to have a man who could do that. "Let me guess which room is yours," she said, changing the subject. She looked up and down the hall. From the apex of the hallway, one extended back and was invisible from the lower level so that was the one she chose. "This has to be it because it's more private, set back from the stairs, and look at these double doors."

"You're right. That is exactly why I chose it. It was just coincidental that it happened to be the master bedroom, anyway." Thorne opened both doors and stepped back to let Natalie look inside. What she saw made her mouth drop.

CHAPTER 10

Nothing in the rest of the house could have prepared her for this room. It was absolutely magnificent. A large fireplace crowded the far corner, and small, black stone statues occupied the white marble mantel along with a black onyx clock. At the bottom of the statues on brass plates, she noticed, the names of several notable artists. Large statues were atop white stands around the room. A white rug covered the entire floor; a black bear rug was in front of the fireplace. A sofa and love seat in periwinkle were in front of another black entertainment center in another area of the room. It was a cozy area, with paintings on the walls in black frames. Pictures of his family in powder-blue frames, matching the sofas, were on top of the entertainment center.

Natalie took her time looking over this room. This was his personal space, and she wanted to know it well. She went over to his king-size bed with its black lacquer frame. "It's big enough for a dozen people," she joked, running her hand over the black and white comforter with squiggly blue lines.

"I like to be comfortable. As you can see, I like a lot of space."

"Does that mean we won't be cuddling tonight?"

"No, it just means that I like my space. Come on, let me show you the bathroom, and you can shower. I have an extra robe around here somewhere." Natalie followed him into the bathroom and made herself not mention that she loved it. It was exactly the sort of bathroom she wanted in her house. As a matter of fact, when they went through her house that first time, she wondered why he hadn't mentioned that she had described this room to a tee.

Natalie stepped into the glass-enclosed shower stall and leisurely soaped her body, trying to rouse herself from the numbness weighing her down. It had been a long day, and fatigue was beginning to creep up on her. She could feel it invading her body. She dragged herself to sit at the vanity table, which was decorated with feminine knickknacks. A small porcelain soap dish, a silver brush and comb set that apparently had never been used; containers of powders, lotions, and perfumes were among the items on the table. After applying body lotion, she put on the large silk robe Thorne had given her and returned to the bedroom.

"I thought you had fallen asleep in there."

"No, I was just enjoying myself. It's beautiful in there."

"Did you notice anything familiar about the bathroom?" He asked, a challenge in his voice.

"Yes, I did. Why didn't you tell me it was exactly like the one I described to you?"

Laughing, Thorne walked over to her. "Because I wanted you to see for yourself how much we have in common—even taste." He kissed her cheek. "You smell good."

"Thank you. You have excellent taste in lotions and perfumes. I used what was on the vanity. I hope no one will mind."

"Why don't you just come out and ask me what you want to know?" Thorne replied, still tasting her cheek and neck.

Natalie was trying to concentrate on his words, but his lips against her skin was making it hard to do. "And what would that be?"

"Either you want to know if they belong to someone else or you want to know how they got there." She didn't reply, so he continued. "To answer your unasked question, the things in the bathroom on the vanity table belong to me. I bought them with Theresa's help. I'm not going to tell you that they haven't been used before, but I only bought them to decorate my bathroom. Okay?"

"Okay," she murmured shakily, feeling somewhat reprimanded. Then she saw that he was also wearing a robe. She touched the silky material and asked, "Where did you bathe?"

"In the downstairs bathroom. I was tempted to join you, but I forced myself to go downstairs."

She ignored his last statement. Besides, the hand resting on her hip was causing her heartbeat to pump madly. She rested her head on his chest and moved closer, wrapping her arms around his waist and pulling him close.

"Um, you smell good, too." Under the thin material of the robes, she could feel him growing against her belly.

They were standing in the middle of the lounge area of his bedroom. Two glasses of wine were next to the lighted candle on the end table. Sam Cooke, her favorite singer, was crooning his ballads of love and pain.

"How did you know?" Natalie whispered softly, totally caught up in the moment.

"Know what?" Thorne brushed the corner of her mouth with his lips. "That you liked Sam Cooke? I like Sam Cooke, so I just gave it a shot. I told you we have a lot in common."

Natalie looked up at Thorne, and his mouth swooped down and captured hers. All the sparks they had felt earlier that day were still there, beckoning for the kiss to deepen until they had to pull apart to catch their breaths. For Natalie, all apprehension went away when she looked into his eyes and saw the depth of passion he held for her. She kissed him again, putting her heart on the line and in his hands.

But Thorne wanted to be sure this was the right time for her. He didn't want to lose her because he was being too impatient to wait until she was ready. When they broke off the first kiss, it had taken all his willpower not to rip off the robe and ravish her on the sofa.

"Natalie, please, tell me to stop now if you're not sure. I may not be able to stop myself later."

"Thorne, I don't want you to stop. Please," she said, standing on her tiptoes and touching her lips to his, "make love to me."

Thorne had heard enough. Kissing her urgently, his hands began to work their magic on her body. He took her neck with one hand and gently rubbed the thumb against her throat until a sob left her lips. His other hand held her breast and caressed and teased the sensitive nipple until it stood straight and stiff.

Riding on a wave of heightened sensuality, Natalie's kisses became more demanding, and her hand went up to play in Thorne's wavy black hair.

As Thorne began kissing his way down her neck, her head fell back to allow him greater access. God only knew how she remained standing when her knees had turned to jelly, Natalie mused.

First, he untied the robe and then slowly pushed it away from her body. Natalie felt momentary panic, but forced herself to hold Thorne's gaze as he stepped back to view her.

Peering at her intently, a knot settled in the pit of his stomach and a lump formed in his throat. Thorne had never before felt what he was feeling for Natalie. She was truly beautiful, but Thorne knew that if she had been extra hairy with an extra body part, he would still want this woman to be his. He had fallen for her; it was as simple as that. A moan escaped his lips as he tried to get himself under control.

"I'm really going to enjoy this. Natalie, you're beautiful."

His approval boosted her confidence and pushed away any lingering doubts she still had. "Thank you, Thorne, but it's not fair for me to still be in the dark."

She released the string to his robe, and took her time spreading apart the robe to reveal his full maleness. He was watching her intently, waiting for a reaction. And a reaction was what he got. Natalie stared at his face then lowered her eyes inch by inch.

At his chest, she stared wordlessly, eyes widening slightly at the sight of his broad shoulders and massive chest, which she expected because his built was evident through his suits and especially his work shirts. His chest was large and his muscles were rippling even though he was absolutely still. *Oh, God, I can't wait to see his back.*

Little fine hairs covered his chest, working their way into an almost invisible line, which she followed to his navel. Just a little past his navel, the hair spread out again and fanned around the most pleasurable-looking male organ she had ever seen.

"Oh, my God," she said before she could stop herself.

"What?" Thorne inquired, chuckling.

Natalie couldn't take her eyes off it. Just gorgeous.

Thorne stood there and allowed her to stare at him. He wasn't surprised by her reaction. It was generally known around the social rumor mill that the brothers were very well endowed.

"Natalie, are you going to look at it all night?" he asked, looking pleased. But Natalie continued taking him in, impressed as much by his obvious confidence as by his size. He stood tall, firm and strong. His thighs and stomach, hips and behind were all rock hard. *Lord, this is a man,* she thought.

"Thorne, what am I supposed to do with that?" she asked with false innocence.

"Don't be silly. You're supposed to enjoy it, and you will."

"Maybe we should stop this. Somebody might get hurt, namely me," she joked.

"Natalie, let's go to the bed." Thorne looked at her as worry surfaced in her eyes. Taking her hand and pulling her close to him, he asked, "Do you think that I would do anything to hurt you? If I begin to hurt you, I will stop."

"I guess those myths they say about you white boys aren't all true, huh?" she said, masking her surprise with good humor.

"I'm living proof," Thorne replied, accepting her compliment.

He drew her against him. His hands rested on her backside and he squeezed and caressed her until he felt her body relax. He kissed her face, ears, and neck. Instead of trying to move her toward the bed, Thorne lowered her onto the sofa and began to fondle her breast.

With her hand in his hair, Natalie forgot her fears, gave way to her feelings, and vowed to enjoy the pleasure Thorne was giving her.

"Natalie, love." Thorne was losing the battle to remain calm and in control as a brief shiver raced through him. He rained light kisses across her stomach and down her hips and thighs. He spread her legs apart on the sofa, parting and playing with her soft nest until he felt her wetness.

Through the sweet moans he heard coming from her, Thorne struggled with all his might to rein in his willpower and retain some self-control. He had never wanted anything or anyone, needed anything or anyone, as much as he needed to be a part of Natalie at this very moment. She was softness and warmth, and he yearned to drive himself into her until he was nestled into her soul and embedded into her heart.

Natalie didn't think she could take much more before she exploded from the tenderness he was showering onto her body. The urgency to reach an unattainable goal began to rise from the pit of her stomach. She could feel the changes her body and mind were making on their journey to become one with him.

"Natalie, come with me," Thorne said between kisses, rising above her and extending his hand. When she saw the desire and anticipation in his gaze, a sigh formed in her throat, and she grabbed onto him ready to be taken wherever he chose to lead her.

The bed was already warm when they slipped between the covers and moved to the center. As Thorne gathered her in his arms and pulled her close to him, she could feel the pressure of him against her hipbone. Her stomach contracted tightly as anxiety slowly began to creep up her spine. He was kissing her face and neck and settling himself between her legs. She could feel the tip of him spread her folds apart and push against her opening.

"Natalie, relax, love," he whispered, his broad shoulders heaving as he pushed his desires aside to concentrate fully on her.

"I . . . I'm sorry, Thorne," she said, surprised to find she had been holding her breath. She turned away, grateful for the semidarkness of the room.

"Do you want me to stop?" he asked chivalrously, silently begging her to say no.

"No, I want to be with you. Thorne, you're, um . . ." He reached into the drawer and retrieved a condom, and she watched as he opened the package and covered himself.

"I'll take it slow, Natalie. I won't hurt you."

She felt the intoxicating sensation of his lips on her neck and ear until she began to relax, then he moved his mouth over hers, devouring its softness.

When her breath began to catch under his ministrations and she was once again swept into the throes of passion, Thorne quickly eased over her and slipped into her. He paused, passion inching through his veins, to let her adjust to him and to get himself under control.

Plunging into her was uppermost in his mind, but he pushed it aside because he had promised her he would take it easy; and even though he knew he wouldn't hurt her, he needed to keep her trust and confidence. Slowly, very slowly, he eased into her, pulling out a little then pushing forward a little more. It was pure hell for him; perspiration broke out on his forehead, but he held on to his control. He felt her relaxing, and it gave him even more pleasure to know he was able to make her enjoy the experience.

Natalie could feel herself opening up to him until finally, he filled her completely. It was torture for her, a sweet torture. Her whole body overheated from the friction he brought into her.

She was so tight around him, Thorne was almost scared to move. God, she felt so good.

"Nat, are you all right?" he whispered cautiously.

"Yes, Thorne. I feel so stupid. You'd think I was a virgin from the way I've been acting," she said, embarrassed by her earlier behavior.

He was looking into her face, into her eyes, asking for her approval before he continued. Natalie smiled up at him, and Thorne actually felt his heart skip a beat. She wrapped her arms around him and rubbed his backside, squeezing his bottom and urging him on. As he began to kiss the corners of her mouth and her sweet lips, the muscles of her passageway contracted around him, and Thorne almost lost it.

"Natalie, you feel so good. Um . . . I love you."

Moving slowly inside her, he tried to make sure she wasn't hurt. When he felt her respond to his easy caress, he quickened the pace and took his strokes longer and deeper. He kissed her face and neck and suckled her breasts while maintaining a steady rhythm.

Thorne drove deeper and deeper into Natalie, losing all control. He was drowning in the passion reflected in her face. Only seconds before he was about to lose himself, Natalie tightened around him and screamed out her release. Thorne could only hold on to her as he buried himself to the hilt and joined her in the glorious light, spilling his seed.

"Oh, God . . . oh, oh, Natalie."

They held each other, kissed each other, and floated together until their passion subsided, and they once again lay side by side on the king-size cloud that was his mattress. "Natalie, you are beautiful; I love you," Thorne said, as he caressed her belly. "I didn't hurt you, did I?"

"No, it was wonderful. It had been such a long time. I'm glad I was with you. Come on, let's take a shower." Natalie sat up and a pain shot through her. She stiffened. "Oh . . ."

"What is it? Are you all right?" He was quickly by her side.

"I'm fine. I think." She moved to the edge of the bed. "Help me up."

"Natalie, should I call a doctor or something?"

"You better not." She gave him an evil look. "I'm fine. Just a little sore, that's all." Seeing a smug look cross his face, she continued. "Don't you look like that! Don't you smile or laugh! What do you expect? It's been a long time, and you're hung like a horse." By the time they made it to the shower, they were both laughing.

"I don't think that most women complain about their boyfriends being well endowed. You're supposed to be thinking of other ways to enjoy me."

"I'm not complaining about you being well endowed. I'm complaining about the soreness, and I've already thought of different ways to enjoy you."

They lit candles around the room and bathed each other in silence, enjoying the easy atmosphere. Afterwards, they relaxed on the sofa and watched a movie before heading back to bed.

CHAPTER 11

A night of mind-blowing intimacies and indescribable pleasures had left Natalie reluctant to rejoin the real world. She was in dreamland and wanted to stay there. Her heart was still beating to the rhythm of their lovemaking as she stood beside him in the private elevator that was taking them on the final leg of their time together.

He pulled her close, randomly kissing her forehead and cheeks; Natalie draped her arms around his waist, enjoying the warmth of his breath on her skin. Neither wanted the moment to end.

"Natalie, I think you're holding something of mine," Thorne said between kisses.

"What? No, I'm not," she replied, not comprehending his meaning.

"Yes, you are. Right here," Thorne said, lifting her hand palm up and tapping the center.

"What are you talking about, Thorne? I'm not holding anything."

"My heart," he said. "My heart is in the palm of your hand."

Natalie looked up, nearly swooning at the intense honesty she saw in his eyes. "Lord, Thorne, that was beautifully said."

"Well, corny but true. I don't know how in the world this happened, but it has. I don't even want to examine it too closely. It's happening. Don't you feel it?"

"Yes, I do. It's kind of scary, but I'm willing to take it one day at a time and enjoy it—if you are."

"Nat, I had better get you home before I take up back in the house and seduce you in the foyer."

"I do have a lot to do today, but I don't think another hour or two will make that much of a difference. What are your plans for today?"

"I just need to stop by a couple of stores before I come by your house tonight. Did I tell you that I had some dates?"

"Some dates?" Natalie asked, curious.

"Yes. I've somehow managed to catch the eye of a couple of adorable young girls. I've been kind of seeing them on the side." He laughed.

"Maybe you didn't know this, but most women don't like to share their men. I hope you have a good excuse for this betrayal," Natalie said jokingly after a moment of hesitation. It couldn't be that bad if he was telling her about it.

"Well, they could hardly give you any competition. You give me things that they couldn't. Then again they are fun, and quite a handful, too," he said, pushing the button to open the elevator door. "I hope they will forgive me for my weakness. I'm going to be pretty late."

"And what is your weakness, might I ask?"

"You, love," Thorne laughed, pulling her back into his penthouse and kissing her with all the passion stored up in his heart.

＝＝

Passion was a strange thing, Natalie mused. It flared up at the oddest times, stayed for the longest times, and had you wishing for it all the time.

Their emotions still barely under control, Natalie and Thorne were once again in the elevator. Their love-making had been so intense, they still felt the energy it had generated.

This time in the elevator, they kept their eyes straight ahead, determined to make it to the garage level before letting their desire overtake them once again.

"I guess your dates will be pretty upset with you," Natalie stated, wondering who the mystery dates really were and if she should be worried.

"You don't sound particularly concerned," he said, smiling mysteriously. He wanted to pull her into his arms, but he fought the urge and shoved his hands into his pockets. "Besides, it's still not too late for us to enjoy an evening together. I'll just skip the shopping trip, or maybe I'll take them with me. You know gifts are the way to a woman's heart."

"You haven't tried to buy my love. They must be pretty special."

"I'm glad I didn't have to buy your love. That means you gave it to me freely; it's more important and special that way." Though quite serious, he thought it wise to lighten up the conversation. "I don't know; my dates are kind of young for my taste. But they have this aunt who really makes my juices flow. Maybe I could talk her into joining us for pizza and the movies." He was smiling brightly.

"Thorne, you made a date with my nieces? They didn't even tell me."

"Actually, I asked them to go skating when I was at the house the other night. We don't have any little girls in our family, just Theresa's son. And he's not even a kid mentally; I think he's smarter than I am. Stephen said that it would be okay. But it's gotten quite late. Our hour or two turned into three. It's easy to lose time when I'm loving you."

Ding.

Natalie and Thorne fell silent when the elevator stopped at Michael's floor. They straightened themselves and waited for the unknown passenger to board. When the doors parted, jaws dropped open and eyes bulged. No one moved for a second, then Tamia burst out laughing and stepped into the elevator.

"Hey, sis," she said nonchalantly. She could have been ordering a cup of coffee. "Hi, Thorne."

"Hi, Tamia. What are you doing here?" Natalie asked, not really wanting or expecting an answer.

It was noon, and here was her sister, who she knew never woke up before one or two if she could possibly avoid it. Then there was the impeccable Michael Philips, hair uncombed, standing stock-still in a pair of flip-flops, an unbuttoned shirt, and jeans. He quickly recovered and stepped into the elevator.

"Oh, I stayed the night with Mike," she said casually. "I see you stayed here last night, too."

"Mike?" Thorne repeated, unaccustomed to hearing the shortened version of his brother's name. He was surprised by the easy use of the name and by the fact that Michael didn't seem to object.

Natalie could tell by the way Michael wouldn't look at her that he was embarrassed, but her sister wasn't. Tamia looked straight ahead and smiled as if it was a normal day in the neighborhood. She glanced at Thorne, who had crossed his arms and was glowering at Michael.

"Um, yes, I did," Natalie finally responded.

"Well, that's great. Now I can catch a ride home with you instead of Mike having to go out."

"Mike?" Thorne repeated, laughing under his breath. His brother looked at him sternly. It didn't matter.

"Sure," Natalie answered. *Am I the only one who sees something wrong with this picture?* she wondered.

Thorne didn't say anything.

Michael was looking at Tamia and wondering why she was so unaffected by their discovery.

Natalie couldn't believe it. Her first impulse was to be mad, because this was her younger sister. But at the same time, Tamia was a grown woman. She didn't really have to answer to Natalie or anyone else, for that matter. Hell, she never did.

Natalie did the only thing she could do under the circumstances. Taking Thorne's hand, she led him to the farthest corner of the suddenly cramped elevator and focused her attention on him.

Thorne looked down at her and winked at her for handling an awkward situation well. He wanted to choke

Michael to death, but he also saw it for what it was—two adults spending adult time together. Weird wasn't quite the word for it, but he was definitely thrown by seeing Michael in such disarray. Be that as it may, it was still none of his business. And he wanted it to stay that way.

When the elevator reached ground level, relief was felt all around. Thorne led Natalie to her car and kissed her good-bye.

"I'll be along shortly. Tell my dates not to be mad at me. I'm only a man," he laughed.

"I'm sure they'll forgive you once you flash those gray eyes at them." She placed her hand on the side of his face, her very touch a reminder of their time together.

Thorne had similar thoughts running through his head as he wrapped her in his arms. There was a lot more he wanted to tell her, but it would have to keep until their next private time together. When, he wondered, had his feelings for Natalie strengthened and grown to such large proportions? Why didn't he realize it when it was happening? And why had it happened so quickly?

He had to admit that the feelings had been strong and deep from the start, but after loving her, talking to her, and listening to her until late into the night, would he ever be able to spend a restful night in his penthouse again? It promised to be the loneliest time in his life.

Thorne held her tightly before helping her into the car. Natalie closed the door and rolled down the window. When he bent down to her, she told him that she loved him and kissed him one last time. Smiling down at her, he sent up a thankful prayer before stepping back from the car door.

Over the hood of the car, he watched Michael and Tamia in a passionate embrace. It shocked and confused him that Michael, conservative and classy, had connected to Tamia, wild child from hell, and not Tamya, the good twin. In the past, all Michael's girlfriends, lovers, even his occasional one-night stands had been women with class and sophistication. Not that Tamia wasn't a nice enough woman. She just seemed to be a little too wild and outgoing for his brother. It kind of brought a smile to his face, though. He just shook his head at them and walked toward the elevator, where he waited for Michael to finish. It seemed like forever before they separated, and when they did, it was only because Natalie was smart enough to blow her horn to get their attention.

It wasn't that Natalie was upset by the surprise her sister and Michael had just delivered. After the initial shock had worn off, it was actually kind of funny. Still, why she felt embarrassed was a mystery to her. It was misplaced and totally uncalled for, but it still threatened to show itself on the surface of her well-controlled demeanor. She was almost afraid to even talk to her sister as she drove her home.

Tamia, she noticed, was also extremely quiet, which was not like her at all. She assumed that she was also embarrassed, which was also not like her. Natalie wanted to ask if something was wrong, but decided it was better to just let the matter rest and move on with the day.

Sunday was a day of true rest. At least that was what Natalie told herself as she stretched across her bed that morning. And as she moved deeper under the covers, she was determined to remain in the bed until it was time for her to go visit Amanda.

The doctor had told her yesterday when she called for her daily check that Amanda was doing much better, but was still being heavily sedated.

An undercover detective had been placed in the hospital to investigate any strange activity that might occur during the evening hours, when only a skeleton staff was on duty. Natalie had found that out yesterday when she came home to an array of unexpected guests.

Feeling footloose and carefree, Natalie had practically floated into her house early Saturday afternoon after dropping off Tamia. She planned to take a long hot bath and relive her night of newfound passion. Thorne would have to deal with the girls on his own, because she had no intention of going back out. She would just lie around and relax while he fulfilled his obligations to his dates.

"Hey, sis. Where you been?" Stephen asked cheerfully as soon as she entered the living room. He was standing next to a beautiful, petite woman with the look on her face that Natalie took for infatuation. She looked around the room and saw a few other people, some of whom she knew, some she didn't.

Stephen saw her raised eyebrow and offered an explanation. "Oh, I'm sorry. Natalie, this is Detective Cassell. Sandra, this is my sister Natalie. You two finally get to meet. This is the detective assigned to your case. She came by yesterday, but you weren't around."

"And again last night," Sandra added, extending her hand to Natalie. "Stephen was nice enough to invite me over for dinner and fun with the girls. They're so adorable."

"Yes, they are. Stephen," Natalie said, "I was under the impression that Thorne was coming to pick up the girls in a few minutes."

"Well, I'll be sorry to disappoint him, but their mother called to say she was coming to get them for an overnighter. She's in the den waiting for them. Before Sandra and Paula came, a couple of the guys and I were just sitting here chillin', watching the ball games. They're about to leave."

"Oh. Well, Thorne is already on his way. He should be here any second. I'm going to hurry upstairs and shower. Tell him to wait; maybe we can find something to do."

"Hey, why don't you two join Sandra and me in a game of spades?"

"Sure, if he doesn't mind. Sandra, did you want to talk to me tonight?" After taking two steps toward the stairs, Natalie turned, remembering that she did have business with the police detective.

"Oh, no," she replied, holding up her hands. "I'm off duty until Monday morning. But I would like to set up a time to meet with you then, unless you'd rather . . ."

"No, it can wait," Natalie said, seeing the hopeful look on Sandra's face.

"Good. Tonight, I plan on enjoying myself."

The shower revived and refreshed Natalie. She heard her nieces' shouts of joy when Thorne finally arrived with a gift for each of them to apologize for missing their date. She quickly came down the stairs.

Being the woman that she was, Natalie suppressed her natural reaction to label Paula, but she knew the kind of woman Paula was. As usual, she was trying to dig her greedy little paws into something that was off limits to her. But one look at Thorne's face as he watched her walk down the stairs revealed the kind of man he was, and she instantly knew that her worries and fears were unwarranted. The love was plain and easy to read.

"Paula, I see you've met my boyfriend Thorne," Natalie said, surprising her ex-sister-in-law so that she took a few steps away from him.

"Yes, I was just wondering what happened to poor Nicholas. I just came to pick up the girls. They're getting their things together. Your brother is preoccupied and isn't giving me any attention, so I decided to entertain your friend until you arrived." She rambled on, a nervous smile hovering on her lips.

"Well, I've arrived. So we'll be seeing you."

Natalie didn't give her time to respond. She simply took Thorne by the hand and led him into the dining room, where Stephen and Sandra waited for them. Paula was left alone standing by the front door.

"I told Sandra you would handle her," Stephen said, smiling. "To be honest, I was hoping to hear a few slaps and punches."

"Now, Stephen, that's not nice," Sandra laughed.

"Well, you were about to, but I decided she wasn't worth it. Besides," she added jokingly, "I could see that Thorne desperately wanted me to rescue him."

Thorne laughed, "I was just in a state of shock. And Stephen, I didn't appreciate your leaving me in there with that barracuda. I thought she was going to attack me."

"Given more time, she would have," Stephen said. "Any man who doesn't give her his full attention seems to be a challenge—and weakness. She has to be noticed. That's probably why she was with me for so long." He sat back in his chair, finally able to make a little sense out of his failed marriage. "I never really paid her much attention. I mean, I married her, but that was because she got pregnant. I stayed with her, but that was because of the kids. I don't know; I guess I loved her, but I never really liked her. I was just there, I guess. I took care of the kids; I paid the bills. You know what? I can't even remember what she did."

"Well, big brother, that's all behind you now," Natalie said. The front door opened, and she heard the kids hollering their good-byes to everyone.

"Wait, Daddy didn't get his kisses," Lindsey said, running into the dining room.

"Thank you, baby. Daddy loves you. I want you both to have a good time."

"We will, Daddy." The girls went around the table to Natalie, Thorne, and Sandra, who were overly flattered to be included in their love. Then they bounced out of the room, giggling.

"I like her for Daddy," Lindsey whispered to her sister loudly. "Don't you, Tracey?"

"Yes, now, shhh, before you jinx the whole thing."

"What does jinx mean?"

"Just forget it. Come on, and don't say anything to Mom about this, okay?"

"Okay, Tracey." Lindsey dutifully followed her older sister to join their mother.

Natalie held back her laughter until she heard the front door shut. Then she and Thorne looked at each other. "Stephen, seems to me like some matchmaking is in the works," she said. They all laughed and settled into an easy conversation.

A card game of spades turned into a competitive knock-down, drag-out war. The simple game led to a simple get-together when Tamia and Tamya showed up with dates, which led to snacks and drinks.

Natalie was confused by Tamia's date. She didn't know what was going on. Tamia was still not being her usual rambunctious self. She didn't even appear to be interested in the guy. A talk was definitely necessary, and as soon as possible. She made a mental note of it because Thorne was insisting that they take a drive so that they could spend some quiet time together before he went home to work.

On their way back to her house, they drove past The Old Sage Room and saw Michael getting into his car with a date. Thorne just shook his head.

"I wonder what's up with those two," Natalie said, tapping her forefinger against her chin, already letting crazy scenarios run through her head.

"I don't know, and I don't care."

"I mean, you saw them together this morning. They could barely keep their hands off one another."

"I don't know, and I don't care," Thorne repeated, not wanting to ponder the situation.

"You're not going to help me on this one, huh?" She turned to look at him; he kept his eyes on the road.

"I don't know, and I don't care."

Natalie finally got the hint, gave up, and proceeded to forget about everything except the remainder of her evening with Thorne.

CHAPTER 12

Most people hate getting out of bed on Monday mornings. It has something to do with metabolism. The body isn't fully able to begin dealing with the work week until Tuesday afternoon. Natalie's body was no exception to the rule. Her Monday was so bad that when she finally crawled into the bed that night she wanted to skip Tuesday altogether.

Not being a stupid person, Natalie realized that when she woke up on Monday, the day was going to be long and tiring. She was meeting with Thorne, Michael, and Theresa at ten for more investigating. Her worries were centered on Thorne and their recent discovery of the birth certificate for a male child born on his birthday to his father and Amanda.

Although they had been blessed with a lovely weekend and he hadn't mentioned the birth certificate at all, she knew it was in the back of his mind the whole time. She couldn't blame him for that. If their positions had been reversed, she probably would have stayed in all weekend and stressed herself out.

Smothering a groan, Natalie dragged herself out of bed promptly at six-fifteen. Her first stop after a luxurious lather was to the house to see how the remodeling was coming along. Disappointment greeted her in the person of Charlie Reynolds, the foreman on duty. It was his unpleasant duty to inform her that work had to be stopped on the house for the day because the truck delivering some of her more important materials had been in an accident en route that morning. The supplier was reordering and re-shipping the supplies, but they wouldn't arrive until the next day.

Okay, she could handle that. *You know sometimes things happen.* It was only one day, and a few of the men were still there doing light work.

Deciding to get on with her day, Natalie next headed to the hospital to visit Amanda, hoping her friend would be alert enough to talk to her. She couldn't wait to tell her about the progress of the investigation; at the same time, she wasn't sure if her friend could handle any surprising news. All hope of conversation was quickly dashed when she stepped onto the floor and was greeted by Sandra. Police were stationed throughout the hospital and in front of Amanda's door because, some time during the night, a man had snuck into her room. He had posed as a nurse doing a routine check on patients. Unfortunately for him, the minute he went into Amanda's room the nurse on duty came around the corner with a tray of medications. The officer told her that her co-worker was in the room, and she informed him that she was the only nurse on duty until morning. It had been at four-ten. The man was apprehended while trying to suffocate Amanda as she slept.

Natalie was frantic with concern and began to shake as dire images appeared before her. She spent an hour talking to Detective Cassell, trying to figure out who would want to harm her friend. Amanda's record was clean, and her friends and colleagues had nothing but accolades for the sick professor. She was respected equally in her profession and by society.

Amanda was resting, and the doctors assured Natalie that her vitals were very good. Natalie sat with Amanda for a short time, again wondering why anyone would want her friend to come to a bad end. More importantly, who could it be?

After two disappointments in a row, Natalie knew her day was ruined. Instead of using the café at the office building, she opted to stop by the corner deli and pick up subs for herself and the Philips' and decided to make an early start of going to the Philips's headquarters.

During the drive over, she encountered a three-car accident that caused traffic to be backed up for several blocks. Natalie sat in the car and contemplated going around, but she was stuck between cars by the time she made up her mind to move. It would have taken her at least forty-five minutes to get to the building that way. So she waited until the road cleared. That only took thirty-five minutes. She was going to be late for her appointment with Thorne and his family yet again.

"So your girlfriend's late again, huh, Thorne?" Michael asked, a suggestion of annoyance in his eyes.

"She wouldn't be Natalie if she wasn't. Don't act like you're surprised by it." He glanced uneasily over his shoulder at his brother.

"I guess I'm not. Listen, I wanted to talk to you about the other night."

"What happened the other night?" Theresa asked, easing into the conversation after talking to her son. She loved to know what was going on in her brothers' lives. It was too bad they seldom let her in on things. Several times she had to rely on her barely-adequate detective skills to find out information.

"Nothing," both men said at the same time.

Theresa looked from one man to the other. "Okay," she said, her voice thick with suspicion. "If you don't want me to know, that's fine. I'm not going to try to be in your business." She started to walk away, then stopped short in faked despair. "But we are a family, I thought we dealt with our problems together. No. No. That's okay." Waving her hands in dismissal, she walked away with stiff dignity. "Keep it to yourselves. I'll just stay over here and let you two talk to each other."

Michael was always the first one to crack under one of her guilt trips. He hated for her to be mad at him. "Okay, Theresa. God, you'd think I was killing you or something."

Theresa smiled and walked back to him. She kissed him on the cheek in gratitude. "Michael, I just have your best interest at heart, and don't use the Lord's name in vain."

Thorne had his arms crossed over his chest, shaking his head at Theresa for once again skillfully succeeding in making Michael feel guilty. It had been a long time since that had worked on him. He almost laughed to himself until she stuck her tongue out at him. To get back at her, Thorne suggested that he and Michael go to dinner that night to talk about the situation. When Michael agreed, he stuck his tongue back out at her.

"I'm sorry I'm late," Natalie shouted, barging into the conference room. "I was really going to be here on time, but there was an accident on the way over."

"Are you all right?" Thorne asked, forgetting about the little game he was playing with his sister. He quickly walked over to Natalie and began checking for himself.

"I'm fine, Thorne. I wasn't in the accident. Good morning, Theresa, Michael," she said as Thorne embraced her in a romantic hug and began to kiss her face.

"Hey, love, I missed you." Thorne replied half in her ear, not caring that his brother and sister were in the room or that they overheard him. He liked showering attention on Natalie.

"I missed you, too," she smiled, still surprised that this important and successful businessman had such a sensitive and sensual side. "But it's only been a few hours."

"I was lonely. You left me to sleep in that big bed all by myself. I don't like it anymore."

"Well, we'll see if I can warm my spot up for you later."

Thorne was about to bend down for a second or third kiss when he was interrupted.

"Um, excuse me, but could we get started here, please? Not all of us are in the lovey-dovey mood this morning."

"Michael, what's wrong?" Natalie asked, concerned but also curious. "You were in the mood Saturday morning and Saturday night. Is everything all right?"

"What do you mean Saturday night?" he hesitated briefly, eyes glowing brilliantly green with wide-eyed innocence.

"Well, we saw you leaving the restaurant with a very attractive blonde. I just assumed that she was your date."

"Yeah, she was." Michael's voice sounded tired and defeated. He looked to Thorne for help, running his fingers through his hair and feeling very uncomfortable at that moment.

Thorne knew a shout for help when he saw one, but the only reason he finally jumped in was because he saw Theresa start to take an interest in the conversation. He was still determined not to let her in on the big secret.

"All right, since everybody is here now, why don't we get started?" He turned to Theresa with a big smile, boldly meeting her eyes. After a sharp intake of breath, she snapped her eyes at him and stalked off to sit at the conference table.

Three hours later, Thorne wished he had never suggested getting started. Natalie wished she had stayed in bed. Michael wished he could wrap his hands around his grandparents' necks. And Theresa wished she could somehow console her older brother.

Thorne's anguish was visible in his eyes, in the lines etched across his forehead, and in the way he tightly clasped his hands in front of him. He couldn't believe the way things were unfolding before his eyes. His whole life had been a lie. He didn't know what to think of his grandmother. *Why had she lied to me?* He didn't know who he was. His hatred for his grandfather grew stronger. And he now knew why his grandfather hated him so much. Now he knew why, all his life, this man had treated him as if he was nothing.

And worse of all, he didn't know what he was supposed to do. His mind was going off into a hundred different directions, and they were all leading him nowhere.

When they officially started the meeting everyone was in good spirits. Only an hour had passed when the mood in the room began to darken.

They already had the birth certificate for the son of Amanda and Matthew. Next, they pulled a birth certificate for Thorne. The birth dates were the same. The father's names were the same. Of course, the mother's names were different. All of that was expected, but what no one could understand was why the file date for the Matthew III person was a few days after his birth, and Thorne's was dated two years after his birth. Everyone was confused about that. Usually, the certificate of birth was filed right after the child was born. So why was Thorne's delayed?

"So what do you think, Thorne, that Dad had two kids on the same day by two different women?"

"That's highly unlikely," he replied, becoming more uncomfortable by the minute as his dismay grew. "Theresa, did you ever look for a birth certificate for a Maria Gamio?"

"No, I thought you said she was from Italy or somewhere."

"I don't know where she might be from. Hell, she might not even exist."

"Well, we didn't find a death certificate for her under Gamio or Philips. Let's try for the birth certificate. It can't hurt."

Natalie stood by the boardroom chalkboard making a list of facts they had uncovered. She didn't know what else to do. Thorne and Michael were brainstorming, and Theresa had the computers under control. This was supposed to be her investigation, but she had to admit that without their help she would never have gotten this far this fast.

"Uh, guys, look at this. It just came over the printer. It's a birth certificate for a Maria Annette Gamio. She was born right here in New Orleans, but look at it," Theresa exclaimed, lifting the paper high for the others to see. "She was born in 1952. That would have made her eleven years old when Thorne was born. And it would only make her forty-seven years old now."

"What the hell is going on? That doesn't make any sense at all," Thorne yelled, despair spreading over his features.

"I know," Theresa consoled. Thorne picked up a stack of papers from the center of the boardroom table and flung them onto the floor.

Michael came up behind Thorne and put a hand on his shoulder in a comforting massage. "Calm down, man. Theresa, how about doing a search for any kind of police record or driver's license on her. Maybe something will come from that."

"Good idea, Michael," Theresa concurred.

"Thorne," Natalie said tentatively, "Drink some of this and calm yourself down, baby." She ran her fingers through his hair. "This may not even be the person we're looking for."

Her concern for him was genuine. She had never seen him so upset. It was almost painful to watch. On the outside, he appeared to be such a strong, confident man, but his vulnerability was becoming ever more apparent.

He held it in as much as possible, but she could see he was worried and maybe a little scared. It scared her, too, and made her mad—mad at whomever would do something like this to a person. It was becoming evident Amanda's missing son was Thorne. If that were true, a whole lot of closet doors were going to be forced open. She hoped he was ready for those skeletons to come out, and prayed he would be strong enough to deal with them.

By noon, the four of them headed out of town to the outskirts of the city. Michael was driving and being nagged by his very impatient brother.

Thorne was anxious to get to the bottom of this big mystery that turned out to be his life. And none of the others could blame him. They offered their support and their love, but kept a wary eye on him and his actions. He was like a volcano about to erupt, so tightly wound was his emotional state. Without knowing which way to turn, what to expect next, and why the people he loved had betrayed him at all, he was left with growing confusion, trying to control his temper and contain his anger.

"Hey, man, could you please just sit back and relax?" Michael said irately when Thorne asked him for the third time if he could go any faster.

"That's easy for you to say. Your whole life isn't turning out to be one big lie. There's no question about who your birth mother was. I'm back at square one, not knowing a damn thing. Who in the hell is she? Where is she? And why the hell didn't she want me?" His pain and confusion deepened and his face clouded with rage.

"But Thorne," Theresa interrupted, trying to avert an argument, "Michael is right, dear. You do need to calm down and relax. Getting all upset and anxious isn't going to get us anywhere. And think about your health. You'll mess around and pop a vein or something at this rate."

Natalie took Thorne's hand, protectively trying to give him what little support she could, but it didn't seem to do any good.

Even though he leaned back and rested his head on her shoulder as the navy SUV moved through the suburbs and further into the countryside, the nervous twitching of his jaw muscle was a very visible sign of his inner turmoil. Natalie worried for Thorne and the effects the outcome of this investigation of theirs would have on him. Before it was all over, his life could very well be changed forever.

≈

"Thorne, Thorne, come back here," Theresa said, pulling on his arm to keep him from moving forward. "You can't just barge into these people's house. Come on, now. Think!"

Thorne abruptly stopped. He had been the first one out of the car and had begun striding toward the front door. In two more steps, he would have reached the first step of the worn-out and rickety old porch, which was badly in need of a repair and paint job. He hadn't even taken a really good look at the house. His only goal was to get to the front door.

"Theresa, I've been thinking all the way over here. Now it's time to get some answers."

"Okay, okay, but let Michael do the talking. He's better at it than either of us." She looked at Thorne with concern, not trusting that he could keep his feelings in check long enough for Michael to get them the answers he so desperately needed. "Do we all agree?"

Everyone nodded and together they gingerly approached the house.

The house was a small. There was no way Thorne or Michael could have stood to their full height in the living room. They both would have ended up practically kneeling on the floor. Through the half-netted, off-balanced screen door, they could see that it was tidy and clean, but hardly big enough for Maria and her six children. They also could see pictures of them all around the room. Sounds coming from the back of the house drew their attention.

As they rounded the side of the house, they saw the oldest children, who appeared too young to have already graduated from school, doing chores; Maria Gamio was hanging clothes off to the side of the house. One child, who looked to be around two or three years old, played quietly on a makeshift swing tied to a large tree limb. The yard was littered with old toys and rusted bikes.

When she noticed Thorne and Michael walking toward her, Maria's face paled and turned nearly as white as one of the sheets she was hanging. She was completely taken aback by how much like his father Michael looked. She hadn't seen either of the usual men in three weeks, and she wasn't due for another drop-off until the following week. It didn't take a hit over the head for her to realize that this was not one of her normally scheduled visits. At first, she nervously thought that she had been found out, and her monthly check would be discontinued. But she instantly calmed herself and prepared to lie to these strangers. Trying to appear comfortable and relaxed, Maria bent to retrieve the last of her wet clothes just as the group reached the clothesline.

Approaching her cautiously, Michael spoke in a respectful tone. "Excuse me, Ms. Gamio, may we speak with you for a moment?"

Maria looked up at Michael. "You must be the youngest son."

"Ma'am, do you know who I am?" Michael asked, surprised.

"Of course, I do. I do get the newspaper. I would have to be blind not to know. Besides, you look just like him." Her eyes shifted to Thorne. "So do you."

"I do?" Thorne asked, knowing he favored his father heavily but strangely needing the confirmation.

Tired of wasting time, she asked, "What is it that I can do for you? I'm very busy." She decided that getting rid of them altogether was her safest bet.

Thorne stepped forward with a copy of his birth certificate and handed it to her.

Michael also stepped forward to begin the questioning, "It seems you know our family. Is there any reason for us to believe that this Maria Gamio and you are not the same person?"

For the first time, Thorne took a good look at the woman whose name was on his birth certificate. Because of the age difference, he knew this was not his mother, but one look at her confirmed it. She was just as light and fair-skinned as Theresa. Her build was slender and willowy, but her shoulders appeared as strong as her demeanor, and there was a hint of greed in her eyes. Given her present state of living, he figured money was scarce.

Thorne made up his mind then that if they sensed the story she gave them was a lie or she refused to help, that he would offer to pay her for information. *No,*

179

this woman was definitely not his mother. So who in the hell was?

"No, I believe this is my name on this birth certificate."

"Ms. Gamio, my name's Michael, this is my sister, Theresa, my brother, Thorne, and his girlfriend, Natalie." Maria looked over the interesting group. "We would like to ask you a few questions."

"Questions about what?" The irritation in Maria's voice barely hid her uneasiness.

"Look, Maria," Thorne said, stepping forward and ignoring Natalie's hand on his arm. "I know you can tell us what we need to know. It's written all over your face." Pausing, he ran his fingers through his already-mussed hair. Then he pulled himself together before finally looking at her directly, pleadingly. "Maria, a lot of questions have suddenly surfaced about my birth. Now we've been trying to figure out most of these answers, but we've gotten nowhere. You can help us; I know this. All we want is a couple of straight answers."

Concentration etched itself on Maria's once-pretty face. Through her armor of toughness and self-interest, Maria felt herself softening toward Thorne, felt sorry for him. After all these years, it was occurring to her for the first time that someone could have been hurt because she had taken money over the years for a little white lie. At the same time, the money that was delivered to her on a regular basis had helped her to provide a better living for her children. She had managed to put one child through one year of college, and another was on his way.

A battle raged on inside her—a battle between right and wrong, good and bad, her children and this one man. There was no way she was going to sacrifice her children's education for a mistake that was made so long ago. She wasn't even exactly sure what the mistake had been. Besides, Thorne looked to be doing all right to her. He had his education, and money on top of that.

Natalie was practically reading her mind as she watched the woman's shifting facial expressions. It was obvious that someone was paying her to stay quiet. It was also obvious that whatever money she received helped her out a great deal. "Thorne," she said, tugging at his arm, "could I speak to you all for a minute? Let's give her some time to decide if she can help us or not."

They turned and looked at her questioningly, but followed her away from where Maria stood debating her conflicts.

"Thorne, we're not going to get an answer from her unless we offer her something. Look at how she's living. She's barely making it, but look at her son." Everyone turned to watch the older boy, now sitting at an old, decrepit picnic table doing homework. "He just picked up a college-level advanced calculus book. Someone is giving her money to stay quiet. If she's using that money to put her kids through college, she's not going to give it up. I'm sorry," she said, looking at Thorne, "but I wouldn't. How about you, Theresa?"

"She's right, Thorne. Sometimes, I think we forget what it's like for people who are struggling to make ends meet. Maybe if we offer her more than she's getting she'll help us out."

"I don't have a problem with that," he answered honestly. "But I wonder who is paying her to stay quiet in the first place." With a plan in place, they walked back toward Maria, ready to deal.

Before they could get too close, she hollered for her children to go in the house and began to walk toward the back door herself.

"I'm sorry, Mr. Philips, but I can't help you," she said, quickly closing the distance to her house.

She almost got away, but Thorne was ready for her to retreat. He stepped in front of her, blocking her off from the house.

"Maria, we understand your dilemma, please believe me. Is someone paying you to remain silent? No, don't answer that question. Look, it doesn't matter. I'm prepared to offer you more for helping me."

He moved out of her path, giving her the opportunity to run inside if she wanted, but Maria stood her ground. She was more than a little interested in his offer, and deep down, she did want to help him.

Michael stepped forward and said, "Okay, if you're willing to hear us out?" he paused for her nod. "Good. Then here's the offer. Your son is in college?"

Again she nodded. "He's in his sophomore year. You have to understand that my only dream is for them to go on and become something."

"I understand," Michael interrupted. He had thought of something that they could easily afford and that no one else was likely to be able to top. "We are willing to take your son for the next three summers as an intern at the Connor Corporation during his summer breaks, fully paying for his continued education, of course, and providing him with a full-time position in one of our organizations upon completion of his studies."

She looked at him in disbelief. "I don't know." Having been brought up by "make-a-deal" parents had taught Maria one thing: The first offer was never the best or the last one. Jumping at this first offer would be a mistake, so she would act the part of the fool for a little longer.

"We are also prepared to set up scholarships for the other five children to attend any institute of higher learning they choose as long as a grade point average of 3.0 is maintained."

Now, Maria thought, this was something she couldn't pass up. She would give them what information they needed and take whatever came her way when her benefactor found out that she no longer held his secret. Quickly, before she had a chance to change her mind, Maria shook Michael's hand and agreed to help them.

They followed her to the back porch and sat on the worn-out lawn furniture, waiting for Maria to come back outside with the fresh lemonade she offered. The sun had finally decided to come out and make an appearance and was beating steadily on their heads.

"Michael, did you have to offer her so much?" Theresa asked, "I mean I'm all for getting to the bottom of this, but that was a little much."

Michael turned to her, saying, "Theresa, I'm surprised at you. I thought you would do anything to help out underprivileged children."

"Well, that's true, but . . ."

"Actually, this is more of an investment than anything else. When Natalie told us to look at the book the kid was reading, I noticed that it was one I myself had used in school. Do you realize how smart that kid has to be to be studying on that level of mathematics in his sophomore year? Well, of course, you wouldn't, but I do. I was in my first year of the master's program before I even tried that book. And look at the other kids."

Everyone once again turned and observed the children, who had just come back outside and were sitting at the makeshift picnic table. The younger kids were reading books; the older ones appeared to be doing schoolwork. Maria explained that the older kids took a summer course at the local college. The youngest, who appeared to be around three or four, was reading aloud *Green Eggs and Ham*. One middle child, who looked to be in high school, was studying advanced chemistry. The older kid had exchanged his calculus book for a thick book that looked to be about biology.

"See," Michael eagerly continued, "these kids are smart; I mean really brilliant. I'd be surprised if they haven't already skipped grades in school. I'm also surprised they haven't already been offered academic scholarships. Their mother probably doesn't know how to go about getting scholarships. This is something we need to look into. All of these kids could be very valuable to the company in the near future."

"As usual, Michael, you're always thinking business," Thorne said.

"I know this is important, too, Thorne. I don't mean to minimize your problem, but—"

"Michael, it's all right. You wouldn't be you if you didn't think the way you do."

Maria came out with refreshments. Michael jumped right in on her. "So do we have a deal, Maria?"

"First, let me say that no matter how badly I feel for what has happened to you, Thorne, the only reason I'm agreeing to do this is for my children. I could get into a lot of trouble for even talking to you, so please don't let anyone know that you got any information from me. And if anything does happen to me, I ask that you look after my children. I need to have your word on that." They could tell that she was afraid of something or someone, but for her children she was willing to risk it.

Thorne's respect for her instantly doubled as he decided that it wasn't right for him to put her in jeopardy like this. It made him feel bad to think that he had compromised her in any way. "Listen, Maria, we don't want you to fear coming into any kind of harm because you talked to us. I mean your children need you more than I need to know the truth from you. We can always look elsewhere for answers. It may take a little longer, but we will find what we need to know."

"No, it's time. There's not much I can tell you anyway. All I know is that about thirty-five years ago I was working for your grandparents in the big house as a cooking assistant. I was young, really young, and should never have been working there, but my mother begged Miss Abby to let me work. We were so poor. I couldn't afford to go to school, but every night I would read at least twenty pages of whatever I could get my hands on. You can see my kids also do a lot of reading. They get that from me, thank the Lord.

"Anyway, one day after we got home from work, Howard Connor came to the door and spoke to my parents. I had seen him up at the house a couple of times. After that day, I never worked in the house again. I went to school and started college. Unfortunately, in my second year, I became pregnant. My parents left me very little when they passed, but my mother told me on her deathbed that if anyone from the Philips family came around to tell them that I understood what they were talking about and that I promised to keep the secret."

Regretfully, she turned her gaze on Thorne and focused on his dull gray eyes. "I don't know what the secret is. I'm sorry. All I know is that a few months after my mother died, Old Matthew came looking for me. He asked me if my parents told me anything, and I said yes. He asked if I would honor their agreement, and I said yes. The following day, and every month since, two men bring me twenty-five hundred dollars. Now that's not a lot of money for my kids and me to live on, but somehow I've managed. This offer you've just given me is too good to be true. With my children's college taken care of, we can live a little better."

"You don't know anything about my parentage?" Thorne asked her, dropping his eyes to hide his pain.

"No, up until a few years after my mother's death I didn't even know that my name was on a birth certificate with you listed as my son. I figure that has something to do with this money we've been receiving all of these years. Heck, I knew I wasn't your real momma."

"Do you remember anything that was going on with my father back then?"

"Hmm . . . let's see. I remember that he used to float around the house so happily. Some mornings, he would walk into the breakfast room absolutely glowing with it. I thought he was the best-looking man I had ever seen in my life. I know half the staff had crushes on him. But from what I could tell he only had eyes for one woman. Now I don't know who she was, but I know that he and his father used to have some pretty heavy and heated arguments about her. I was only there for about a year when he moved completely out. Some of the staff said that they had heard that he had gotten married, but I don't know. I was rather young." Maria looked off into the sky for a brief second as if trying to pull something from another time.

"Do you remember anything else?" Michael pressed further.

"I was just thinking about the one argument that I had seen for myself. He and Old Matthew looked as if they were about to go for each other's throats, but Miss Abby stepped in and held them both at bay. Old Matthew said that he hadn't raised him all these years for him to sleep with dogs. Miss Abby told Old Matthew that he hadn't raised Matthew at all. And Matthew said he would do as he pleased, that he didn't need Old Matthew's money to raise his family. He would stay with the woman he loved, and that she was a hell of a better person than he was. Matthew said that . . . oh, I can't think of her name. He called her something that started with an M. Well, that she gave him more love than anyone ever had besides his mother. At that point, Miss Abby told him that he had her love and support with anything that he wanted to do. She said that all of their money belonged to her; and therefore, it belonged to him and his family. I had never seen Old Matthew so mad. I got up out of there as fast as I could before he could see me."

"You don't remember anything more?" Theresa asked, feeling proud of her grandmother for supporting her son unconditionally.

"I'm sorry, that's all I know. I hope it's a help to you."

"Don't worry; you did help us out some. And you helped us to get to know our father a little better." Thorne glanced at his sister and brother and squeezed Natalie's hand, which he had been holding since Maria had started her story. "We already felt that he was a good man. You just helped to confirm that. Thank you."

"You're welcome. Still, I wish I knew more. I want you to know that your father and your grandmother were both good people. And I apologize for the part I had in this deception."

"Thank you, Ms. Gamio," Michael stepped in and gave the older woman a firm handshake and reassuring nod. "We know you helped us all that you could. Now I would like to have a word with your son before we leave. His name?"

"Christopher."

CHAPTER 13

The ride home was in silence. Everyone was busy running the amazing story that Maria told them back through their minds, trying to piece together what was turning out to be one hell of a jigsaw puzzle.

So Matthew had been in love with someone that Old Matthew had considered way beneath them. Whether it was for economical, social, or ethnic reasons, it was unacceptable to him. Because they knew of his racist ways, it was safe to consider that the person's race was the bone of contention as far as Old Matthew was concerned.

Although Thorne was grateful for the information Maria gave them, he realized that he was basically still in the same spot. All their visit did was to confirm their beliefs about their father, confirm what they believed about her not being Thorne's biological mother, and enable Michael to scout out new talent for the company.

His impatience grew stronger as a wave of anxiety shot through him. The need for the truth filled him completely as he sat in the back seat of the SUV mulling over pieces of his memory, trying to remember just a hint, a small flicker of his mother. But no picture ever emerged, not a voice or a scent, not a phrase or a familiar song.

Regardless of this outcome, Thorne intended to continue his search; he wanted to know the whole truth, and as soon as possible. He needed to know who his mother was, who he was. *It would be easy enough to just go to Amanda's hospital room,* he thought. *Amanda, MANDY.*

Thorne sprang forward, nearly knocking Natalie into the back of the front seat; she had drifted off to sleep against him. He had been so deep in thought he had forgotten she was leaning against him.

"Mandy," he said in a harsh, raw tone.

"Huh? Thorne, what are you talking about?" Natalie and Theresa asked at the same time, both looking confused.

"Mandy. That's what Dad used to call her," he said, jubilantly, sounding as if he had solved an ancient puzzle.

"Thorne," Michael began, pulling into the Connor Corporation garage, "man, what in the world are you saying?"

"Remember, Maria said that Dad used to call this woman by a name that started with an M. Mandy, short for Amanda. Don't you see?"

"Well, that sure would answer a lot of questions and make a lot of sense. Do you think that Amanda may really be the woman? And if so, she could be your mother." Natalie felt him tense up as if what she said had led him to another possibility. But he quietly relaxed. "Would you be all right with that?"

"Natalie, right now, all I want to do is get to the bottom of this." He didn't really want to talk about all of the possibilities. One step at a time. He didn't honestly know how he would feel about it. That would mean a lot of different things. "It's late, gang, let's call it a night. I want to think about something else for the rest of the night. Tomorrow will come soon enough." Everyone climbed out of the SUV, and Thorne kissed Theresa on the cheek and shook hands with Michael. "Hey, guys, thanks again for helping us out with this."

"Thorne, what did we say? What's yours is ours, right? Your problem, our problem; your money, our money; your wife, our wife," Michael joked, putting his arm around Natalie's shoulder.

Theresa and Natalie laughed as Thorne chased Michael around a half-dozen cars— unsuccessfully. Even though they both wore oxfords, Thorne's caused him to slide rather than run on the cement. "Keep your hands off, Michael." He finally caught up with his brother, but couldn't get a hold of him.

"I was just kidding, Thorne," Michael said breathlessly, holding his hands up in surrender, ready to end the chase. "I wouldn't put my hands anywhere Natalie didn't want them," he said, flashing a dazzling smile.

"Wait until I catch you." After a few more minutes of roughhousing, the tired foursome walked toward the welcoming elevator, only to stop short at the sight of Tamia crouching in a corner outside of the elevator.

"Oh, my God, Tamia," Natalie stammered when she saw her.

Shocked by her sister's appearance, she hesitated briefly, but before she could act, Michael crouched down and pulled Tamia into his arms, concern visible on his face. He checked her face and hands and kept asking her if she was hurt anywhere.

Tamia kept her eyes lowered to hide her embarrassment. The side of her face was slightly bruised, and her shirtsleeve was torn completely off. Natalie went to her sister's side, hot tears sliding down her cheeks.

"Tamia, baby, try to calm down. What happened?" Natalie asked, smoothing Tamia's hair away from her face. Tamia turned her face further into Michael's shoulder, seeking both comfort and cover.

Michael tightened his hold possessively. Inside, his fury was growing, causing his features to harden; his eyes became sparkling flashes of Irish emeralds. He didn't speak, afraid that his anger would frighten her.

"Tamia," Natalie asked again, "what happened?"

"Let's get her up into the house first," Thorne wisely suggested, keeping an eye on his brother, who he knew almost as well as his own hand.

Michael lifted her effortlessly off the floor and held her protectively for the ride to his penthouse.

Natalie, upset by the sight and the lack of answers, started to cry softly as Thorne held her, whispering in her ear that her sister was okay and that Michael would take care of her. But she didn't want to be consoled; she wanted revenge. This wasn't the first time this scene had played itself out in front of her. She knew who the culprit was, even without Tamia confirming it.

Michael stood silently with Tamia in his arms, the vein on the side of his jaw beating furiously. He was enraged, and whoever had hurt her was going to pay. It didn't matter that they argued constantly after three minutes on the phone—only two in person—or that he couldn't stand being around her half the time. He was going to get whoever hurt his baby.

When the elevator doors opened to his penthouse, Michael went straight to the bedroom. Pulling back the bedsheets, he placed her in the warm bed and then got a washcloth from the bathroom. He began to gently wipe her face.

Noticing that it was almost seven, Natalie called the restaurant because she knew that Tamya would be looking for her twin.

"Girl, I'm so glad you called. David Rogers came in here earlier. He asked Tamia to step outside and talk to him for a minute. I tried to tell her not to go, but she said she would be all right. I could tell that he had been drinking." Tamya's voice was quaking with emotion. "Natalie, I haven't seen her since, and that was about an hour and a half ago."

"Calm, down, Tamya. She's with me. When we got to the Connor building, she was waiting near the elevator. I don't know yet exactly what happened, but she's pretty shaken up. Have you talked to Stephen?"

"Yeah, he went looking for David. I think you and Thorne might want to go to David's house. Stephen just left about fifteen minutes ago. I'd hate to see him get himself into trouble when he's finally happy again."

"Okay, listen, are you all right at the restaurant? Do you need help?"

"No, it's slow, and I already called Karen and asked her to come in. Just take care of Tamia and find Stephen. I love you, and tell her, too."

Natalie hung up the phone and turned back to Tamia, her hands on her hips and ready for the square off. Tamia had stopped crying and was pulling herself together. *Good,* Natalie thought.

"I'm sorry," she sadly whispered; her pride was seriously bruised.

Michael paused and stared at her, suddenly realizing that his problems and his imperfect personal life paled in comparison to the challenges she presented; she well could be his biggest problem yet, even his biggest downfall. That was a scary thought. "Come on, girl, don't be ridiculous," Michael said, trying to ease her guilt and shame.

"No. For real, Mike." Grabbing his arm, she finished sincerely, "I really appreciate this."

"*Mike?*" Theresa repeated.

Thorne looked at her sideways and smiled, then shook his head to stop her from laughing.

"Oh, I'm sorry. Hi," Tamia said, finally noticing Theresa. "I'm Tamia, Natalie's sister." Tamia extended her hand to Theresa, who easily accepted it.

"I'm Theresa, *Mike's* sister." She glanced at Michael, daring him to say something about her using his new name. "You don't have anything to apologize for. It seems that you know Michael pretty well. I've never been able to call him by a nickname." Theresa smiled, sending her brother a look laden with unasked questions. What with her traveling so much, she barely had time to dabble in her brothers' personal lives. She was learning a lot about both of them lately.

"Oh, yeah, we're good friends. He's my boy."

"Your *boy*?"

"Yeah, you know. Like . . . we're just good friends," Giving up trying to explain, Tamia decided to just keep it simple.

"So what's going on?" Theresa asked, immediately liking this girl who reminded her a lot of herself back in her rambunctious days.

Tamia turned and looked at Natalie, "I just got into a little scuffle."

"Don't you do that," Natalie said impatiently.

"What?" Tamia asked innocently. Surely, Natalie was not about to put her business out there like that.

"Make excuses for that no-good bastard. I just got off the phone with Tamya. Did David hit you? Did he?!" Natalie was angry with David, but it was transferring over to Tamia very quickly. "I can't believe you're going to do this!"

Tamia sat there without answering and then turned to Michael. She saw his anger and wanted to prevent what was about to happen; the stark fury in his eyes spelled trouble. His hand was in a tight fist around the cloth, and his cheeks had turned crimson. And he was so handsome. *I shouldn't have come here,* Tamia thought. He was her golden warrior, and he was ready to run to her rescue. But she couldn't allow him to do that. He was Michael Philips, head of one of the top corporations in the country. She wouldn't let him lower himself and stoop to David's level.

"Well, did he?" Natalie asked again. "That ass-whipping we gave him the last time wasn't enough? Did you know that Stephen has already left to look for him? He thinks you're still with him."

By now, Natalie was furious at, and frustrated with, her sister. The girl was actually going to sit there and act as if nothing had happened after they had just found her damn near hysterical.

"I don't want to talk about it. Just go and get Stephen before something happens."

Michael stood over the bed. Not trusting himself, he had mostly remained silent since they found her. The emotions swirling about him frightened more than surprised him. He was having a hard time controlling his anger, and he found that disorienting. No, it wasn't. It was making him face up to some facts that he'd rather let stay hidden. He blocked Natalie and Theresa from her line of vision.

"Tamia," he said, teeth clenched, "maybe you had better tell me where I can find this David fellow."

"No," she replied stubbornly.

"Tell me, now, Tamia," Michael warned a second time.

"No!" she retorted, her voice rising.

"Look, dammit, Thorne and I will go and get your brother." With his hands on his hips and his legs spread wide, Michael was seething. "Where in the hell is this guy who likes to put his hands on you?"

"Mike, don't," she pleaded, knowing he had reached his limit.

"I'll tell you," Natalie said, stepping forward.

Tamia looked at her in disbelief. She could not believe the betrayal.

Natalie was not going to back down. "I don't care if you get mad or not, Tamia. I don't want Stephen down there by himself, and somebody needs to whip David's ass. Every time he gets a little drunk he comes looking for you. You haven't even been together for over a year, and still, he comes looking for you to fight. I'm tired of it."

"Natalie, please, I don't want Mike and Thorne to get into any trouble."

"Don't worry about us, Tamia," Thorne interjected. "We can take care of ourselves."

Natalie jotted down David's address and the name of the bar that he frequented. "Here and be careful. It's a rough neighborhood." She kissed Thorne, then said to Tamia, "And don't look at me like that. I'm only doing this because I love you."

"Mike, please don't go down there," Tamia pleaded, again grabbing his arm. "Please. I'm all right. He only got one good hit in."

"That was one too many," Michael replied, his anger resurging.

"I fought back!" Tamia cried hysterically. "I swear. Natalie, you know I did!"

"I know you did, but you won't stop him from coming back," Natalie said, her tone taking on a new chilly edge.

"Oh, God. Mike, please," Tamia begged one last time as Mike kissed her forehead and walked with Thorne out of the room. Her tears choked her. "See, Natalie, what if something happens to him? I'll never forgive myself."

"Tamia, what in the world is wrong with you? Any other time, you'd be on the bandwagon ready to go whip David's behind right along with them."

"Natalie, I don't know. I really like him, you know. I don't want anything to happen to him." She lay back on the pillows and dabbed at her eyes. "I can't stand him, and all we do is argue, but I can't get him off my mind. Oh, Lord. What is wrong with me?" she finally asked.

"Sounds like love, Tamia. But don't be mad at Natalie. She couldn't have stopped him or Thorne. From the moment Michael first saw you like this, they had already made up their minds what they were going to do. Sometimes you have to step back and let a man be a man. Michael must care for you a lot, too. I haven't seen him this mad, especially over a woman, in a long time. As a matter of fact, I don't think Michael has ever gotten this upset over any woman other than me."

"Okay, let's just get you cleaned up," Natalie suggested, trying to ease the tense atmosphere. "I assume you'll be staying here tonight. The least you could do is be presentable when he comes back. I'm sure you're not too tired to reward him for his gallantry."

"Ha, ha. Very funny." Tamia suddenly paused and, looking more closely at the two other women, said, "Well, I guess it wouldn't hurt to freshen up." They all laughed, beginning to feel better about the night's events.

They helped her get cleaned up and then the three watched DVDs until each had drifted off to sleep across the huge bed. They awakened to the sound of loud voices punctuated by even louder laughter.

"Well, what do we have here? Look, three sleeping beauties," Thorne said from the doorway of the bedroom, laughing raucously. The boisterous trio seemed unable or unwilling to settle down.

"This is the last time I'm going to tell you three menaces-to-society to quiet down," Sandra said, pushing her way to the front of the group. Addressing the women in a pleading voice, she said, "Excuse me, ladies. Do you want to claim these three so I can get them off my hands?"

"What happened?" Tamia asked, roused by concern for Michael's welfare. She quickly sat up, eager to hear all the details.

Followed by his cohorts, Michael stumbled into the huge bedroom. They all had quite a bit to drink, judging from the smell of beer emanating from their bodies.

Michael's hair was tousled, and his usually impressive double-breasted suit was beyond repair. Buttons were missing, and dirt and grass stains were all over the knee and elbow areas. His left hand was wrapped in a bandage.

Thorne's sweater sleeve was ripped, and he had stains on his jeans. Stephen's clothes weren't too badly messed up, but his left eye was hugely swollen.

Theresa sat up on the bed as Natalie ran to Thorne's side, and Tamia went to Michael's. "So what did you do to that poor man?" she asked nonchalantly.

"Poor man?" Michael snorted, patting his swollen lip. "That 'poor man' got the beating of his life for messing with my baby." He slumped onto the sofa in the far corner of his bedroom, pulling Tamia onto his lap. They sank into its cushions, and Michael, emboldened by liquor, forgot about everyone in the room and began nuzzling her neck.

It was obvious that she wasn't getting any more out of him, so Theresa turned to Thorne. "What happened, Thorne?"

"Oh." He lifted his eyes from Natalie's cleavage, where he had been concentrating for the past few minutes. "Um, when we got there, we saw Stephen walking into the corner bar that Natalie told us about. By the time I parked and we went inside, he had already confronted David, but he was surrounded by a lot of David's friends. So Michael and I naturally stepped in to assist."

"Naturally," she echoed, expecting nothing less out of her brothers.

"What David didn't know was that I employ half the men in that area on construction jobs. When some of the men saw who we were, they backed off immediately. Michael told David he was Tamia's new boyfriend and handled him. Stephen and I only had to take care of a few strays." He pulled Natalie to him. "Come here, love."

"So, Thorne . . . Thorne," Theresa began, trying to get him to focus. "Thorne, so why do you three smell like a brewery? Hi, by the way, I'm Theresa, the sister of these knuckleheads."

"Hi, I'm Stephen, and this is, um, Sandra, my, um, friend." Stephen quickly gave up trying to put the detective into some category.

"Hi, I'm a detective with the NOPD," Sandra said. "Lucky for them, I was around when they were hauled in for disorderly conduct, destruction of property, inciting a riot, intent to do bodily harm, and offensive touching. I managed to get them all off on everything except the offensive touching because they beat the guys up pretty bad. But it's a misdemeanor and involves payment of a fine only. They were already kind of drunk when I got to them. Both Mr. Rogers and the bar owner pressed charges. But when the bar owner was told the repairs would be made by Connor Construction and a minimal amount paid to him for damaged property and interruption of business, Mr. Davis, the proprietor, decided to drop his charges."

"After the fighting was over, we decided to enjoy the rest of the evening. You know, we had ourselves a little boy's night out," Stephen explained. "The police picked us up when we were leaving to come back here."

"I hope you make your 'nights out' few and far between if you're going to be acting like this." Theresa looked around the room. Michael had fallen asleep on the sofa, and Thorne was whispering into Natalie's ear. For the first time in years, she felt lonely, and she didn't like it. "Well, I'm going home. I'll see you both in the office first thing in the morning," she said on her way out. "It was nice meeting you both," she said to Sandra and Stephen.

"Thorne, we're heading out, too. I'll give you a call later. Oh, please remind Michael to get his car tomorrow." Stephen stopped on his way to the door. "And, hey, thanks for having my back tonight, man."

"No problem. It's been a long time since we've been able to get out and let loose. Go get some steak for that eye." They shook hands.

"All right."

Thorne was practically sleepwalking on the way to his house. Natalie had managed to get him into the bedroom, where he collapsed on the leather couch. That suited her just fine because he was too messed up to take a shower, and he was not getting into bed with her smelling like a brewery.

CHAPTER 14

It was Friday afternoon and Thorne sat alone in the office of his mansion, Gladewinds. He heard the phone ringing but didn't answer it—didn't intend to. It was as if he was in a trance-like state. He sat in his black leather chair, his thoughts running amuck.

His sudden retreat to his country home was necessary, he thought, for his mental stability. He needed to get away from the chaos that had become his life. Of course, Thorne knew that he couldn't run forever, but he seriously needed a time-out. He had taken this little breather to form a plan for restoring some measure of order to his life.

The caller ID showed calls from his brother, sister, and Natalie. Over the last few days, they each called numerous times. But he had no desire to talk to anyone; he needed quiet time to think, period.

In one short month, his life had changed dramatically. He had been a single, fun-loving guy, a very wealthy man who enjoyed most aspects of life. He had never wanted for female companionship, and he ran a very, very successful business that he loved. He had a close-knit family and all the luxuries and privileges one man could possibly want in life. But now, he was confused, a virtual stranger in his own skin. So many changes—some good, some bad—had come his way. Too fast, too soon.

He was in love with a wonderful woman. He honestly and truly loved Natalie, of that he was certain. Finally, God had brought a woman into his life who was only concerned with his happiness and well-being. His money and power didn't matter to her at all. In fact, when he was with her, Thorne sensed that she held all the power. She was everything that he wanted and needed in a mate. And he could see her as his life partner.

But how could he be with her, make her happy, or give her the love and support that she needed when he was so totally lost? He didn't know who he was or what he was about. He had learned that his whole life had been nothing more than one unbroken lie.

Hatred was what Thorne was feeling right now. He didn't understand why his grandmother would lie to him or why his cousin, Howard, had participated in the lie. So many questions still needed answers. His father had obviously had some part in the creation of his new identity. Ever since he could remember, his name had been Thorne, always Thorne. Nobody had ever called him Matthew. The name didn't even fit him. He wasn't a Matthew.

Thorne closed his eyes, and his nostrils flared with fury as he relived for the umpteenth time how the truth of his birth had unfolded.

Thorne awakened Tuesday with a slight hangover. He showered and dressed and then went downstairs to make a quick breakfast. Natalie was still sound asleep.

He had already decided what he was going to do. There was only one surefire way of getting to the bottom of everything. Going to his grandfather wasn't an option; it would hinder more than help him in his quest for the truth. Old Matthew had long since washed his hands of his grandson, and vice versa. If Thorne were to see him now, he was sure that he would be arrested for attempted murder before it was all over.

Howard was out of the country on vacation. But as soon as he stepped foot back into the country, they were going to have a long sit-down. Meanwhile, only one person could help provide answers to his questions.

Feeling good about his decision, he wanted to start his day off on a positive note. He woke Natalie with a plate of bacon, eggs, toast, and coffee to apologize for falling asleep on her the night before. As she ate, he retold the previous night's account of their little scuffle with David and his boys, being sure to make himself sound like a superhero, complete with action-sequence moves.

"Come on now, Thorne," Natalie said, giggling at the absurdity of his tale. "You really threw the guy all the way across the room?"

"What? You don't believe me?" he asked, feigning offense.

"I just find it hard to believe, that's all."

"Well, I did it," he laughed, keeping his fingers crossed under the blanket.

"I'm just glad that none of you were seriously hurt last night. What are you doing?" she asked, feeling his hand skim over her thigh as she took a sip of coffee.

"What? I'm just trying to apologize," Thorne answered, still caressing her thigh.

"You already apologized," she said in mock harshness.

"But I don't think that I was sincere enough the first time," he smoothly countered.

Natalie tried to ignore the hand exploring the hollow area behind her knees and continued to eat her breakfast. He slowly made a path up her hip and across her waist until he could feel the beginnings of her nest just below the band of her bikini briefs.

"You have a lot to apologize for, you know," Natalie said in a low voice, moving the breakfast tray to the floor.

"I'm willing to do whatever you need me to do, love."

Nestling down under the covers, Natalie turned towards him in the bed. She put her hands on his chest, massaging the muscles as she marveled at the magnificent man in her arms.

Thorne pulled her closer, locking her to his body as he buried his face against her throat.

The urgency of the moment quickly wrapped around them like a warm blanket, sending shivers of excitement through them. Thorne rolled her over to lie astride him. His hands moved gently over her backside as he worked her briefs down her legs.

Slowly caressing her back and neck, he gently pulled on her hair so that she lifted her head and gave him access to her neck.

Natalie was more than willing to be Thorne's plaything. His skin next to hers sent shivers of delight through her. Moans of ecstasy escaped her lips as he skillfully lulled her into a state of euphoria with his mouth and hands. Her breast tingled against the spray of hair that covered his chest as he lifted her and began to lower her onto him.

"Thorne . . ." Clearing her throat, she suddenly stopped moving.

"Don't worry, Nat, I won't hurt you," he said, feeling her hesitation. His lips brushed against hers as he spoke.

"I know, but . . ."

"We'll take it easy. If you aren't comfortable, we'll change," he assured her. "Besides, you have total control of the situation."

Natalie could felt his hardness pressed against her. He felt so damn good. She liked the way he rubbed against her, the way his tongue felt on her neck, breast, and shoulders. Eventually, she wanted more, needed more than his touches. Her body melted against his, his expert touch sending her to even higher levels of ecstasy.

Thorne held himself steady as he anticipated her descent onto his waiting length. Her hesitation and apprehension were fleeting, so his arousal grew strong as passion pounded the blood through his body, chest, and head. His pulse quickened when her hand surrounded him.

Natalie eased down onto him very slowly. She felt herself stretching to accommodate him. Trying to relax, she took several deep breaths as her discomfort became unbearable.

"Wait . . . wait," she gasped, after she felt she couldn't take the pressure. "Thorne, I think we need something."

"What do you mean?" he asked, masking his inner turmoil with a deceptive calm. The condom was in place; he was ready for her.

"I don't know, lubricant or something," she suggested, trying to make it easier for both of them.

"Oh, I got something in the bathroom. Hold on." She rolled off him, and Thorne jumped out of the bed in a shot. Natalie laughed as he streaked across the room butt naked, rushing into the bathroom in all his handsome glory. As he banged the cabinet door shut, she tried to remember exactly when he had removed his clothes. Not that she was complaining. She liked what she saw—a nice tight body covered with firm skin, muscle upon muscle.

Thorne applied the lubricant over his condom and hurriedly repositioned himself on the bed, swinging her into the circle of his arms in the process.

She grimly set about concentrating on rebuilding their passion. She kissed him on his face and softly nibbled his chin and chest so that he wouldn't be so focused on his main goal.

In turn, he fondled each of her heavy globes until the peaks tightened into small knots. When they were both relaxed and enjoying the foreplay, she easily slid onto him. The quickness of the entry made them both gasp, Thorne recovering first.

After holding Natalie to him for a brief second, Thorne slowly began to move from side to side, thrilled by the moist tightness engulfing him. Natalie tried to lift herself, but found it difficult as her lower body vibrated with liquid fire. Instead, she leaned forward against him until together they found the tempo that bound them together. She gradually worked her hips faster. Before long, Thorne was helping her to move over him. The pace quickened until Thorne changed the direction of their speed, wanting to prolong their lovemaking.

He sat up so that they would be facing each other and wrapped her legs around him, holding her close to give them both a chance to catch their breaths and to slow things down. Natalie found that she liked this position better and began to move over him, his raw sensuousness carrying her to greater heights until the muscles of her canal contracted around him as she reached her climax. Thorne lowered his face into her shoulder, locked his arms around her waist, and groaned out his release, no longer fighting to hold back his true feelings.

"I love you, Nat," he whispered in her ear, holding her tight as contentment flowed over them.

"I love you, too," she sighed, savoring the feeling of complete satisfaction that he gave her. Kissing him slowly, her heart filled with love for him, sweetly drowning all of her doubts and fears.

Later, while they made love under the steamy stream of hot water cascading from the showerhead, Thorne told her that he loved her again. Now that his true feelings had been revealed to him, he couldn't expect to be able to simply make them fade away.

Thorne thought about his feelings for Natalie and many other things as he sat musing in his office. He wondered what he was going to do about her—her and the woman who had identified herself as his mother.

CHAPTER 15

The walk down the corridor that led to Amanda's hospital room was one of the longest Thorne had ever taken. Approaching the door, he could feel his fears beginning to tighten around his neck like a noose, and he wondered if he was about to hang himself by letting this woman into his life.

With his hand frozen on the knob, for the first time in his life, Thorne hesitated before making his next move. His life was already changing. He was changing. Never before had he second-guessed his decisions. He was a strong, smart man who helped to run one of the most successful companies in the country, but he was scared as hell of what waited on the other side of the door.

When he told her of his intentions, Natalie called ahead to the hospital to make sure that Amanda was doing better and up for company. She was afraid that her seeing Thorne would somehow trigger another relapse. However, the doctor assured her that Amanda was doing much better, and they had significantly reduced her medication. Amanda was very lucid and had been asking for her.

She wanted to go into the room with Thorne, but recognized that it was something that he needed to do alone. So she nervously sat in the metal hallway chair and watched him standing by the door doing battle with his thoughts. She only prayed that he would make the right decision and walk into the room. The truth needed to be told, and if Amanda was his mother, he needed to hear it from her.

Amanda turned her head slowly toward the opening hospital door. She hated to be bothered by those pesky nurses when she had so much on her mind. For once, her head wasn't throbbing, her back wasn't hurting, and she wasn't half delirious from the medicine they kept shooting into her IV. She wanted to stay that way, at least until Natalie came by to visit.

In fact, she was ready to leave this godforsaken place and return to the comfort of her own home. The doctor wanted to run this test and that test. She didn't need any more tests. Nothing was wrong with her, but she couldn't seem to convince him of that.

"Excuse me," Thorne muttered uneasily, cautiously stepping into the room.

Amanda gasped when she saw him, and her hand flew up to her chest. The crossword puzzle book that she had been working on slipped out of her hand and fell to the floor.

"I'm sorry. I didn't mean to startle you," Thorne quickly apologized. Frightened anticipation touched his spine, causing him to want to bolt from the room. Another brief round of second-guessing made him hesitate, but it quickly passed. He had to do this.

Amanda didn't say anything. Tears slowly slid down her right cheek. She couldn't believe what she was seeing. It was like looking at a ghost. Had he come back to her?

"Matthew?" she whispered unbelievably. No, it couldn't be. They must have slipped her some more of that awful medicine. It had her mind going back to the past.

"No, my name is Thorne, Thorne Philips," he answered.

"I'm sorry," Amanda said, shaking her head from side to side, trying to contain her confusion. She wiped away the wayward tears. "I thought you were someone else, someone that I knew a long time ago. You look so much like him."

Thorne slowly crossed the room. He took the chair that was at the far window and moved it closer to the bed. "Do you mind if I talk with you for a moment?"

"Of course, not, Matt . . . I mean, Thorne." Amanda still wasn't sure whom she was talking to, or if she was talking to anyone at all. But she did know that she was looking into the face of the only man she had ever loved. If he was a ghost, she thanked the Lord for this visit; if he wasn't, she would just have to be declared certifiable. But she was going to enjoy his company. He could be who-ever he wanted to be.

His first plan of action was to barge in and say what he had to say, yell at her a bit, accuse her of lying, and then offer her money to just go away. It had worked countless times in the business world, but when he saw her lying there in the bed, pale and weak, he knew he couldn't treat her that way. This wasn't a business merger, and she wasn't an adversary. So who was she exactly?

He knew she was Natalie's friend, but he still didn't want his life to be affected by this turn of events. But his heart had softened a little. He couldn't just barge in and curse at this frail-looking woman. Regardless of whether she was his mother or not, she was going to get his respect.

Natalie said that her friend was strong and demanding, but this woman didn't resemble that description at all. Only the small glint in her charcoal eyes let Thorne know that she was indeed a fighter. Her body was small and thin; her hair was a little unkempt and unruly, but he saw conviction and strength in her eyes.

"Did you know Matthew Philips?" Thorne asked.

"Yes," Amanda said, wondering if this man could be related to her Matthew in some way. "He was my first husband. Are you one of his sons?" she asked, thinking a little more rationally.

"Yes, I am his eldest son," Thorne said, watching her closely. Before she could speak, Thorne continued, "A mutual friend of ours, Natalie Davidson, surprised me with the news that you had once been married to my father. Of course, I didn't believe it until we obtained copies of the marriage license and such."

"You're her gentleman friend, the one she was trying to tell me about. So handsome. You look just like your father. I always missed talking to him. But I suppose you're here because you want to stop Natalie from looking for my son."

Thorne was beginning to see the strong woman that Natalie had talked about. Amanda seemed to grow stronger right before his eyes. She was sitting upright without adjusting her bed or using pillows, and her eyes were lit with determination.

"No, ma'am, I told Natalie that I would help her with this search, and I will, no matter what the outcome."

"What do you mean by that?" she asked.

"Well, Natalie, my brother and sister and I have been doing a little research. We found the birth certificate for your son, Matthew Charles Philips III."

Amanda's laughter was hearty. "I always hated the fact that I had to name my son that. Matthew and I argued for a long time over that name. I didn't want my baby named after that racist, good-for-nothing father of his."

Thorne didn't interrupt; that she was clearly reliving the past.

"But that's what he wanted. I was so crazy in love with Matthew. And when our baby was born, he was so proud. He loved that little boy. He wouldn't have cared if our son were black, blue, purple, or red. Matthew was such a good father. I used to watch them roll around on the floor in front of the TV and watch cartoons together. Then he would bathe Little Matt and fall asleep with him sprawled across his chest, like breathing together."

This time, Thorne was the one who pulled a tissue out of the little cardboard box and wiped the tears from Amanda's eyes. She had lost a lot, and Thorne knew grief when he saw it. But he couldn't let himself soften for this lady. That would stop him from achieving his goals.

"Um . . . Amanda," Thorne began, intruding softly on the woman's thoughts, "the problem that I have here, um, with this whole investigation of ours, is that the date that appears on your son's birth certificate is the same as mine."

"What?" Amanda looked at him closely, blinking in bafflement.

"Yeah, your son appears to have been born on the same day as me," Thorne repeated.

"No, that can't be right. Matthew and I were married. He was a good man. He didn't cheat on me. He loved me," Amanda replied, refusing to believe that Matthew could have deceived her in such a way.

"Yes, of course he did. I knew my father well enough before he passed away to know that." Thorne paused. "See, I don't exactly know what happened or how, but I believe that my birth certificate is a fraud."

"Thorne, people don't just go around forging birth certificates. What makes you think so?" Amanda asked, wondering where he was going with his reasoning.

"Well, the name of the lady that my grandparents told me was my mother, Maria Annette Gamio, is actually the name of a woman who lives just on the outside of the city. We went and visited her yesterday. She said that she didn't know why her name was on my birth certificate, but that she was being paid to keep it a secret. It was an arrangement made years ago between her parents and my grandparents."

"Well, if she isn't your real mother, then who is?" Amanda asked. She felt so sorry for this man, who apparently had become an innocent pawn in someone's cruel game of chess. It seemed that no one had given any thought to how this young man might feel in the future. She had made the same mistake herself. Amanda thought about her own son. How would he feel when she found him? Would he hate her for not thinking about his future feelings?

"I'm not sure, but I've been thinking about this for a couple of days, and it makes sense to me that you may be my real mother."

Now it was Amanda's turn to be cautious. She didn't say anything, because before she opened her heart up to be broken, she wanted to be just a little surer. She had wanted to find her son for so long. Fear was the only thing that had kept her from trying sooner. Fear of rejection. And now here was this man waltzing into her hospital room telling her that he was her son. She wasn't ready to buy it.

"What makes you so sure?" she asked, now suspicious of his real purpose for being there.

"Well, as I said, I'm not sure, but it just makes sense. My birth date is the same as your son's, right? But my birth certificate wasn't filed until two years after I was born, which is around the same time that you left. I don't know why that is, but just listen to me." Thorne framed his face between his hands. "No, *look* at me. I'm not fair-skinned like my brother and sister. I mean, yeah, I look like a tanned white man, but it's a permanent tan. That's why I so easily believed that my mother was Italian. But I could also be the product of an interracial marriage. That would explain why my grandfather hates me so much. I'm a constant reminder of the one and only time that he couldn't control someone or something."

"Thorne . . ."

"No, let me finish," he said, standing up and moving closer to her bed. Thorne felt as if he were grasping at straws. He wasn't sure what he was doing. All of this was going to have to come to a head sooner or later, and he would rather just have everything out in the open. "There's an easy enough way to settle this."

"And what would that be?" Amanda asked curiously. She wanted this puzzle solved, too. It would be easy enough to wish that Thorne was her son, but she had to know for sure.

"Let's just get a blood test done. I'll pay for one right now. That way at least one of my questions will be answered."

"Thorne, are you sure that you're ready to have your questions answered? Don't get me wrong. I would love for it to be proven that you are in fact my Little Matthew, but are you really ready for the consequences of this discovery? Have you really thought about what this could mean? And what if it leaks out that I am your mother? What about your business, your friends? Would you be able to deal with knowing that you're not white or Italian, but actually biracial? These are things that you might want to think about first." Amanda wanted him to be her son, but from being older and wiser she knew that it would be a very hard adjustment for him. She liked Thorne and the way he carried himself. He was a good, strong man. His disposition showed her that much.

Thorne was amazed and surprised that Amanda would care if he could handle this situation. He was a complete stranger to her, but still she wanted to be sure that *he* was ready for the truth. His admiration for this lady grew, and he made another decision: He and Amanda would be good friends after this whole thing was over, whether she was his mother or not.

"I don't have any friends. And my business has nothing to do with this. It speaks for itself. All I know is that right now I don't know anything about myself. I'm like a lost dog that somebody found on the street and took to the animal shelter with no name tag."

"Thorne . . ." Amanda began, reaching for his arm.

"No, it's true," he said, moving away from her and toward the window. He leaned with his forehead against the cool glass, his hands shoved deep into his pockets. "And I can't stand it."

"Okay, let's do it," Amanda replied, feeling that she had to help ease his pain even in the least way.

"Good. I'll call a friend of mine who works here on the staff. She's a good person. I trust her to keep the results to herself. Is it okay if I ask her to do it right away? We—Natalie is outside—can wait for the results."

"Yes, of course. One more needle can't kill me, I suppose," she joked, a flash of humor crossing her face.

"Thank you," Thorne said. "I know this can't be easy for you, either." He looked into the eyes of this stranger. He liked her.

Except for the shuffle of Thorne's shoes as he walked back and forth in front of the window in Amanda's room and the flipping of pages as Natalie pretended to be reading a magazine, the hospital room was totally quiet. Nobody talked while they waited for Dr. Miller to show up with the test results. When Thorne called her, she said that it would take only a couple of minutes once the blood was drawn, but an hour had already passed.

Thorne's face was beginning to show signs of strain; his patience was wearing thin. He didn't know how much longer he could stand waiting for his possible identity to be revealed. For the umpteenth time, he ran his hand through his dark, wavy mass of hair.

Amanda lay back against her bed pillow, having decided to just pray for a positive outcome. After all, it was now in the hands of the Lord.

"Amanda, do you want something to drink?" Natalie asked, bored to death and looking for something to do.

"No, dear, I'm all right. Check on your young man. He's the one falling apart."

Thorne overheard the exchange, but ignored it. He continued walking back and forth with his head down, thinking.

"Baby, why don't you have a seat?" Natalie suggested.

"No, Nat, I'm all right," he replied without inflection.

"But, baby . . ."

"Natalie, please . . ." Thorne stopped abruptly and looked at her. He didn't want to take his frustrations out on Natalie. None of this was her fault. If anything, he guessed that he should have been thanking her, but now was just not the time. When he spoke again, his voice was tender, almost a murmur. "I'm sorry. But I just need to be left alone."

"Would you like me to call Michael and Theresa?" she asked, still trying to help him through this stressful situation.

"Yeah . . . no . . . no, I'll talk to them later."

"Well, I need to do something. I can't just sit around here like this. We're acting as if we're at . . ." Natalie stopped talking when she heard the door to the room open.

A tall, sexy brunette walked into the room and headed straight for Thorne. "Hi, Thorne," she said in a low drawl.

Thorne cut her off. Her facial expression said she was a little too happy to see him. She had been in the middle of something when he called her earlier, so one of her assistants came up to take their blood. He also saw the look on Natalie's face, which made him act quickly. He was already going through enough.

"Hello, Tabitha," Thorne couldn't escape her hug, but he made it as brief as he possibly could. "Let me introduce you." Clearing his throat, he stepped away from the doctor and moved closer to Natalie's side. "Dr. Tabitha Miller, this is Natalie Davidson, my girlfriend." The look that passed between the two women before they spoke was unmistakable. "And this is her friend, Amanda Henry. Amanda's the lady who I think may be my mother."

"Hello, Amanda. How are you feeling today?" Quickly switching back to doctor mode, Tabitha approached the side of the bed. After Amanda murmured her answer, she continued. "I have the results of your tests. I'm sorry it took so long, but I wanted to deliver them myself."

"I bet she did," Natalie whispered, stepping closer to Thorne.

"Behave yourself, Nat," Thorne warned, smiling down at her. "Okay, doc," he said, turning his attention to Tabitha, "what does it say?"

"Well, beyond a shadow of a doubt, Thorne, Amanda is your biological mother. I can understand that this is a lot to deal with right now. If you would like, I can contact one of the hospital's counselors or psychologists."

"No, that won't be necessary. Thanks a lot, Tabitha. Just bill my office, would you?"

Tabitha watched as Natalie hugged Amanda, who wept openly, rocking back and forth. "Maybe I should call her doctor in."

"No, I'm all right. Thank you, Jesus. I'm just fine now." Amanda smiled at her, trying hard to push back her tears. "Thank you, doctor."

"Amanda, I'm going to go out with the doctor so that you and Thorne can talk for a minute. Will you be all right?" Natalie asked, realizing that the two had more talking to do.

"Yes, and Natalie, thank you, too, so very much," she said to her friend.

Natalie kissed her on the cheek and then went over to Thorne. "Are you all right?" she asked him.

"Well, at least now I know part of the truth." He was still upset and more confused than before. He now had a whole new set of questions to ask. "Nat, you stay in here. If it hadn't been for you, none of this would have happened."

"Are you sure?" she asked, kissing the side of his face softly. He nodded.

"Yes, I think we both need you," Thorne replied. Natalie returned to the room's only chair. "Well, now we know," he said, edging closer to Amanda's bedside. His hands were shoved back deep into his pockets.

"Yes, we do. Now what?" Amanda asked, her face a study in strength, serenity.

"I don't know. I have a lot to think about, a lot I want to know about." Thorne gripped the railing on the side of her bed, using it to support some of his weight.

"Thorne, let me explain something to you first off. I'm sorry that you had to find out about me this way. I never really thought about how much it would change your life. I guess I was being selfish and stubborn. But I needed to find you. I never stopped loving you. Never. And I hope you believe that."

Amanda reached for one of Thorne's hands and held it tightly. For the first time in thirty-four years, she was touching her son. He was so handsome. Her son. She thought of all of the times that she had seen pictures of him in the newspapers or on the magazine covers and thought that maybe he could be her son. Although she had never believed Old Matthew's stories of her son dying with his father, she should have tried much harder to contact Miss Abby for verification. All of this could have been avoided if she had just tried. This was her son.

Thorne wasn't sure how he was supposed to feel. He was glad that he had found his real mother, but why was he mourning the memory of a woman who had never existed and that he had never known?

For years, he had held onto a certain image of his mother, had made himself believe that she loved him. And deep in his heart he had believed it had been his fault that she was gone. He had lived with the horrifying notion that he had killed his mother at birth for damn near his whole life. And now here was his mother, who was saying that she loved him and always had. Thorne wasn't quite sure that he was ready to jump in and be the son that she wanted.

"Why did you leave me, us?" he asked tersely, trying with all his might to keep his anger under control.

Amanda patted the side of her bed and moved her leg to make room for Thorne to sit, choosing to ignore the fury brewing in his eyes. She saw him hesitate, but he sat. Before she began to speak, Amanda touched his face, ran her fingers through his hair, and wiped her eyes.

"Thorne, do you know what it's like to make the greatest sacrifice?"

"No, I don't," he answered, after briefly pondering the question.

"No, I didn't either until I met your father. We seemed to hit it off right away. God, back in those days, there was so much hatred and racism going around. Even though we were here in New Orleans with its mixture of cultures and lifestyles, there were still some things that some people considered taboo. Your dad and his friends used to come down to this little juke joint where I was working with some of my friends. We used to sing and wait tables. He flirted with me outrageously. At first, I figured that he was just looking for a good time. I mean, all of the girls knew who he was. So I figured that he was some spoiled rich kid coming down into the bayou to let off steam or to defy his parents. He was a little rebellious."

Thorne listened intently.

"At first, I tried not to pay him any attention. But he wouldn't give up. He kept coming around until I finally wanted him just as much as he wanted me. His friends used to help us sneak out together. They had all gotten together and rented an apartment in the city so that they could be closer on the weekends. I guess it was also to get away from their big family mansions and relax a while. I was scared, but to be honest, it was an adventure. We had such a good time together. Before long, it was love. I mean real love. And all of our friends saw it. They were all helping us to spend time together. I was lying to my family; he was lying to his, just so we could be together. Then I got pregnant . . . with you."

She turned and looked at him.

"Everything changed after that. Matthew changed. He wanted you from the start. He proudly told people that he had a baby on the way. It was as if he didn't understand how things were. Or maybe he just didn't care. His friends even gave him a party to congratulate him on becoming a father. They loved him, you know. He had a lot of friends. Your father was a good man." She paused, remembering her beloved.

"Let's see, he told Miss Abby first. She was actually happy for him. They loved each other a lot. She just wanted him to be happy. Your father had bought me a little cottage so that I could be comfortable; of course, he was there, too, more often than not. Miss Abby even came over to visit me a number of times. She was excited about the birth of her first grandbaby. I think she waited until I was in my seventh month before she told Old Matthew. He probably already knew because word traveled around fast. And she only told him then because your father insisted that we be married before you were born."

"I'm sure that didn't go well," Thorne said, eager to hear more. He was mesmerized by the story that Amanda was telling, almost as if he were a kid, and this was one of their nightly bedtime stories.

Amanda laughed, "No, it didn't go well at all. But with Miss Abby's help, we were married. And we were so happy for a while, but every day I blamed myself for the hatred that was brewing between Matthew and his father. Matthew couldn't go into his parents' home without being harassed by his father. Eventually, the fathers of his friends found out and made them dissociate from him. Some of them still found little ways to see him secretly, but it was very hard. He was being treated differently at restaurants and clubs that he had been going to all his life. You were his only joy. When he held you, his gray eyes just sparkled. He loved you so much, Thorne."

Thorne remained silent.

"That's what I mean about making the greatest sacrifice. Your father gave up his life, everything that he had ever known, his whole way of living, for me, for us. I felt so guilty, and I loved him enough to try to give that back to him. I admit part of it was selfishness because I didn't have it easy, either. My family completely disowned me. It was fine when I was just lying up with the white man and bringing home money to my parents so that they could have the things that they wanted in life. See, my father was a drunk, and when I brought him money, it was one night easier for my mother, younger sisters, and me. He would go out to the bar, and we wouldn't see him until noon the next day. Ha, I got so good at trying to make him stay away that I would divide the money up so that it would last him the week. When Matthew bought me that cottage, I didn't even look back. All I took with me was about ten dresses and my three pairs of shoes, but that was a lot back then."

They both laughed.

"Believe me, Ma . . . Thorne, leaving you and your father was the hardest thing I ever had to do. But I didn't want Matthew to live isolated like that. He wasn't used to it. And I loved him so much for trying it for me. When I left, you were asleep on his chest. I didn't know where I was going, but I thought that you would both be better off without me. Miss Abby loved you so much. I knew she wouldn't let anything happen to you. Besides, she was the one with all the money, anyway. Matthew told me that it was her family whose money your grandfather let people around town think was his own."

"But . . ." Thorne started to interrupt but decided against it.

"Thorne, you were so light. I knew that you could pass. And I figured that you would get into the best schools and have a much better life than I could have given you. I knew that Miss Abby would have taken care of us, but I didn't want you to be labeled as a mixed kid. Times were so hard back then."

"I didn't want to pass. I wanted, needed a mother. I understand that you thought that you were making the right choice, but you were so wrong." Thorne's anger finally surfaced. "You could have at least stayed in contact with me, or let me know something."

"Thorne, I stayed in contact with Miss Abby in the beginning. She understood what I was going through. She never told Matthew that she had heard from me. It would only have made it that much harder for him to move on. She sent me pictures of you, and even money occasionally to make sure that I stayed on my feet. I just saved it. Eventually, Miss Abby put me through college. If it weren't for her a lot of things would have gone very wrong in my life. I never knew that your name had been changed, and I don't understand why it was done, but knowing Miss Abby there had to have been a good reason.

"Your father and I never spoke to each other. But I missed him so much, then we accidentally bumped into each other two years after I left. He was in Philadelphia on a business trip. Deep down, I always thought that Miss Abby had sent him up there on purpose. I was working at this lounge that he happened to visit. He later told me that Miss Abby had suggested the place to him."

"Anyway, nothing had changed; I was still very much in love with him. He stayed with me that night. We were up until all hours of the morning talking about you and the past. He showed me pictures of you and told me how things were down here. We even talked about me visiting you. But I was scared. I didn't think you would remember me. Maybe I was being selfish again."

Thorne handed her another tissue as she continued her story.

"After that, we stayed in contact for a few years. He would come to Philadelphia maybe six or seven times a year. I think that we were just trying to hold on to our past. The last time he visited he told me that he was engaged to Susan. We kept in contact for a few more years, then I never heard from him again."

"That must have been around the time of the accident. He and Susan both died."

"Yes, I know that now. Thorne, I did try to contact Miss Abby after that, but Old Matthew put his lawyers on me. I couldn't get within 100 feet of that house by the time they were done with me. They *advised* me that you had died in the accident and to stay away from Miss Abby as I no longer had any ties to the family. I didn't believe them, but I did stay away, for far too long. I've seen pictures of you and your siblings in papers and magazines. And the articles describe you as Matthew's oldest son from a previous marriage. They mentioned your mother had died during childbirth. I didn't know how many children Matthew had after I left. Eventually, I guess it was easier for me to believe Old Matthew's story.

It stopped me from having to deal with my own guilt. But when this happened to me, I asked Natalie to find you. When I had this last accident, I was afraid that I would never get to see you and apologize. I know that it's too little too late, but, Thorne, I do apologize, and I do realize that my decision was a bad one. That's why I begged Natalie to find you."

"Well, she sure did do that," Thorne laughed, looking over his shoulder at her.

"Do you love her?" Amanda whispered.

Thorne smiled down at his mother for the first time, "Yes, I do." He wasn't sure if Natalie had heard the question, but she had heard his answer.

"Well, now can you tell me about yourself?" she asked.

"There's really nothing to tell," he replied.

"Then that's exactly what I want to know."

CHAPTER 16

Somewhere deep in his subconscious, Thorne could feel the brandy glass slipping out of his hand. He jerked fully awake and tried to focus on his surroundings. The portrait over the marble fireplace of his great-grandfather, Jacob Howard Connor, reminded him that he was still lying in the same spot he had been in four hours earlier.

The family study was a large room at the back of the Gladewinds mansion. Most of the more valuable pieces of the family's art collection were kept here. The room also boasted large paintings of numerous figures in the Connor ancestral lineage dating back to the 1800s. Attired in costumes associated with a given period, they were depicted enjoying different sporting or cultural activities. The portraits suggested his ancestors had remarkable strength, grace, and dignity in their various pursuits.

"None of you are like me . . ." he said, scrambling to his feet. He looked from one picture to the next, each one reminding him of the irony of his situation. His anger grew. Here he was with a fortune built up over the years and left to him by people who had lied to him, people he had trusted, people who he should hate right now.

Crossing over to the fireplace, he tossed the glass into the dark hole as hard as he could, the sound of the shattering glass doing little to ease his agitated state. Taking a deep breath, he made another decision—to get the whole truth.

Matthew Philips was sitting on his bed on the second floor of the west wing of the expansive estate of Southend. The back rub his nurse was giving him gave him time to let his mind review the plan he had in mind for his grandchildren. Although he didn't legally own the estate, he had reigned as its lord and master for the past sixty years. A simple thing like a will wasn't going to change that. Nor was he going to let a simple old woman, a mistake from the past, come and destroy his plans.

The first thing he had to do was get in his grandchildren's good graces. Theresa would be the easiest of the three; her maternal instincts could be used against her. Then he would use her to get to Michael, who tended to side with her when she began to get upset. The last one would be the hardest, but with the help of the other two, Thorne wouldn't be that hard to win over, either.

He should have known that she was going to do something like leave him out of the will. They had never had a real marriage, and practically hated each other from the start. He hadn't known what he was getting himself into. On their first date, she had practically raped him, and he had thought he was getting a good deal. Even though they didn't have much in common, she was a pretty enough girl. He thought that she had a wild side

231

that nobody else knew about. So he dated her and agreed to marry her after her father came to his house claiming that he had gotten her knocked up. But after the wedding day, she never let him touch her again, never even shared his bed.

They argued about it constantly until he realized that he could get his pleasures elsewhere, both inside and outside of the household. Although he was reduced to having his needs met by employees, servants, widows, and a string of prostitutes, it was a means to an end for his sake. The rest of his anger he took out by spending as much of her money as he could get away with.

Each muscle of his back began to relax under the ministrations of his live-in nurse. At eighty, even though he couldn't perform up to his old sexual level, he put his money to good use, employing women who would do everything he asked for the right price. After she finished with his back, she complied with his wish to have the front massaged as well. This was a nightly ritual.

Resting his head on the soft down comforter, he closed his eyes slightly and got as comfortable as possible. With the lights dimmed and the wind blowing through the slats of the open window causing the ceiling-to-floor curtains to sway gently, the atmosphere was set for an evening of erotic pleasures.

"Did you hear that?" he asked, almost he had heard footsteps.

"No, Matthew . . . you must relax," Sophia whispered coolly, pushing his shoulders back down against the bed cover. She turned his head toward the open door leading out of the bedroom to begin working on his shoulders and neck.

Old Matthew obeyed, closing his eyes against his better judgment.

~~~

Thorne walked down the hall none too quietly, mumbling to himself and holding his hand tightly. His knuckles were badly scraped and swollen from his fight with the security guards.

His drunken state had betrayed him into thinking he could just walk into his grandfather's residence without confrontation. Unfortunately, the guards had seen him and tried to prevent him from entering the estate. He was smart enough to know when he was fighting a losing battle after three of the men wrestled him to the ground and escorted him off the premises.

But they didn't know that Thorne had been sneaking on and off this property on a regular basis since early childhood. He simply drove to the back of the grounds, found the loose plank on the back fence he and Michael put there years ago, and squeezed through the opening. Then he walked through the gardens, up the back lawn, down the service entrance, and opened the window to the laundry room. It was never locked.

As he walked through the estate, not knowing which way to turn to find his grandfather, his steely determination showed no signs of softening. Instead, he went from room to room peering through doorways, looking for his prey.

He stumbled on Old Matthew getting a back rub only ten minutes into his search. Thorne stood outside the doorway seething with his hatred for the man in front of him, trying to remain focused as a mist of red haze drifted across his vision. Pushing the door further open caused it to squeak.

Old Matthew looked up just as Thorne crossed the threshold, approaching him at a rapid pace.

"What the . . ." Old Matthew jumped up from the bed only to stumble sideways and lean back over it. "Matthew, is that you?" He asked, knowing full well that it was his grandson. He clutched his chest.

"Stop playing games with me, old man. You know who I am," Thorne answered through clenched teeth.

"Oh, God, Matthew are you all right?" Sophia went to Matthew, trying to ease him down to the bed. Hysterical and unsure of Thorne's intent, she reached for the security panel and began frantically pushing the red button.

Old Matthew continued clutching his chest; his mouth was hanging loosely as Thorne's movement slowed. "Son . . ." he sighed before collapsing in his nurse's arms.

Sophia screamed, sure that Old Matthew had just died in her arms. Letting him fall to the floor, she began blindly bouncing around the room, forgetting all about CPR. Nowhere in her job description was there anything about dealing with dead people. She wasn't even a real nurse.

"Shut up, damn it," Thorne yelled, pushing past her to kneel down next to Old Matthew.

"Step away from him now, Thorne," Jason Ryder, one of his grandfather's security men said from the doorway, a pistol aimed at Thorne's back.

"I'm just tryin' ta help 'im," Thorne replied, his words badly slurred.

"Back away, Thorne, or I'm going to have to shoot," he lied, wanting to avoid a confrontation.

"All 'ight, Jay," Thorne said, putting his hands over his head and lifting off the floor to move away from his unconscious grandfather. He could hear the sound of sirens as two police patrol cars pulled onto the arched driveway of the palatial estate.

Inside the crowded jail cell, Thorne sat on an empty bench with his head resting against the dirty cement wall covered with graffiti, still feeling the aftereffects of his alcoholic binge. He didn't pay attention to the complaints of his cellmates or the pungent odor of urine from the filthy commode that assaulted the air around him. The pounding in his head wasn't due to the snoring of the slumbering man on the left dressed in a too small rumpled clown costume or to the taunting coming from the drag queen sitting to his right. It was due to the verbal whipping he was giving himself mentally as he waited for the police officer to take him in front of a judge.

He should have known better than to try to drown his problems in alcohol. Instead of getting the answers that he wanted, he had landed in jail. Refusing to place the blame for his actions on anyone or anything else, he swallowed what little pride he had left and acknowledged that this was entirely his fault.

Burying his head in his hands, Thorne took a deep breath and wiped the single fresh tear from his eye. Now was not the time, and definitely not the place, for his emotions to be on display. But he didn't like feeling the way he was feeling. He didn't like the betrayal that hung over his head the last couple of days. Not only from his mother, whom he didn't know, but from his grandmother, who was his light, his strength and backbone for so many years.

He absentmindedly scratched at the thick beard that had grown in from days of not shaving. That was something else he didn't like. It was only a more vivid reminder of how he had lost control of himself. That something could push him this far over the edge wounded his pride.

He was a man with literally thousands of families relying on his sound judgment and leadership abilities to survive. His employees counted on him, but why should they if he let things cause him to totally dissociate himself from his company and his family?

It took some convincing, but his mother agreed to stay at his penthouse, but as soon as she moved in and was comfortable, he left for Gladewinds. His siblings had been calling, but he wasn't answering. And he was putting the woman he loved through hell by not returning her calls. And why did he do this? Because his own insecurities had him doing the one thing he had never done before—hide from a problem.

"Ahmmm . . ." Michael cleared his voice a second time, trying to draw Thorne out of the deep thoughts were causing his brows to draw together tightly. "Hey, man . . . Thorne . . . Thorne, man, do you hear me?"

Finally, turning his eyes to the sound of his name, Thorne saw his brother standing on the other side of the steel bars, dressed in jeans and a crisp white T-shirt. Shame and regret closed in on him as he watched his brother waiting for him to move closer.

"What's up, man? You going to stay in there all night?" Michael had never seen his brother in such a state of disarray. He wasn't thinking about the ripped black dress shirt or the wrinkled, grass-stained jeans, but the disheveled hair, the dark circles around his eyes, and the ton of facial hair covering his naturally strong features. Thorne had always been the one with the firm grasp on his surroundings. This wasn't the brother he was used to being around. "Thorne, man, come on. I've already talked to the officer-in-charge. They're dropping the charges. Let's go." As uncomfortable as his brother felt in jail, Michael's discomfort for him was stronger.

"You shouldn't have come here, Michael."

"What are you talking about, man? Look, let's just go home and get out of here."

"I didn't want you to see me like this." Thorne waited as the officer opened the cell door to allow him to exit. "I'm really . . ."

"Don't worry about it, man. Now let's go," Michael said, placing a hand on his shoulder and escorting him out of the station to his SUV parked at the curb.

～

The ride back to Gladewinds was long and quiet with Michael trying to carry on a one-sided conversation with Thorne, who seemed to have disappeared within himself.

"Okay, man. Tell me, what were you thinking?"

"Nothing."

"Well, why did you go over there?"

"I wanted to."

"For what?"

"I don't want to talk about it," Thorne said in a nasty tone.

"Well, I think you should. Thorne, there are things going on here that are affecting all of us—me, Theresa, and especially Natalie. I think you need to get over this and get on with your life."

"I said that I don't want to talk about it."

"But you're hurting the people who love you, and you act like you don't know it."

"I'm hurting, Michael," he said, turning his back on his brother and looking out the passenger side window.

CHAPTER 17

At about ten, Stephen stumbled through the front door and tossed his door keys into the dish on the coffee table. Thirsty from the half-pint of ice cream he had shared with Sandra, he went to the kitchen, his mind set on a tall glass of iced water.

Feeling positive about the direction of his new relationship, he approached the kitchen door with a bounce but stopped abruptly when he saw the outline of someone sitting at the table. Flicking on the light, he saw that it was Natalie leaning on her arms, a cup of untouched hot chocolate beside her. Only the steady heaving of her shoulders told him she was awake.

"Natalie?"

She didn't move.

"Natalie?"

Startled, Natalie immediately placed a hand over her face, more to keep Stephen from seeing her puffy red eyes than to block out the light.

"Huh?"

"What's up?" he asked, already well aware of the problem. Thorne. Thorne was causing his sister to sit around crying herself to death.

"Nothing," she sighed, resting her head back on her arms.

"Well, it sure does seem like something's wrong. Why are you sitting here in the dark by yourself?" Stephen moved towards her.

"I'm fine, Stephen. I really just want to be left alone, please." The front of her head felt swollen from the constant pounding going on inside. "Please, I have a headache," she whispered in her depression.

"Maybe it has something to do with all the crying." Instead of leaving her as she asked, he pulled a chair next to her and leaned on it.

As the chair scraped against the floor, she ground her teeth to ward off the sound, but this only made her head ache even more. "Oh, God, Stephen, please," she moaned. Her stomach began to loudly protest its emptiness.

Hearing the growl, Stephen asked, his anger mounting, "Have you eaten anything today, Natalie?"

Her head moved slowly from side to side against her arm, her whole body engulfed in tides of weariness and despair.

"Do you want me to make you something?"

"No, I'll be all right."

"Natalie . . ."

"I'll be all right, Stephen." Her voice was just as unconvincing as her posture.

Fury swelled up in him. Sure it was true that Thorne was going through his own problems these days, and they were pretty big ones, but you don't just up and shut yourself off from the world—especially not from your girlfriend, and especially when it was his sister. She was hurting, and the only person who could stop it was the one person who caused it in the first place. Boy, if he could get his hands around Thorne's neck, he'd break it in half, or at least give it his best shot.

Naturally, his brotherly instincts kicked in, and all he wanted to do was let her know that it would get better. And he knew that it would. Maybe Thorne just needed time to get past this. That was what Michael had told him earlier when they met up for a quick basketball game, which Thorne was supposed to participate in.

"Natalie, honey, why don't you go upstairs and lie down? It's late, and you need to get some rest," he softly coaxed. "Not getting any sleep won't help you any."

"No, Stephen, go ahead. I'm all right," she weakly replied.

Stephen sat down in the chair he had been leaning on. "You don't sound all right."

"I just don't understand, Stephen." She finally looked up at him with desperation in her voice and sorrow in her eyes. "I don't understand why he would push me away. He won't answer my calls. I don't even know where he is. Theresa told me that he hasn't been to the office all week. She and Michael haven't seen him either."

"Well, I'm not saying that what he's doing is right, but think of it from his side of things for a minute." Stephen fell silent, giving her a chance to refocus. "He's probably confused as heck and mad as hell. Natalie, after all these years, Thorne not only found out that his real mother is alive, but that she's black, which means he's black, or mixed, which means the same thing as black in this country. He has to sit back and reconfigure his whole being. He's lost, Natalie. Or at least, I know that I would be. On top of that, he was lied to by his grandmother and his father, the two people that he trusted the most in the world. He has to view everything so differently, and he has to be ready for people to view him differently, too."

"I know that, Stephen, but I'm willing to help him with all of that. I love him, and he's not even giving me the benefit of the doubt."

"But, Natalie, maybe it's not about you. All of Thorne's life everything he has gotten has been given to him on a silver platter."

"That's not true. He's worked hard to get the respect that people give him," she quickly interrupted, defending her man.

"Let me finish. I'm not trying to take anything away from Thorne. He's a good man. I know that. And yeah, he is a hard worker, that's why people follow him like they do. He's fair, and he's honest. But Thorne has never had any real problems in his life that he knows about. I mean, this is the first time that there has ever been a crisis that can't be fixed by trade, service, or money. This is something that he has to deal with on his own, in his head, and in his heart. And it's a doozie."

"Oh, my God, Stephen, I feel so bad for him. It's just crazy that he has to go through this. I wish I had never agreed to find Amanda's son."

"Well, don't be hard on yourself. You were doing a favor for a friend, and Thorne needed to know. In the long run, this will all work out. You'll see. Thorne's a strong man. He'll get himself together and make the right decision."

"I just hope it's soon. I don't know how much more of this I can take. Do you want some hot chocolate?" Natalie got up from the table, needing to move, and walked to the sink to make fresh cups of chocolate, hers having gone cold.

"Um . . . have you heard from Nicholas lately?" Stephan asked cautiously.

"No, and I hope that I don't."

"Well, just for your information, I saw him today. He was having lunch at that new eatery on Bourbon. He was with Samantha Little."

"I'm not surprised. She's been after him for a while. I think that he was probably already seeing her anyway. She called his cellphone enough."

"I just wanted to let you know so that you wouldn't be too surprised if you ran across them yourself."

"Thanks, bro, but believe me when I tell you that I'm long over Nicholas, and maybe this means that he's long over me, too. I wish him the best."

"I never thought that I would see the day that you finally got rid of him. You really love Thorne that much?"

"I do. I never cared about Nicholas the way I do for Thorne. The friendship was okay, but I could never commit to more. And I told you how crazy he acted at the restaurant that day, right?" Her brother nodded. "God only knows what a marriage to him would have put me through."

Stephen laughed, "I don't think that Nicholas would have acted up that badly, but if he did, you know I would have handled all of that. At any rate, I must tell you how glad I am that you did let him go. We didn't want to see you end up with him. And granted, I wasn't too happy when I saw you waltz in with a white man that first night at Noah's Ark, but I must admit that Thorne grew on me. I like him. And I also like Michael and Theresa. You would have some nice in-laws. Hell, you could definitely do a lot worse. Thorne being black now is just a little icing on the cake for me."

Natalie whirled around so fast that she forgot she had the filled spoon in her hand and accidentally spilled hot chocolate powder all over the kitchen floor. "I can't believe that you even said that, Stephen."

"Said what? The truth?" He stared back at her.

"You know that makes you just about as racist as everyone else you've been talking about."

"Let's face it, Natalie. And I know deep down inside there's a little part of you that sees it, too. You might not be willing to admit it, but a little load has been lifted off your shoulders."

"That's not true, Stephen, and I resent that you're trying to put me in a category."

"Okay, fine, then. Let me say it like this. Instead of dating a white man and/or bringing one into the family, you're now with a black man. And I personally like that. I won't apologize for it, as ignorant as it may seem. And let me say for the record that I was ready to accept Thorne as a white man, but I'm more comfortable that he's black."

"And I say it again, you're an asshole," Natalie's temper was blazing, and she decided to let it burn, her headache briefly forgotten. "Don't judge Thorne by the mistakes that you've made in the past. That's the stupidest thing I've ever heard. First of all, I loved Thorne when he was white. I love him the same now. I had sex with Thorne when I thought he was white, and I loved it."

"I don't need to hear all of that," Stephen interrupted.

"Oh, shut up. I'm not going to let you or anyone else think that his color has anything to do with my love for him. When we walked down the street together, sure, we got a couple of stares, and guess what, we'll still get them because his skin color is not going to change. He's still Thorne Philips. His picture has still been on damn near every popular magazine ever published. People are still going to know who he is."

"True, but when this story gets out, and it will, he's going to be getting more attention than ever."

"Well, that's something else that I'm willing to help him with."

"If he lets you," Stephen finished her thought.

"Yeah, if he lets me."

"Don't worry, sis. Thorne can't hide for long. You know they have the company picnic and fundraiser coming up next weekend."

"Oh, yeah, Thorne told me about that a few weeks ago. Did they hire the girls to cater it?"

"Theresa did. They said she's putting the picnic together. Michael's real busy without Thorne. What's up with him and Tamia, anyway?"

"I don't know. Whatever's going on, they're keeping it pretty well under wraps. She's still dating other people, and so is he."

"Strange, isn't it—how you fight the thing that you want the most. I used to do that. Either they're too much alike, or they're too different."

"I don't know, but I saw how much they cared for each other the day that we found her in the garage. Thorne and I were both caught off guard by that."

"Natalie, have a seat," Stephen said, growing serious. "Now, listen. I've been sitting here debating whether or not to tell you this. But I love you, and I think that you should know," he paused for a second before finishing, "and I don't want you to get upset or go into hysterics or anything like that."

"What is it?" Natalie asked, standing back up. She was ready to run, but didn't know in which direction to take off.

"Sit down," Stephen demanded, pointing to her chair. When she did as he asked, he continued, "I was with Michael today. We were supposed to play basketball this afternoon at the gym. He told me that he saw Thorne two nights ago. He said that the police had called him telling him to come and pick Thorne up from the station."

"What? What happened?" she asked, her hand moving up from her throat to cover her mouth. Again, she was about to get up, but a look from Stephen stilled her.

"Michael said that he hadn't heard from Thorne either since last week when you two called him after leaving the hospital and told him what had happened. He said that he was supposed to meet with Thorne that next morning, but Thorne canceled and then wouldn't return any of his calls. I guess he was basically doing the same to all three of you. Anyway, the police called him, and he went down to the station and found out that Thorne had been brought in for breaking and entering, destruction of property, and attempting to do bodily harm. They couldn't get in contact with their cousin, Howard, because he was still on vacation. In fact, he should be back in the country sometime today."

"Yeah, yeah. What happened, Stephen?" she prodded.

"Right. Apparently, Thorne had gone to the mansion to talk to Old Matthew, and his guards or whoever wouldn't let Thorne in to see him. So, being Thorne, he got into a little tussle with two of them before some others came and finally threw him off the property."

"Was he hurt?"

"He's fine, Natalie. Michael said that he left the house then snuck in through one of the windows in one of the other wings. Old Matthew was so surprised to see Thorne walking toward him and his nurse or lover, whatever she is, that he had a slight stroke. Michael said they told him Old Matthew was rambling on about his son coming back to haunt him. I guess Thorne really caught him off guard. Anyway, Thorne was arrested because the woman Old Matthew was with told the security guards and the police that Thorne grabbed him before his stroke."

"But is Thorne all right?" Natalie asked anxiously.

"He's fine, Natalie, I mean, physically. He had a few scrapes from the fight with the guards, but besides that he's okay. Now, mentally, that's a different story altogether."

"What do you mean?"

"I mean that Michael said that when he got to the police station, Thorne was a wreck. He hadn't shaven and looked like a madman. He's going through some serious stuff, Natalie."

"I know, Stephen. Why do you think I'm trying to get to him? What happened after that?"

"Well, they had to drop the charges for breaking and entering because it's a family-owned estate, and you can't break into your own home. The window that was busted was basically his, too. And Thorne said that he never laid a hand on Old Matthew like he wanted to. It was his word against the woman's. Who do you think the police sided with? Michael took him home and tried to talk to him, but he said that he didn't know if he got through to Thorne or not."

"I've got to call him, Stephen. I have to talk to him. This is crazy. He shouldn't have to go through this all alone," Natalie said as she stood up from the table, her mind all set.

"Well, don't call now. It's three in the morning. Let him sleep. Just go to bed. You look like you need some sleep yourself."

"Yeah, you're right. I called Amanda today. She hasn't heard from him either. She's almost at her wit's end, too. She keeps blaming herself."

"Well, at least she's more comfortable. It was good of him to decide to move her to his penthouse. I was a little surprised that he did it, but that's what a good man would have done."

"No, Thorne was just being Thorne. He's going to take care of his mother regardless. When he did that, I thought he had everything under control."

"Natalie, I don't think Thorne's problem is with Amanda being his mother, or with him now being black. I really think that he can handle that. His problems are, first, being lied to; second, having to re-identify with himself and who he is."

"Well, first thing tomorrow, I will be banging on that door. I know he's at Gladewinds. Amanda said she was going crazy in that big penthouse all alone. He made her promise not to leave and to only let me and the nurse in."

"Well, I'm going to bed. I had a late, great, and very tiring night," he said with a smile.

Briefly perking up, Natalie asked hopefully, "So I take it you and Sandra are getting along pretty well?"

"Very well, sis," he replied.

"Then maybe, just maybe . . ."

"Let it go. I'm taking this one nice and slow. For your information, I really like Sandra a lot, and so do the kids. Yeah, I'm just going to let this one take its course." Stephen bent over his sister, and giving her a quick peck on her forehead. "Good night, Natalie," he said, and headed for the stairs.

"Good night, Stephen." She cleared the kitchen table and washed the coffee mugs. If she wanted to get a good start in the morning, it was indeed her bedtime, too. And the first thing on her early morning agenda was to take the long ride to Thorne's estate to see what was going on with him.

Michael sat in the family room of the main wing of Gladewinds, Thorne's newly renovated estate. He sat on the plush cushions at one end of the new sectional sofa with his legs stretched out and his feet resting on the matching ottoman. As he sipped his brandy, Michael's trained eyes examined the craftsmanship of the work recently completed by one of Thorne's crews. They had done a very good job. But of course it was for the boss, so they would have done the best job possible, not that they usually didn't.

Thorne was Michael's main concern. He was very worried about his brother and his displays of anger, something that was usually alien to his personality. If Thorne didn't get around it soon, Michael was afraid that it would slowly but surely destroy him. However, the more relaxed he became sitting on the soft cushions, the more his mind kept returning to Tamia. And although he tried to fight it, Tamia became his focal point.

That damn girl, he thought. He had to get her off his mind. But the harder he tried, the more he thought about her. It was silly—these little games they kept playing with each other. First, she wanted him, then she didn't want him. He wanted her all the time and was just too stubborn to admit it to either her or to himself.

Lately, he found himself more often than ever riding past Noah's Ark. Or maybe he was just paying a lot more attention to it, hoping to catch a glimpse of her. When he saw her out with another man, he was immediately enraged. Once, he was about to walk over to her and her escort and create a scene. But the I-dare-you look she gave him made him realize that it was just what she wanted him to do; so, to get the upper hand, he turned and walked the other way. Games, games, games.

Even his problem with the flight attendant was no longer in the forefront of his mind. She had called the office for him two days ago asking if she could see him. How she got the number directly to his office was a mystery; it wasn't listed in the employee directory. He explained to her that as a president of the company, any kind of relationship would be inappropriate. She protested and threatened to file a sexual harassment suit against him.

He counteracted the threat by simply reciting the names of a number of other upper-management employees who had the pleasure of taking a flight on that particular aircraft, including a female vice president. In the end, she opted to keep her job instead of pursuing the matter further.

Michael was going through some things himself, but he knew that his problems were minuscule compared to Thorne's. His brother came into the family room and went directly to the bar to fix himself a drink.

"After the other night, I wouldn't expect you to be needing another one of those any time soon," he commented. He didn't really expect a response. By the look of things, Thorne still wasn't back to his normal self. He had shaved and showered, but the heavy bags under his eyes were quite visible.

"About as well as can be expected for a man who has no identity," Thorne replied.

"Do you want something to eat? Ms. Alden is making me an omelet. Should I call and ask her to make it two?"

"No."

"Man, you have to eat something. When was the last time you ate anything?" Michael asked, picking up the phone.

"I don't know," Thorne answered honestly.

"Yes, Ms. Alden, could you please make Thorne an omelet, too. We'll be in the family room. You can call us when it's ready. Thank you." Michael turned back to his brother. "Thorne, that's not good. You have to eat."

"Michael, I don't have time to think about eating. Do you realize how fucked up my life is right now?"

"Thorne, you're not the only person who has been affected by all this, you know. I told you that the other night. I can see what you're going through, and I'm worried as hell about you; so are Theresa and Natalie. Stephen told me yesterday what she's going through because you haven't called to let her know that you're all right."

"Because I'm not all right, Michael."

"Thorne, you have to get past this. And that's what I'm here for—to help you." Michael paused, looking at his brother. He knew that the best way to get everything out of Thorne was to piss him off enough to make him snap. "So," he continued, "you just found your real momma. She's a nice woman, by the way. I met her a couple of days ago when I stopped by the penthouse. But she's black." Michael looked at him.

"Yeah, so?" Thorne asked, sitting up.

"Well, you know that means that you're black, too, right?" he asked, knowing he was on the right track.

"Yeah, so?" Thorne stood, towering over his brother. "Just what are you trying to say, Michael?"

"Well, I just thought that you would be a little pissed off at having found out that you were actually mixed, that's all."

"And just why would that piss me off?" Thorne asked. His voice sharpened with a steely edge.

"Maybe I'm wrong. Let's just forget that I said anything."

"Forget, my ass. If you have something to say, Michael, say it."

"It's nothing, Thorne. If it doesn't bother you, hell, it's cool with me."

"Hold the hell up. Am I supposed to be mad because I'm a black man? Is that what you're saying? Should I be upset because I found my mother, and I really like her, but she's black? Michael, I'm not now, nor have I ever been, prejudiced. And I didn't think that you were, either." Thorne began to prowl around the room furiously.

That's when Michael knew he had him.

"Let me tell you something." Thorne was pointing at him from a distance, but Michael knew that before long he would be up in his face. He was ready. "I happen to like my mother, and I happen to be very glad that she finally came looking for me. I hope to have the chance to grow to love her very much. I don't care about her being black. She could be red, green, yellow, or purple for all I care. And I don't care about being black myself. I have a problem with being lied to all these years by people I loved and I thought loved me. I have a problem with now trying to struggle to learn to be something I know nothing about being. Michael, I don't know about being black. I know of the struggles of black people, but that was from what our grandmother taught us. I've grown up feeling that I should hate my own ancestors for their mistreatment of black people. But now I've turned into one of those oppressed people who my ancestors mistreated. I can't even . . ." Thorne clamped his hands to either side of his head, his body shaking with rage.

"Whoa . . . brother, calm down. First of all, please have a seat before you pass out or something." Michael put a hand on his shoulder. "This can't be good for your blood pressure. Look at you; your face is all red, and you're sweating. Let's calm down a bit."

Thorne sat down and let Michael pour him another drink. His brother was right; he had to calm down.

"Thorne, I think that you might be taking this whole being a black man thing a little bit too far. First of all, you need to just concentrate on being Thorne. You don't have to know how to be black. Just be yourself. That's who we all love. Now listen," Michael said, handing Thorne his drink. "I'm your younger brother, I always have been, and I always will be. I don't care about you being black. You know that Theresa and I aren't like that. We love you. There are no color lines."

Michael sat next to Thorne and faced him. "Man, I love you. You are the head of our company, the head of our family. Thorne, if you fall apart, we all do. We're in this together. Look around you, Thorne. Me, Theresa, and especially Natalie are all in your corner. I can understand you being mad at our grandmother and even our father, but you're messing up something that could be part of a great future for you, and that's Natalie."

"Natalie doesn't want me. What for? I'm so messed up and confused right now."

"You know what, Thorne? It's time for you to stop feeling so damn sorry for yourself. I'm tired of it."

Michael was starting to get back to his old self. He decided that if he wanted his brother to stop pitying himself, then he had to stop it, too. If Thorne needed a little tough love, then he was just the one to give it to him.

"So you were lied to, so what? So you're biracial, so what? So you found your mother, and she's black, so what? Damn, at least you have a mother. At least you know her, or have a chance to get to know her." For the first time, Michael let his own hurt show through for just a minute. He never showed how much he missed his own mother, but Thorne needed to realize how lucky he was.

"Michael, I'm sorry. I didn't mean to be inconsiderate."

"Thorne, all I'm saying is that you need to take advantage of this opportunity. You can't let your hatred ruin this for you. You got Amanda and Natalie, and they love you. You got me and Theresa, and we love you."

"I'm being a fool, aren't I?" Thorne asked, already knowing the answer.

"No, you're just being human. But don't take too long getting things straight. Hell, I'm learning a lot lately about being a fool myself."

"Oh, yeah, who for?" he asked, again knowing the answer.

"Tamia. Man, it's such a long story I don't even feel like going into it right now. Let's go eat." They got up and started toward the kitchen.

"Falling hard for her, huh?" Thorne asked.

"Harder than I want to admit. It must be something about those Davidson women."

Entering the front entrance hall, they saw Natalie standing at the door. She looked around the door and was trying to peek into the side windows at the entry hall, but couldn't see through Thorne's new, heavily tinted windows. Still, being Natalie, she didn't give up trying to see into the house.

"Here's yours now, bro," Michael laughed, shaking his head.

"She's so nosy. Look at her," Thorne laughed.

"Well, I'll go so that you can handle your business."

"Okay, and hey, Michael, thanks for the talk, man," he said, holding his hand out to his brother.

Thorne let Natalie stand outside a little longer before opening the door.

CHAPTER 18

"Look, Natalie, I'm not going to argue with you about this," Thorne said, slamming his untouched glass of brandy on the coffee table.

Natalie jumped just a little, surprised at his anger and the force with which he had slammed the glass.

"Thorne, would you just calm down and listen to me? Damn, I only came out here to check to see how you were doing. It has been a week; Amanda and I are worried about you. You just dropped off the face of the planet without so much as a phone call to anyone." He sat back on the sofa and ran his hands over his face. "Thorne, we care about you."

"Well, I don't want you to care about me," he snapped, his voice anxious and full of uncertainty. "I don't want to be cared about."

"You don't mean that," Natalie replied defiantly, hurt by the comment.

"Yes, I do, Natalie." Thorne stood and turned away from her. He couldn't stand to see what he was doing to her. Couldn't stand to do it, but in his heart, he knew it was something that needed to be done.

He fled to his country estate when he realized he couldn't do it, but she had followed him, so now was the time. He had to let her go for her own sake. It was the only way he could help her right now.

Thorne was a mess, and he knew it. He didn't want her pity, and if she stayed with him now, he was sure it would be for that reason.

He stood by the huge bay window that took an entire wall of the study and told her exactly how he felt. "Believe me, Natalie, this is very hard for me to do, but I don't want to see you anymore." Thorne paused when he heard her gasp, but struggled not to face her. "I don't think that I can be the man that you need, Natalie. I'm not sure who I am anymore. I'm not sure of anything right now."

"Thorne . . ."

"No, I have to say that I'm sorry for making you go through this these last couple of days, and I'm sorry that I couldn't tell you sooner, but it's for the best."

"Thorne, why can't you just talk to me? Why do you have to push me away? I've always been here for you. You know that." Natalie was almost begging for him to see what he was doing. He couldn't just leave her like that and expect all their hurt to go away. "I can't believe that you're the same man that I fell in love with. You're not even going to fight this, not even going to try."

Why did she have to say that?

Just when it seemed that she had finally gotten through to him, he whirled around and stared at her with those amazing eyes. They didn't sparkle anymore. They were dull and lifeless, and she could see his hurt and pain in them. Thorne was tired and defeated. She hated seeing him that way.

"That's because I'm not the same man, Natalie. I don't have any idea of who the hell I am. I'm like a lost soul or something. I'm not afraid to admit that I'm confused and afraid. I'm not Thorne Philips anymore. Now I'm Matthew Philips III. And I don't know who the hell he is. I can't be the man that you love, because I'm not that man anymore. I'm a stranger even to myself, so how can you know me?"

Thorne turned back to the window, and a single tear escaped those gray eyes. His past was ruining his future, and he didn't know how to stop it.

"Natalie, I have to let you go. I have to. I'm sorry that you don't understand, but I have to find a way to get rid of my hatred right now. I don't want to end up hating you, too."

"But, Thorne, I just wish you would let me help you. Amanda . . ."

"Amanda," Thorne said. "Natalie, I don't know that woman. She's my biological mother, but I don't know a damn thing about her. I put her up in the penthouse because she's my mother, and I don't want any harm to come to her, but I don't know her."

"So get to know her, Thorne," she said, coming behind him and putting her hand on his shoulder. She could feel his tension. "Who says that you can't get to know Amanda? You could even come to love her. She's not trying to rush you, but wants to get to know you, too—as her son."

"I have to get to know myself first."

"So do that, too. What's so hard about it? Whether you're Thorne or Matthew, your heart is still the same. Your family is the same, and your friends are the same.

Unless you're worried about what this will do to your company. I mean, maybe the same people you've dealt with in the past won't like it when they find out that they're actually dealing with a black man."

"I told you before, I don't care what people think of me. I know how to run my business. I know the kind of business I run. My reputation will speak for itself."

"Well, then, what's the problem?" she asked.

"The problem is that I don't have all of the answers. And until I do, I'm not going to be able to function right for anybody. I've taken a leave of absence from the company until I can get myself together."

"So you want to take a leave from me, too? That's how you're going to handle this problem? By running away from it . . . from me?"

"I don't run from anything," Thorne snapped.

"Okay," Natalie said, picking up her jacket and purse from the sofa. "Fine, if that's how you want it. It can be over between us. Good luck with your problems. I can't stand being around you while you're feeling sorry for yourself." Infuriated wasn't the word for what she was feeling; it was more like devastation. She couldn't believe that he was going to let her go that easily.

Thorne let her parting shot bounce off him. It wounded his pride a little to hear it from her, but his decision was for the best.

Natalie was in denial even as she saw him watch her put her jacket on and fling her purse over her shoulder without making a move to stop her. She was still in denial even as she heard him walking behind to the front-entrance hall without trying to stop her from leaving. She turned the knob and stepped into the reality of the situation when she ended up standing on the other side of the door in the exact same spot where her mission had begun.

And that hurt her.

Thorne stood on the other side of the door for what seemed like an hour before he heard the sound of her car's tires against the gravel in the driveway. He stood there a while longer, trying to convince himself that he had done the right thing.

He loved her. He loved her; it was that simple. But he couldn't allow anything to cause him to bring her pain, and he truly believed that until he could get himself together, that would be the likely outcome. He had seen the tears build up in the corners of her eyes when she tried to understand and accept his wishes. He had seen her brief hesitation when she reached for the doorknob. Thorne wanted to stop her and pull her into his arms. He needed her, needed to draw on some of that strength she was offering. But he didn't.

And that hurt him.

The three siblings sat wordless in the waiting area of the Connor law firm, drinking coffee. They did not need words to convey to each other how uncomfortable they all were.

Theresa appeared to be the ultimate in high-society chic and poise in her crisp, tan linen suit. She sat with her legs crossed at the ankles, but the constant wiggling of one foot gave her away.

Michael, too, was sleek and elegant in his Dolce & Gabbana tailored three-piece double-breasted suit, but he kept getting up and walking to a nearby window and looking out.

Thorne wore an expensive but simple printed shirt and black slacks. His only show of nerves was running his fingers through his hair every two or three minutes. These little shows of discomfort aside, the three siblings appeared to be business as usual.

At least they did until Howard personally came out to the lobby to greet them. He didn't do this too often. His receptionists knew that he only did it for important clients, and the other employees were aware of this pattern, too. So when the top boss came out of his office, they knew that whomever he greeted was to be taken notice of.

Most people already knew who the trio were; those who didn't made sure to educate themselves. The mostly female workforce had already taken stock of Thorne and Michael. Two had even been bold enough to tell Michael to let them know if they could do anything for him. This he quickly dismissed. At any other time, he might have welcomed their attentions, but not today. He was there solely to conduct business with Howard. Besides, he still couldn't get crazy Tamia off his mind.

On the way to Howard's office, Theresa made notes of people who paid particular interest to them. They had to be careful with whom they conducted business. She was sure that Michael and Thorne were doing the same. Well, maybe not Thorne. His face was a rock solid void, virtually unreadable.

Howard Connor was a first cousin to Abigail Connor Philips, their grandmother, and it was her parents, his aunt and uncle, who mainly raised him, which made him more of a brother to her than a cousin. Most of the time it was just the two of them running around on that vast estate of Southend. Because he was almost fifteen years her junior, most of the time he was getting on her nerves. But they loved each other.

Miss Abby had inherited the bulk of her father's massive fortune, but he had been sure to include Howard in his final will and testament. With his not-so-meager inheritance, Howard had successfully built a small law firm into one of the country's most profitable consultant firms. His clients ranged from wealthy sheiks, presidents, and kings, popular actors, singers, and business executives to socialites and professional athletes. He also had over twenty smaller offices across the country that dealt specifically with providing legal aid to those who couldn't afford the high cost of legal representation.

Because he was fair and trustworthy more so than that he was family kept Howard and his firm solidly in the employ of the Connor Corporation. He handled most of the company's business personally, but four of his six sons worked beside him. They were also well trained and highly qualified lawyers. Eventually, the practice would be passed on to them.

Howard was the best at what he did, taking care of both professional and personal needs of his client. He had a kind and caring heart, and he knew when it was time to be honest.

Now was one of those times. Looking over his extraordinarily huge handcrafted oak desk, he examined the three faces in front of him. Michael was tense, and his usual impatience showed itself on his face. Waiting never was his strong suit. Theresa's concern for her older brother was most evident. She kept glancing over at him as if she expected him to leap up any second. And when he turned to Thorne, he could see that her concern was justified. He was clearly at the very end of the thin rope that was holding him together. Thorne's face was full of questions, and Howard could see that he wasn't leaving without answers.

It was time to give them all what they needed.

"Okay, I can tell by the looks on your faces that a lot has happened since I last saw you at the reading of your grandmother's will," he began. Howard pushed the intercom button on the black panel on his desk, saying, "Rachel, please hold all my calls until I give you further notice."

Thorne didn't wait any longer. He couldn't. "Howard, there has been a lot going on. A lot of things have come to light. And you're the only person we can think of who may know the answers to our questions."

"So tell me what you need." he asked Thorne.

Michael stood and walked to Howard's desk, "We want to know the truth about what happened."

"Michael, sit down," Thorne urged. "It's not going to help matters any by jumping down Howard's throat. He already knows what we want to know."

"No, it's okay, Thorne," Howard said, waving his hand nonchalantly, noticing Theresa's hand reaching over to comfort Thorne.

"Well, can you answer our questions?" Michael asked. "Thorne's been going through hell lately. And I just don't think it's fair."

Michael's comment impressed Howard. It never failed to amaze him how much the three siblings looked after each other, stood by each other. He admired that, and hoped that his owns sons would tighten the ties that bound them to each other.

"Okay, Thorne," he said, "let's get started. First of all, let me apologize for my own part in the deception regarding your birth. And I know it may be a little hard for you to understand or accept right now, but what was done was done for your own good."

"You're right, I do find that hard to believe," Thorne replied. "Whose decision was it, exactly?"

"The final decision was your grandmother's, but believe me, she put up a hell of a fight. She and I talked about it long and hard for many a night. And it troubled her, but the choice that she made ensured your welfare, education, and inheritance." He stood up and walked over to the built-in entertainment center. Opening the sliding doors and turning on the television set, he continued: "This, um, decision that your grandmother made caused her a lot of heartache and pain.

She knew that one day the truth would come out. Granted, neither of us thought that it would be this soon after her death, but what's done is done. So now, we move forward."

"Howard," Theresa interrupted, "you mean to tell me that if Thorne's biological mother hadn't decided to start a search for him, he may have never known, not even from you?"

Howard turned around and faced the three siblings. "If Amanda hadn't looked for Thorne, no, you wouldn't have found out about this. Not now, anyway . . . and definitely not from me. I swore to your grandmother that I would carry this to the grave with me, and I would have. As you know, I loved your grandmother. She was my big sister. And she loved you guys so very much. Your best interest was always her main concern."

"You don't have to sell us on grandmother's love, Howard," Michael said. "We just want to understand the purpose of all this so that Thorne can move past it and get on with his life. He has a good life, a good family, and a good woman. But look at him, he's in such a stupor that he's in danger of missing out on most of it."

"Could you please stop talking about me as if I weren't here?" Thorne objected. "Look, I'm fine. Yeah, I was messed up for a minute, and I admit that I've made some mistakes due to all this anger built up inside me, but I plan to rectify them. Just shed some light on this for us, Howard."

"I can do better than that, Thorne," he replied, closing his private safe, which was hidden behind a huge oil painting of his deceased mother. "I will give you the lady's words from her own mouth."

He held in his hands a VHS videotape. He walked back to the television, pushed a few buttons, and slipped the tape into the empty slot. Before he pushed play, Howard turned and faced the group once more. "Your grandmother insisted that if and when the time ever came, she be able to explain her side of things for herself."

Thorne, Theresa, and Michael sat forward, anxiously anticipating what was about to be revealed to them. And with a flash of light, Abigail Connor Philips came into view, as vibrant as ever.

Absent were the countless signs of old age and the disfigurements caused by the arthritis that haunted her the last years of her life. They saw the grandmother they remembered, the one they wanted to run to when times were bad. The grandmother who gave them hugs and kisses and candy with love.

CHAPTER 19

"Hello, loves. If you're watching this video, and no doubt it's the three of you together, then my worst nightmare has come true," Abigail began, looking sadly into the camera. "First off, let me apologize to you all, but especially to you, Thorne." She looked to her left. "I can hear you outside playing in the gardens right now. You sound so happy and playful. Thorne, I can hear you shouting orders to Michael. You are so good at being a leader."

Abigail paused and looked down at her hands before continuing. "I want you to always be happy and playful. You know, so many mistakes have been made in my life that sometimes I find it hard to count them, but I know that your father was never one of them. He was the greatest joy of my life. And when he passed, I thanked him for you little ones." She paused again.

"This is so hard for me, but I must explain to you why your father and I did the things we did. The decisions we made were for your benefit. Your father and I had to make sure that Old Matthew couldn't get his hands on your money. I know that it sounds ridiculous and maybe even stingy, but just listen to me.

"I grew up the product of very strict, over-achieving parents. I was an only child until Howard came to live with us. Well, to make a long story short, when I was about seventeen years old, my family hired a new house-keeper by the name of Margaret. Margaret came to live with us in the servants' quarters with her son, Michael, who was eighteen. He was hired to help the drivers and tend the gardens. Michael and I became fast friends. He even took Howard under his wing, more often than not.

"Soon," Abigail paused, smiling, "Michael was my best friend. We hung together from the time I got out of school until I went to bed.

"The year before this, my parents began throwing lavish parties at the house in an attempt to bring me into society's eye. I didn't like it. I hated the people, couldn't comprehend their views, and liked their sons even less. But around the time Michael and I were becoming friends, my father decided it was time for me to marry. In addition, the idea of me palling around with a Negro was absolutely unbearable. See, he was of the same mindset as Old Matthew.

"Our family had millions of dollars, old money, passed down from generation to generation, but I was as miserable as a child could be. That just goes to show you that money really can't buy happiness."

The siblings listened intently to what their grand-mother was saying. All three had thoughts running through their minds, but none felt anything but sadness and sympathy for her loneliness. They simply couldn't fathom it. As far back as they could remember it had been the three of them. Even Thorne had numerous play-mates before Michael and Theresa came along; Nicholas had been one of them.

"Before either of us knew what was happening," she was saying, "Michael and I began a torrid affair. I was in love with him from the start, even though it was forbidden. Slavery was over, but black people still weren't treated much better. I never wanted to lose what I had with him. During the days and the evenings, my father had me going on dates with one of his associates' many available sons, but I was daydreaming about Michael. At nights I would sneak out to the servants' quarters to be with him. We had decided that it was safer for me to go to him than vice versa. Can you imagine what would have happened to him if he had been caught in the house? I'm sure that many of the servants knew what was going on, but they never would have told on him. In most ways, the bonds that held them close were so much stronger than ours.

"Everything was going pretty well until I got pregnant," Abigail paused and wiped at the tears forming in her eye.

Theresa wiped her own eyes just as a hand reached into the frame and gripped their grandmother's shoulder. A colored hand. It rubbed her shoulder gently, by its action urging her to continue. All three saw how that one hand gave her so much strength.

"Listen, I had to do what I did so that things could remain constant in my life. So when I found out that I was pregnant, I married the first guy that I could. Luckily, Old Matthew had been begging me to marry him from the moment we met. I couldn't stand him, mind you, and I knew that all he wanted was to get his hands on my father's money. But I had to do it. Michael and I sat down and thought up a plan that we prayed would work, and unfortunately, it did."

Abigail reached up and squeezed the light-brown hand still resting on her shoulder.

"The next time that I went out with Old Matthew, I practically forced myself on him. I had to in order to make him think that he had fathered my child. Once that was finished, I waited about two weeks then told my mother what had happened. And just as I expected, Old Matthew was all too happy to oblige my father's order of marriage. And so we were married. But I hated Old Matthew and never shared a marriage bed with him. We each had our own bedrooms and basically our own lives. I'm sure that by the time you see this tape you would have heard all the rumors about him and his mistresses. I'm sure he'll have many more. I want you to know that it's all right.

"See, by doing this, I was able to keep my family together, my real family, that is. Me, Michael, and our son. Michael and I had a beautiful baby boy, Matthew Jr. That's what I had to name him. And that's okay, too, because a name is such a little part of whom the real person turns out to be. And Michael got to have his son around him, watch him grow, and even be a part of his life. I love Michael so much that I had to give him that." She finally pulled Michael in front of the camera with her. He took a seat next to her on a sofa that looked to be an office of some kind.

As the man they came to know and love as Mr. Morris, their gardener, came into view, the joy on Abigail's face was not missed by any of her grandchildren. They looked at each other and then back to the television screen.

"Thorne, Michael, and Theresa, this is your real grandfather, Michael Morris. I know it comes as a big surprise, and it did to your father as well, but he did know the truth before he passed away. Right after he told me that Amanda was pregnant with Thorne, we had a long talk, and I told him the truth. Matthew was beginning to have some doubts about the way things might turn out for him and Amanda. So I told him; we both told him because we didn't want him to make a mistake in his decisions. And we wanted him to know that we were both behind him one hundred percent. I think after he got used to the idea, he liked knowing that Old Matthew wasn't his father. But he kept our secret because he knew that if the truth came out, Old Matthew would send Michael away or, worse, cause him to come to harm. Old Matthew's friends were known for doing things like that.

"After Matthew found out the truth, he changed. He became more positive and blessed— yes, that's the word." She squeezed Mr. Morris's hand. "I think he realized how blessed his life really was. He turned into a totally different man, a better man. See, that's the key word—man.

"Thorne, it doesn't matter what color you are; what runs through your veins is red blood. That makes you human; we all are. It's how you treat others and how you treat your family that counts. People will look up to you and love you because you're a good person. And that's all that really matters. Your father realized that, and he did his best to be the best he could. He did right by you because he loved you and your mother. Times changed a little, and I had some of the right people in my pocket. So I helped them to marry. It was the right thing for them to do. Michael was my driver. That was all anyone knew of him. So he was able to be with me everywhere I went and able to attend his son's wedding. Michael never told Amanda for his own reasons. But, they were so happy together."

"Now I don't know what made your real mother leave, Thorne. My best guess is that she just couldn't take the pressure. But I want you to know that she had stayed in contact with me for a couple of years, and she would always ask about you. I lost contact with her right around the time that your father passed away. But before all of that, let me tell you the real reason I had your name changed."

Thorne took a deep breath as he prepared himself to finally hear the truth. So far, everything their grandmother had told them had been a shock. But as far as he was concerned, it wasn't what he needed to know. What he needed were answers to his questions.

Mr. Morris sat forward and looked into the camera. "Thorne, I know that I'm probably not the person that you want to hear this from, and right now, all you know me as Mr. Morris. I want you to know how much I love you kids. And I am and always will be so pleased to have been your grandfather. Forgive me if I make you all feel a little uncomfortable, but I just have to tell you all the things that I've always wanted to tell you. I love you all a great deal. And, Michael, I was even more proud when your father named you after me. And I must also apologize for my part in this if you were hurt in any way. Thorne, I am the one who told your grandmother to change your name."

"See, Thorne," Abigail interrupted, but was stopped by Mr. Morris with the slightest pressure applied to her hand.

Then something happened that the three siblings had never seen before in all the years their grandmother was alive. She actually sat back quietly and gave Mr. Morris the floor. Thorne sat forward, amazed.

"Thorne, not long after your mother left, Matthew came to me, upset and distraught. He had a very hard time dealing with things after she left. He couldn't understand why she went away. Of course, I kind of knew what she was going through. The love that I felt for your grandmother was never public. I didn't have to deal with rejection from society in general, a society that already held a low regard for me because I was Negro. Your mother had to deal with her rejection and the rejection of your father. Even though he seemed not to care about himself, it broke her heart to see what he was going through."

"When she left, Old Matthew began to badger Matthew terribly about giving you away. He kept saying that he wasn't supporting no half-breed and so on, when in actuality, he was being supported himself. However, he was the head of the household according to the law. Matthew was not going to give you up. But at the same time he was falling apart. He was in no position at the time to take care of you. So I told him to go to Old Matthew with the idea of saying that Amanda came back and took Matthew III with her. At the same time, the rumor was to be started that Matthew had gotten the daughter of one of the servants pregnant. The girl had the baby, and then gave it to Abby to raise. It basically only served to save Old Matthew some face. That hound dog only cared about what his Klan buddies thought of him.

"At any rate, Matthew must have been convincing enough, because by the next morning the rumors had already been started. Now Abby had a maid who had accidentally discovered us one day in a hug near the washing room. It was our mistake, but to keep her quiet, Abby fired her, paid her and agreed to continue supporting her family if she allowed us to use her daughter's name. We used the name to put on your new birth certificate. I'm sure you know it's a fake by now."

Miss Abby squeezed his hand and continued, "Thorne, all of you, we know that it seems like a lot of lies and deception going on, but believe me, it was all necessary in order for you to have your inheritance. There was no way I was going to let Old Matthew have anything that is ours.

"Your father went away for about a year, just traveling the country, trying to get over your mother. But that never truly happened. When he returned, he began working for me and began dating again. I sent him to Philadelphia, because that was where I knew your mother was, in an attempt to see if they could rekindle the old flame. I believe they did for a while, but by that time so much had already happened. I know for a fact that he made many return visits. They still loved each other, but I think it was more friendship than anything else at that point. He never really forgave her for leaving, but he always had a place for her in his heart.

"Soon, your father met and married Sue Ann Davis, and before I knew it I had two more bundles of joy. I love you three more than you'll ever know. But once they had their home established, Matthew felt bad about you being here with us for so long, Thorne, and he wanted to take you back home with him. That's what they were coming to do the night of the accident. You three had stayed with me the weekend, and your father and Susan were coming to pick you up, all of you, to take you home. They had argued about it a lot, especially after Sue Ann was told the truth about Matthew's first marriage having been to a black woman. Susan's upbringing forced her to resent your father for that, and then for him to want to bring his son into the home was totally unacceptable. She never knew about Matthew's true father. It was best that she didn't know. She would never have been able to keep her mouth shut. Eventually, she would have told that nosy mother of hers, and that would have jeopardized Michael. Matthew wasn't going to let that happen.

"Matthew told me at the hospital before he died that they were fighting in the car on the way over. The car hit a side rail on Malden Road and went over the hill. Sadly, Sue Ann was killed instantly. Her neck was broken.

Matthew lived until the next afternoon. He died in my arms, the same way he had come into my life."

Theresa dabbed at the tears streaming down her face. The video ended with Mr. Morris, their grandfather, holding their grandmother in his wide strong arms and kissing her gently on her temple. It was a relief to know that her grandmother had found true love despite the life she had endured with Old Matthew. Theresa was happy for her grandmother, and she envied her for having found something she herself had been unable to find.

As soon as Howard stopped the tape, the three released a collective sigh. He silently walked over to the metal trash bin, broke the cassette open, pulled out the tape, and let it fall into the trashcan. Then he lit a match and watched it burn. The weight that had been resting on his shoulders visibly lifted. He didn't say a word until the last piece of tape had become ashes.

"You can understand the promise that was made to your grandmother. I had to destroy the tape. It was only for your viewing. I have now fulfilled my duty."

"Howard," Thorne commented, "you always do. You were so loyal to her."

"Thorne, she was loyal to me. She helped me in so many ways. My loyalty to her is my pleasure. Now, is there anything that you have questions about? I'm here to help you."

"It must have been so very hard on them to keep their love a secret for such a long time," Theresa, the constant romantic, commented.

"Yes, it was. But if they hadn't kept it a secret, Michael would have been killed. You do realize that, don't you? Their love was unbelievably strong. And it was only God who made it possible for Matthew to pass. His birth was never questioned by Old Matthew."

"So," Michael interrupted, "that's why she used to always walk down to the cottage and talk to Mr. Morris, I mean, our grandfather?"

"Yes, they had to be sneaky back in the day, but by the time you were in your twenties they were old enough not to have to sneak so much. It just appeared to be two old friends drinking tea or having lunch. She would always tell people that she kept him around for the company or that he reminded her of the old days. Of course, they bought it."

"And that's how she knew everything that we were up to," Thorne said. "I can remember telling Mr. Morris things that I would never tell anyone else. He always had good advice, not that I always listened to it."

"Exactly. They had quite a little system going on when it came to you three. And I think it kept them young, trying to outsmart you," Howard replied.

"You know," Theresa interrupted, "Mr. Morris died not long before Grandmother did. Thorne, you were out of the country on a business trip, but I can remember her asking me to fly back home to attend the funeral."

"Yeah, and the whole time he was sick, she went down to that cottage, staying for days. When I asked her why she didn't let one of the maids attend to him, she said that he was her oldest friend and that she needed to be there for him. And you know, you never disagreed."

"Well," Howard stood and walked to the window, "your grandmother was a wonderful woman. She loved Michael Morris, and he loved her. I loved them both." He walked around to his desk and opened a folder. "Before Michael died, he had me draw him up a will also. See, his mother had saved and saved her whole life as well. She didn't really have to spend anything because she lived on the estate; he did, too. So we drew up this will, and he wrote this letter. He never thought that you would get to see it because he never really thought that the truth would come out, but he wanted it known that he had also provided for his grandkids." Howard's eyes shined with pride and admiration. "So in the event that I showed you this video, I was also to give you this letter. Thorne, being the eldest, I hand it to you."

Thorne slowly opened the envelope. What other surprises could this day hold for him? It was only nine in the morning and already he had more knowledge than he had been prepared to absorb. After a quick glance at his siblings, he realized the need to get it all out in the open now.

⌐

"'My Dear Three Musketeers,'" Thorne began. He remembered being called that by Mr. Morris when he was a kid. "'I hope that this letter finds you healthy and in good spirits. If you're reading this letter, then you know the truth about me and my relationship to you. And I, for one, am glad of it. All the days I played with you in the gardens when you were kids, listened to your problems as teens, and watched you grow into adults were my greatest joys and pleasures. The day my son named his son after me was a blessed day.'" Thorne looked at Michael and continued reading.

"'But that would have been nothing compared to the day that I could have told you that I was your grandfather and loved you as such. Sadly, I know that day will never come in my lifetime. But I write this letter with the wish that it could be so in yours. I hope that the fact that you are part Negro is no great shock to you. Abby and I have taught you so that you have respect not only for your races, but also for the races of all others. I pray that those lessons hold fast.'

"'At any rate, I wanted to tell you of my joy at having been a part of your lives, and I wish that I could have been more. God sees fit to place us where we're needed the most, and I accept my role. Now my old buddy, Howard, has to talk to you about something that is very dear and important to me. Your devoted grandfather, Michael Morris.'"

Thorne put down the paper and looked at Howard. "Okay, now what, Howard? More surprises?"

"You know how old folks are, Thorne." He stood and went back to his safe. When he turned back around, he was holding what appeared to be an old strongbox. "They hold on to everything."

Howard set the box down on his desk and produced the key to open it. The small box creaked when opened, spilling a small amount of dust onto the desktop. Howard turned the box around and handed it to Thorne.

"As the eldest, Thorne," he began, "I release these into your custody."

Thorne took the box and set it down in front of them. Before reaching into the box, he glanced at Michael and Theresa.

"Go ahead, Thorne," Michael whispered anxiously, "lift the cloth."

Thorne did as he was told and pulled back the thick velvet cloth, revealing a dull-colored, rather long gold necklace. The wear on the metal was obvious. It was made of heavy solid-gold blocked links that had been visibly marked and dented. The necklace appeared to be quite old. Thorne cautiously pulled the heavy necklace from the box.

Just when Thorne thought the necklace would never end, the shape of the block links changed to diamond-shaped, flat pieces of gold, each containing large precious stones. On each side of the chain was matching stones of diamond, ruby, emerald, and sapphire. The necklace was beautifully handcrafted, and the jewels were set deep into the metal. He held it up high and examined it before passing it onto Michael. Theresa let out a deep breath as Thorne reached back into the box for the rest of the treasure.

Once all of the jewelry was out of the old box and resting on the velvet cloth, Howard began to explain as best he could their unexpected prize.

"Okay, now, where do I begin?" he asked, pausing to look at his young cousins. "Before you are the royal jewels of what was once the Tribe of Umergodia. As folklore has it, this was once a wealthy tribe of peaceful people living in the low mountains of West Africa until they somehow became involved in a massive war between two rival tribes. With the war of the neighboring tribes quickly invading their land, many of the Umergodia tribe left the lands, leaving the village vulnerable. The war finally came to their lands. A large majority of the people of the Umergodia tribe were either killed or enslaved. Now, according to your grandfather, his great-great grandfather was the youngest prince of the tribe. He watched as his parents and elder brothers were killed during the war. The only survivors in his family were his older sister and himself. These jewels have been passed down from generation to generation to the oldest male child. Somehow, he and his sister managed to sneak them out of Africa and into this country with them. They didn't come to America on slave ships, but were quickly indentured once they arrived. The jewels have continued to be passed down through the generations secretly."

Howard looked at the siblings, who were finding the story just as hard to believe as he had when he first heard it. "I know what you're thinking. I couldn't believe it either, at first. But the proof is right in front of you. Somehow, your ancestors managed to keep these jewels away from their employers for over two hundred years. I've had them in my possession since your father died. Michael gave them to Matthew the night that he and Abby told him the truth, but they kept them locked up in the cottage. After your father died, Michael couldn't bear to have them near him. So he left them in my safe-keeping to give to Thorne when it was time."

"But, Howard," Theresa interrupted, "what if . . ."

Howard put a hand up to silence her. "We don't have to think about any what ifs, Theresa. Things are now as they were meant to be. The truth is out, and I think that you'll all be the better for it. The jewels consist of the necklace, which belonged to the chief; the diamond and gold earrings, which belonged to his queen; and the wedding band set, which they wore during their reign—all of which total approximately two hundred million dollars. That was at last appraisal. Now it's up to you to decide what to do with them. But I warn you, and please believe me; these are a missing fortune for some, an antique collector's greatest find. Many have been searching for these jewels, not knowing they were in the custody of the rightful owners."

"What do you mean, Howard?" Michael asked.

"Well, for one," he said, looking directly at Thorne. "You have to stay away from Old Matthew. Like your grandmother said in the video, he's getting his. He's dying a lonely, old, and poor man. His worst nightmare has come true. He has a set income, which is very meager, and he can't go around town living the good life any longer. The little bit of money that was left to him by his own father was gone years ago."

Howard laughed a little before beginning yet another story. "It seems that Old Matthew's father wasn't anything like his son. He had numerous mistresses, both white and black, and was very generous to them all. His wife had already passed away at the time of his death, so he left each of his mistresses a piece of land and a good bit of money for his quote-unquote other families. Would you like to guess who his first illegitimate child was?" Howard sat back in his chair and looked at the siblings, who looked back in amazement.

"Um, Thorne, now we know who we truly got our looks from," Michael said with a laugh.

"But I know that Old Matthew was the one who was trying to hurt my real mother, and I know he was also the one who was threatening Natalie," Thorne replied angrily. All he wanted to do was get his big hands around that old good-for-nothing's throat.

"And that might be true, Thorne," Howard agreed. "But let the police handle that. The more you involve Old Matthew in your life, the more you're giving him a reason to be there. Just let old dogs lie."

"He's right, Thorne," Theresa said. "We all need to stay as far away from him as possible. We have everything that our grandparents left for us, and we have their love. That's more than enough."

"Besides, Thorne," Michael put in, "I think its time for you, for all of us, to look to the future. In the last few months, our family has almost doubled. We have found a mother, learned of a grandfather, gained a possible sister-in-law. Man, we need to take advantage of that. We missed out on not knowing that Mr. Morris was our real grandfather. You don't want to miss out on anything else, do you?"

Thorne leaned back in his chair and let his head fall back. He took in the advice he had just received and decided that they were all right. He did have a bright future to look forward to. He had the answers he wanted, or at least the ones he needed. And even though everything didn't make sense right now, it would in time. A good woman whom he loved was waiting for him. It was time for him to settle down and start some family traditions of his own.

Suddenly, he sat up and looked around. Damn her, he thought. He had never thought about stuff like that before meeting Natalie. He glanced at Michael and realized his brother had practically read his mind.

"Well, if you're going to get her, you had better go," Michael laughed. "Don't expect her to wait around forever. You got to get her while the getting is good."

"No, I have something else in mind," Thorne replied with a wink. "Right now, we have to decide what to do with these jewels."

"Well," Theresa said, "according to the history of the jewels, they're yours, Thorne. You are the eldest male."

"Right, so put them in a safe and let's go," Michael suggested.

"True, but I'm ready to change history. I can do that, can't I, Howard? I mean, they are mine, right?"

"You can do whatever you want to, Thorne, as long as the jewels stay in your family."

"Well, then, I think that we need to decide what we are going to do with them. First, I would like to contact one of the museums or the university and enlist their help finding out more about the Umergodia tribe and these jewels."

"Maybe we could display them in a museum," Theresa suggested.

"Maybe," Thorne agreed.

"Well, I don't think it would be wise to carry these around without security," Michael said. "They need to be put away for safekeeping. Howard, can we keep them here until we can make arrangements to have them moved?"

"Sure," Howard answered, "but I doubt that anyone would be the wiser if you walked out of here with them in your back pocket. Just call me when you're ready to move them."

"Thanks. Look, I hate to be rude, but," Michael replied, glancing at his watch. "I have to go. I have a lunch date with Tamia."

"So how's that going, anyway, Michael?" Theresa asked.

"Theresa, you know Michael doesn't like to talk about his women," Thorne suggested, trying to give his brother a way out.

"Whatever, Thorne," Theresa said, but looked to Michael for an answer.

"You kids and your wonderful young lives," Howard laughed. "I remember when I was in my heyday. Whatever you do, just make sure that you don't let the right one get away. That's my word of advice. Now if you'll excuse me, I have to get ready for my next client."

They all stood and shook hands with Howard. They were at the door when Michael paused and turned back to Howard, a curious look on his face.

"Wait, Howard," Michael began, "I don't understand something. If Old Matthew's father was Mr. Morris' father, then how is it that he received the jewels? I thought they were passed from son to son."

"No, they're passed to the first-born male in each generation. Michael's mother had a brother, who was in possession of the jewels, but he didn't have a son before she did. In fact, I believe he had all daughters."

"I guess that explains it. Have a good day, Howard," Thorne said as they left the office.

CHAPTER 20

After a few days of begging from Amanda, Natalie had finally relented and was visiting her friend at Thorne's penthouse. Since being rejected by Thorne, she had shut herself off from the world, wrapping herself in her satin pajamas and her favorite blanket and lying on the sofa. Some days she was buried so deep in her misery not even the joyous greeting from her nieces could brighten her mood.

But today, this very morning, she had finally forced it out of her system. Tired of self-pity and disgusted with the unhealthy changes in her person, Natalie focused her determination on getting past her pain. To Stephen's delight, she donned her pink two-piece capri set, a white T-shirt and sandals and made a stop at Starbucks. A tall glass of french vanilla cappuccino was just what she needed to get her started on her way.

"Come in, baby," Amanda greeted her cheerfully as soon as the elevator door opened. Walking toward Natalie, her arms opened wide and sympathy leaped into her heart for her best friend. She was dressed elegantly in a black lounging gown with matching slippers. As soon as she put her arms around Natalie's waist, her suspicion of weight loss was confirmed. Holding her at arm's length, she looked her over closely. The heavy dark circles under her eyes no doubt came from lack of sleep and continual crying.

Natalie put her head down shamefacedly. All their past talks came to the forefront of her mind. The nights they stayed up talking about the power of women, about the strength of black women—all women—came into focus, and she remembered a speech Amanda had given to her Women's Sexuality study group.

A man can only do to you what you allow him to do. If your heart is broken, you allowed it to happen. If your money is gone, you allowed him to take it. If he beats you constantly, it's because you didn't put a stop to it the first time. Be true to yourself; only then can you expect a man to be true to you. When you command respect, you get respect. But respect starts where, ladies? In yourself.

"Head up, lady. You know better than that," Amanda said, taking hold of Natalie's hand and leading her into the living room. "Natalie, I must say that I am very disappointed in you, my love."

"I know. I'm a mess."

"No, baby. You're human. There's nothing any of us can do about that. Why haven't you called me? I've been locked up in this big old place all by myself going crazy."

"I know. I'm sorry, Amanda. I just couldn't ... can't seem to get myself together." She could feel them coming—tears she had fought to control welled up in her eyes.

Amanda gently squeezed the hand she was holding. "Natalie, it's all right, baby. You don't have to try to be strong for me. I know what you're going through. I haven't heard from him either."

Giving in to her frustration, Natalie let the floodgates open. "Amanda . . . I don't . . . know what to . . . do."

"It's all right, baby," Amanda consoled her, tears also welling in her own eyes. "I wish there was something I could do. But you just have to have faith that everything's going to be all right."

"I'm tired of waiting around for him to come back to me. He said that he didn't want me, Amanda."

"But you know that's not true. Thorne's just been going through a lot. He's probably said a million things that he doesn't mean right now. Just give him time. Don't harden your heart because of something said in a heated moment."

"I went to him," Natalie said, blotting her eyes with a tissue. "I went to him, and he turned me away."

"He didn't mean it, Natalie. As soon as he gets his head right, Thorne will be apologizing for everything he has said or done over the last couple of days. You know he loves you."

"If he loved me, he would have let me help him."

"He's a man, Natalie. Since when has a man willingly let any woman help him? You love him, don't you, Natalie?"

"Of course, I do . . . with all my heart."

"Don't you think that love deserves a chance to grow?"

"Amanda, I can't take this pain that I'm feeling. I don't like being left out, pushed away. I've been miserable for the past few days, walking around like a zombie, not talking, not eating, and crying all the time. I haven't even been getting dressed."

"I know . . . I talked to Stephen the other day. He told me that you weren't doing too well." She hugged her again. "Oh, baby, all I can say is that it will get better."

"No, it won't. I can't keep coming here to see you. This is his place. Just sitting here makes me remember the times we spent together here. I haven't been to the new house. I know he's not there, but it just reminds me too much of him. His crew, his name all over the trucks—everything reminds me of him."

"Natalie, listen to yourself. Thorne hasn't gone and is not going. He just needs some time to himself. He has a lot to deal with. But that doesn't mean that you have to let yourself go. It doesn't mean that you should stay in the house in mourning. All relationships go through their ups and downs. And, yes, it hurts like hell at first, but once things work themselves out, you two will talk about it and get through this."

"I don't think so. Maybe it's best this way. Maybe we shouldn't be together."

"I don't believe that, and neither do you."

"Well, I'm not going to sit around like a sick puppy anymore." Feeling slightly renewed and invigorated, she hit herself on the leg and stood up over Amanda.

"Good." Amanda clapped her hands, eagerly cheering her friend on.

"And I'm not going to be lying around crying all day, either."

"And you shouldn't."

"As a matter of fact, I'm about to take myself on a much-deserved shopping spree, right now. Would you like to join me?" She extended her hand, pulling Amanda into a standing position.

"I wish I could, baby, but that nurse will be here any minute for my therapy. I can't miss it. It's the most relaxing time of the day for me. But I want you to go out there and enjoy the rest of the day. Buy yourself something really expensive. That always makes me feel better."

"I love you, Amanda," Natalie smiled down at her, feeling good for the first time in days.

"I love you, too, Natalie. And remember, I'm your friend. No matter what happens between you and my son, I'm your friend." She hugged her again as they walked to the elevator. "You keep that smile bright."

The ding of the elevator bell startled both of them.

"That's my nurse. She is running a little early today."

Inside the elevator, Thorne waited patiently for the door to open. He rushed home as soon as he left Howard's office, full of optimism and ready to move forward with his life. Feeling past the grieving and the deception that amounted to lies told to him by his grandmother, Thorne only wanted to begin concentrating on a relationship with his mother. The majority of his questions had been answered; he was assured of a love that he briefly doubted. Now it was time to cherish the remaining time he had with Amanda, Mandy, Mom.

He felt a moment of uncomfortable surprise when the doors opened and he came face to face with Natalie and Amanda. Natalie was the last person he expected to see. He was unprepared to talk to her, didn't know what to say, and the words that randomly formed in his head never made it to his mouth.

As for Natalie, she wished the door would close. After standing rooted for an uncomfortable minute, she and Thorne cautiously walked past each other, barely making eye contact and mumbling their greetings. Her partially repaired heart broke all over again. Waiting for the door to close, she stared at the white marble floor of the foyer and concentrated on not letting a single tear fall.

Once the door closed, the dam broke and she rode the elevator to the garage level accompanied by convulsive sobs that wracked her weak frame.

"Hello, Thorne," Amanda said sternly, although she was happy and relieved to see him safe and sound.

"Hello," Thorne whispered, running his hand through shoulder-length hair badly in need of a cut. He stared at the elevator door until he heard it moving.

"Didn't expect you back this soon. Am I to assume that things are better now?" she asked inquisitively.

"Yes, you may. How have you been?"

"Doing well. Thank you for asking. The nurse you sent has been taking very good care of me. In fact, I'm expecting her any minute."

"I'm glad to hear that. Was Natalie here visiting?" That was a stupid question, he knew, but he had to open up the topic somehow.

"Of course," Amanda replied, turning and walking toward the kitchen. She smiled when he followed.

"How is she?"

"Oh, she's doing fine."

"She doesn't look fine. Has she lost weight?" he asked, pulling out a stool and sitting at the kitchen counter. He watched her stirring a stew simmering in a pot on the stove. His stomach began to rumble.

"That's what usually happens when you stop eating."

"She stopped eating? That looks good." His stomach rumbled again.

"Didn't you?" She put the spoon down and watched him closely. "Usually, when people go through emotional imbalances in their lives, their desire to eat is the first thing to go."

"Are you talking as a teacher or as a mother?" he asked. She reached into the cupboard for two bowls.

"Both. Now, listen up. Thorne, when two people find themselves in love, it's important that they give each other a certain level of respect."

"I don't know a lot about love. I've only recently found myself in that state, so it's kind of new to me."

"Nevertheless, love is respect. When you push the people who love you out of your life, you hurt them. It's not an easy thing to make up for."

"If you're referring to Natalie and me, I would prefer you stayed out of it."

Silence hung over the counter for a second as she contemplated his wish. Maybe she was overstepping her boundaries as his newly discovered mother. "Okay, if that's what you want, I will."

That was easy enough, Thorne thought. But to continue his relationship with Natalie, wasn't he going to have to completely accept himself? Was he ready to do that? Why else had he come home if not to face his future head on?

Clearing his throat, Thorne looked up at Amanda, who was faking attention on her bowl of stew. Thorne knew that she wasn't the least bit interested in what was on her spoon. He watched her closely, rehashing all that he had learned about himself in the past week, all that he had learned about her love for his father, his father's love for her, and the love that his grandparents had for each other. That was the kind of love he wanted to have, the kind he could have with Natalie. But how was he going to right the mistake he made by turning her away? He needed some advice.

"Mom?" He softly whispered the word that rolled thick and virginally off his tongue. Instantly, he realized that he had never used the word before; never, in thirty-six years, had that word come from his mouth. His grandmother was called Grandma. Suddenly, it hit him, and he let go of what little restraint he had left. Tears of frustration, of pain, and of happiness fell from his eyes, mixing together in a pool of relief. "Mom," he said again, stronger, firmer.

Amanda rounded the short countertop easily and went to him. Her own tears fell happily for both herself and her son as she pulled him into her arms and let him vent the rest of his emotional tide. He needed her—her baby, her little boy, her Little Matthew needed her to hold him again as she had so many years ago.

"Oh, I'm so sorry I caused you all this pain, baby. But it's going to be all right now. Mommy is here," Amanda was crooning.

Thorne grabbed her around the waist roughly and held on to his mother, his eyes tightly shut. And for the first time, he was okay. The guilt he harbored for his mother's death was gone; he didn't have to worry about being alone. He had someone who loved him unconditionally. He had his mother.

CHAPTER 21

"Woman, would you please just take it," Thorne finally demanded, disappearing into the walk-in closet of his penthouse apartment bedroom.

"But, Thorne," Amanda said, following closely. She wore a two-piece mint green cotton tunic pantsuit. "This is simply too much. It's too extravagant. Really, what am I going to do with another full-length mink coat in the middle of August?" She released a long, exasperated sigh. Arguing with him never did any good. She should know better by now.

"Then throw it into the closet until December. Now can I please get ready? The employee picnic will be over by the time we get there."

"Thorne, you have to stop buying me things. Where am I going to wear this?" she asked, raising it high in the air as if he had never seen it.

"Mother, please. There will be more than enough places for you to wear that thing. I like buying you things, okay?" He leaned down and kissed her on the forehead. "That's what sons are supposed to do, right?" Then he yelled to his brother, who was in the living room waiting for them, "Michael, would you come get her, please? She's at it again."

Michael came bouncing down the hall dressed in a pair of tan khakis and a yellow polo shirt, eager to get his day started. "What's the problem, Thorne? Come on, man, we're going to be late."

"She's at it again. I need to get dressed," he replied.

"Now, Mom, you agreed to let us take care of you," Michael said, leading Amanda out of the bedroom. "You have to live up to your end of the bargain."

"You're just as bad as he is. I put that diamond bracelet in a safe-deposit box down at the bank. You can't leave stuff like that just laying around." She accepted Michael's quick peck on the cheek.

"That's all right. Thorne has just given me something else to top," he laughed, helping her to the sofa. "But I'll wait to see what Theresa brings in with her. She just called and said that she and Mikey will be up any second."

"You kids have to stop this. I might start enjoying it," she laughed.

"That's the whole idea, Mom. *Mom*," Michael paused, "I love the sound of that. Theresa and I never really knew our own mother. Are you sure you don't mind us sharing you with Thorne?"

"Of course not. Maybe if I hadn't been so stupid, I would have had more kids myself." Amanda said, swiping away a stray tear that had managed to escape.

She didn't know what had brought on her son's sudden change, but she loved it. And she thanked the Lord that she didn't have to worry about him any longer. Thorne seemed to be himself again, not that she knew how he had been before they met. But for her part, now he was the most loving and attentive son she could have possibly asked to have.

Since moving back into the penthouse, Thorne had accepted that what had happened to him was a plus, not a minus. He didn't focus on the lies or the deceit anymore. Questions that used to plague him and harden his heart had been answered. Not all of the details were clear, and some never would be, but he knew enough about his past to be okay with his future.

He was still himself, and no amount of lies or secrets—and certainly no skin color—was going to change that. He didn't mind that his mother was black; he never did. He didn't care that he was black; it was his blessing. He and his siblings all shared in the discovery of their race.

Walking into the living room and watching his mother open yet another gift from her new grandson, Thorne thought he needed to do one more thing, and his life would be complete.

His attitude and his actions had been very negative toward Natalie because they had been negative toward himself. It was very unlike him to act as he had. But this had been the first time in his life that he had been dealt a hand of cards that he couldn't bet on. He only hoped that she would understand his dilemma and forgive him.

He had come home, and had regrouped with his family, had gone back to work, and had been calling Stephen daily to check on Natalie. At first her brother didn't respond well to Thorne's calls, but after Thorne talked to him and explained his feelings for Natalie, Stephen tried his best to let him know how she was doing without abusing the trust she had in him. However, each report ended with the same admonition: *If you really wanted to know, you would call her yourself.*

Thorne couldn't count the number of times he had set out to do exactly that. But every time he tried, his nerves caused him to choke. But he couldn't stop trying.

Now he was back to his old self. He had confidence in himself, his family, and his decisions. And Thorne had decided not to let her go. He had made up his mind to do everything in his power to regain her trust and belief in him. But most of all, he just wanted to love her.

"Okay, guys," he cheerfully addressed the room, "are you ready to go to Gladewinds for this year's company picnic?"

Everyone turned to him and smiled.

"Thorne, look at this lovely necklace my grandbaby just gave me. It's so beautiful," Amanda said, brushing away tears. Speaking to Theresa's lanky eight-year-old son, who was dressed exactly like his Uncle Michael, she said, "Mikey, I think this is the best gift I've ever gotten in my whole life." She hugged the boy and kissed his forehead.

"Well, it's just how I feel is all," he replied honestly. This earned him another quick hug.

"All right, let's go before someone else pulls out a gift," Michael urged. He hit his nephew playfully on the back of his head. "You knew I wanted her to like my gift best."

This set off a little wrestling match that ended when Thorne, in Levi jeans and navy polo shirt, placed both Michaels in matching headlocks and headed for the elevator.

"Theresa, I want to apologize for not being able to help you with the plans for the picnic this year," Thorne remarked during the ride to his estate.

"It wasn't any trouble, Thorne."

"Yeah, I'm sorry, too," Michael added. "But with Thorne out, I had additional workload."

"As I said, it wasn't any trouble. Honestly, I had a whole committee of people working on the project. I had a lot of help with the activity planning. All I did was sit around and give orders. The caterers were cheaper than I had expected, and I even had enough left over to hire a security detail, just in case."

From the front seat of his brother's sky blue Lincoln Navigator, Thorne remarked, "You sound as if it was fun. Is this going to be the next area of business for us to look into? Party planning?"

"No, but it was fun, Thorne. This year's picnic is going to be a ball. Did you two get to sign up for any of the activities? Well, Thorne, I'm sure you didn't. Did you, Michael? I had sign-up sheets posted all over the buildings."

"I saw them; but no, I didn't have time."

"Well, don't worry about that. I'm sure there will be time before each race for new entries."

Thorne turned and cautiously looked at his sister. He knew Theresa almost too well.

She looked nice and comfortable in her paisley-printed summer dress, but something was up her sleeve. Anticipation was in every word she spoke. Sitting in the back seat, she looked like a little kid about to burst.

"What kinds of games did you pick this year, Theresa?" Amanda asked. "I'm ready for a lot of fun." Thorne turned around again. Something was definitely up.

"Well, we have the usual stuff like the egg toss and the three-legged race. For the pie throw, of course, Thorne, Michael, and myself will be the targets of choice. The employees will have a chance to get back at their bosses. That was a last-minute decision," she explained after Michael gave her a look. "Don't worry, Michael, there will be overalls for us to put on. You won't get your khakis messy." Theresa loved teasing Michael about his exceptionally refined style of dress. "We also added a dunking banquette this year. Thorne, you were elected as the biggest draw for that. Sorry. And believe it or not, we have a kissing booth. The proceeds from that will go to a local charity called Living for Our Future. It's a fairly new organization that maintains a recreational area, computer lab, and library for kids in the area. I thought it was a good idea."

"That is a good idea," Michael said good-naturedly, "I hope you found someone good for the kissing banquette. I would hate to—"

"Oh, don't worry, I hand-picked them myself. We're going to have a couple of girls up there to help attract more donations."

Thorne again looked at his sister. This time she stuck her tongue out at him.

He couldn't tell what was going on in her head, so he decided to pass time talking to his nephew about school and his latest science project. When Michael joined in, Thorne soon found that he was outmatched and decided to just sit back and enjoy the ride rather than overwork his brain cells.

The conversation eventually changed from science and math to television and sports, and everyone was able to participate and enjoy the leisurely ride into the country.

My family, Thorne thought. He was relaxed and enjoying himself immensely. And to think, he had almost let this slip by. Mandy, his mother. He caught her eye in the mirror of his sun visor and knew that he loved her, and when her eyes met his and she put her hand on his shoulder, he saw how much she loved him.

This was his new self, his new life. And it was only the beginning.

A soft wind gently caressed Natalie's face as she and her sisters walked through the large steel gates into the massive front lawn of Thorne's Gladewinds. Theresa had recruited her help in planning the company picnic, and she had seen more of this place than she cared to.

There was a time when she thought this could have ended up being her family home, the home that she and Thorne would make for their children. Now it was just a harsh reminder of a failed relationship that she was foolish enough to rush into without thinking. But that's how love was supposed to be—spontaneous, right?

She had agreed to assist Theresa when she still thought she and Thorne still had a chance. And when she realized that it was over, she still felt obliged to honor her commitment. Well, actually, Theresa wouldn't allow her to back out. So here she was walking across the yard of her ex-boyfriend's estate, checking in with the different booth managers and trying to make sure *his* day went well. He probably wouldn't even show up.

Tamia and Tamya had been hired to provide the food and beverages. They were busy setting up the picnic tables and making sure their employees were doing their jobs. Once people started arriving, they would have other jobs to attend to.

Natalie was very happy with the way they had decided to set up the picnic. She and Theresa had hired a group of teenagers from the local high school to set up a valet service and attend to the cars. Behind the house was a pool area and a beautiful garden that could be used for small social events. Further back was, Natalie guessed, about ten acres that wasn't being used. That is where they set up for the employee picnic.

Signs had been posted along the road for employees to follow to the right of the acreage for parking. To the left, tents were set up for the food and picnic tables. And in the middle Natalie had positioned the various booths to allow for the flow of the crowd. Hopefully, everything will go according to plan and there wouldn't be any blockage in the area.

There was plenty of space further behind the booths for the blow-up castle, haunted house, and the little rides for the younger crowd. A very good job had been done, even if Natalie said so herself. As a precaution she had hired a few of Sandra's police officer friends for security purposes, but she didn't expect any real trouble.

By the time the first guests began arriving, the food was being prepared, and the booths were manned.

"Natalie, you really outdid yourself," Theresa marveled when she found her inside one of the booths putting up more prizes.

"Thank you, Theresa," she replied. Her pink velour jogging pants hugged her body perfectly.

"Hon, I hope you weren't planning on hiding out here all day," Theresa said, knowing that was exactly her plan.

"Oh, no, I just want to keep things running smoothly."

"Uh-huh. Well, just so you know, Thorne is here, and he's in a very good mood. I think he's back to his old self. I really wish you would go find him. I think he's looking for you, too."

"No, I think I'm the last person he wants to see. How is Amanda?" she asked, changing the subject.

"Oh, great. She's looking for you, too." Theresa gave her arm a little squeeze. "Okay, I'll let you hide for a little longer, but you still have to introduce the start of the games after the speech from the president."

Natalie just turned away. She would introduce the start of the games and then leave; until then, she would just stay out of Mr. Thorne Philips' way and hope for no incidents.

That's what Natalie was thinking when the first incident happened.

⟋⟍

The picnic had been underway for a solid hour. Then Thorne and Michael were unexpectedly called into the study of the house for an emergency phone call from one of the oil refineries in Texas. The phone call lasted two hours, but the problem had been resolved.

When they returned to the picnic area, they found that the kissing booth had opened and that lines were about forty men deep. As they walked closer, Thorne noticed that the men were also switching from one line to another.

"Michael," he said jokingly, "they must have picked some real lookers for these lines to be this long."

"Yeah," Michael agreed. "So what do you say? Should we stand in line like everyone else, or should we pull rank and cut in?"

"Well, I don't know if that would be fair, but let's cut in. I want to see what all this ruckus is about," Thorne laughed.

They started walking through the line of employees, joking with the fellows and being badgered along the way.

"Hey, Bob, is it that good?" Thorne asked, knowing the man was married.

"Hey, boss, it's worth getting hollered at by the wife. I told her it was for a good cause, but I've been in line twice."

"Come on, boss," another man protested. "The line starts back there."

"David," Michael said, shaking the man's hand. "We have to check things out. Nothing but the best for our staff."

"Well, then, you outdid yourselves this time." The other men in line laughed.

"Oh, no," Thorne whispered when he saw the front of the line. Michael was still joking with some of the guys and wasn't looking ahead, but Thorne knew this wasn't going to be good. "Hey, Michael," he said, "let's just wait here and chill with the guys for a minute."

"Don't be silly, Thorne. Keep it moving, man." He still wasn't paying attention.

"Um . . . let's just wait. Hey, Charles, man, how's things going?"

"Good, Thorne. Just trying to get to the front of the line, man."

"Yeah," Michael said, "me, too." That's when he finally looked up and saw what Thorne had been trying to hide from him. "What the hell?" he said, half to himself, half to Thorne.

"Oh, damn," Thorne said, trying to follow closely behind his brother. "Michael, wait a minute."

Michael's long strides took him to the front of the booth in no time. His cursing and shoving caused a bit of a stir among the men at the front. But when they saw who it was, they were more curious than peeved.

Tamia and Tamya had provoked quite a commotion since opening their kissing booth. Their goal was to collect as much money for their charity as they could in the next two hours. What nobody knew was that another set of twins would then take their place. Male twins, Dominique and Dimitri, were German-born body-builders/models who had started the charity two years ago. They were good friends of the girls, and would bring in more money from the female employees. To be successful, you had to think from both sides of the bowl.

The girls were pulling in big bucks and having a lot of fun. Because they were both flirtatious, the men kept coming back. It didn't hurt that they were looking exceptionally beautiful in matching tank tops and tight-fitting blue jeans. Their hair was pulled back in long ponytails, and both had applied just the right amount of makeup, causing their bronze skin to glow in the afternoon sunlight.

They were receiving more than a fair share of invitations to movies, dinners, and plays, but always politely declined the offers. It was nice just to be asked, especially by such handsome and successful men. The kisses were kept brief and impersonal, but each man was made to feel it was the best kiss he had ever received.

Their lines stayed long, and they were on their second hour. Some of the faces were new, as people were still arriving, but many of the men just kept getting back in line. The girls grew tired, but it was for a good cause. So to kill time, they began to flirt more.

"You've been in my line four times already," Tamia said, smiling at the man she came to know as Tim Popovich.

"I guess that I can't get enough of you. But, to be honest, I've been in your sister's line twice, too. And I plan to come back."

"Got a thing for twins, do you?" she laughed.

"I like you more," he replied seriously.

"Okay, Mr. Big Spender, let's get this over with," she said, taking his five dollars and placing it in the steel box in front of her. She didn't particularly like where he was going with his conversation. Then she leaned forward, allowing the top of her breast to show and offering him her lips.

Tamya saw Michael's fast approach, but not in time to warn her sister. She stepped back instinctively when she saw murder in his eyes. Tamya yelled her sister's name just as Michael jerked Tim back from the booth.

Tim spun around, about to retaliate when he saw that it was Michael with Thorne close behind. But Michael wasn't even looking at him; he was throwing killer daggers at the beauty behind the banquette. *Damn*, Tim thought, *he hadn't even gotten her name.*

"It's all right, Tim," Thorne said, going over to the confused man. "Just step back here for a minute."

Tamia opened her eyes in time to see Michael pull Tim aside and step in front of her. She stepped back, too.

Quickly, she recovered. "Hey, Mike," she said, trying to be as nonchalant as possible. Michael had noticed she did that often.

"What the hell is going on here, Tamia?"

"What do you mean?" she asked innocently.

"What did I say?"

"We're running a kissing booth, Mike. It's kind of obvious."

"Don't be smart, damn it. Why are you up here kissing all of these damn men?"

"Mike, please. You're starting to cause a scene."

"I don't give a damn about a scene," he countered, slamming his fist down on the banquette.

"Michael," Tamya interrupted, "this is for a really good cause."

Michael turned his angry eyes on her. "Look, Tamya, I already know about the cause. It is a good cause." He turned back to Tamia. "Come on. I'm not playing. Close up this side of the booth. Now!"

Tamia just stood there looking at him. She wasn't going to let him do this to her. Not in front of all these people.

Michael watched her; he knew what she was up to. The challenge was flashing in her eyes. "Don't do it, Tamia," he ground out between his teeth. "Don't even try to fight me on this. Now I don't care if Tamya keeps her side open, but you're done for the day. I'm not playing."

He was serious. Tamia knew it. Sometimes you had to choose your battles, but it was still hard for her to let this one go.

"Tamya," Michael was saying to her sister, "I'm sorry. I know that Roger is a pretty understanding guy, but I'm not. I'm very selfish. It's my nature." Then he turned back to Tamia. "And I told you that. Why are you doing this to me? You knew that I would snap."

"Mike, it's for charity," she replied.

By this time, Theresa, Amanda, and Natalie had gotten to the scene.

Natalie saw the big smile on Thorne's face and almost forgot what she was there for. She couldn't see past him. Then he turned to her; she quickly looked away.

"Michael, what's going on?" she asked.

"Natalie, I'm glad you're here," Michael said. "Tell your sister to close down the booth."

"Why would I do that? She's doing a great job," Natalie said, looking from one to the other. Meanwhile, the crowd was steadily growing.

"Because I asked her to. Look, Natalie, I'm not going to stand for my girlfriend being up here kissing every man that I employ. That's crazy. Find somebody else."

"Oh, I didn't realize you two were going together," Natalie said, laughing.

"I didn't know that either, Michael," Theresa said. "I wouldn't have asked her to do this if I had known."

"I didn't know we were going together, either, Mike. You said that you never wanted to see me again after we went out to dinner last week," Tamia said. She leaned forward, one hand firmly supporting her against the table.

"You know what I mean," he said, looking at Thorne. Michael had walked himself right into it. Thorne couldn't help him out of this one.

Thorne just hunched his shoulders and continued listening like everybody else.

"Well," Michael finally said, "we do. This booth is closed," he said to the line of men waiting behind him. "You all have to move over to the next line." Then he turned to Natalie, pulled out ten one hundred dollar bills and asked, "Will this do for the rest of her time?"

"Good thinking, Michael. It will do," she replied, handing the money to Tamia, who put it in the steel box. "You're closed. Tamya, get busy, girl. You have ten more minutes of work to do."

"Ten minutes?" Michael asked.

"Yeah, the girls are done here in ten minutes. Their replacements are over there." Natalie pointed to the other twins, who had a group of women hanging around them.

"Looks like you got got, Brother," Thorne said laughing.

It sounded good to Natalie to hear him laugh again.

"Well," Michael said, looking at Tamia, "I guess it was worth it."

"What do you mean, you guess?" she asked.

"I don't know, Tamia. You may be the death of me. Let's go and get something to eat." Michael took her hand and led her away from the booth. Everyone watched as the couple walked off.

Amanda laughed. "That's a love-hate relationship if I ever saw one. But sometimes those are the best kind."

"You're right, Mother," Thorne said, coming up behind her and putting his arm around her shoulders. He looked at Natalie. She was still beautiful, and he still loved her. "Hey, Nat."

"Hi, Thorne. Amanda, I'll see you later. I have to finish over there," she said, quickly walking away when she saw Thorne about to say more to her.

"Damn," he said quietly, watching her walk off.

"Give it a minute, son. Your time will come." Amanda patted his hand and smiled up at him. "Trust me. You might have to work a little harder, but it will come."

CHAPTER 22

Around 4:00 P.M., the crew cleared away the food and set out desserts and beverages. Most of the booths were closed, and all the prizes were given out. The monies collected for various charities were tallied and put away. It was time for the president's speech and the competitions.

Theresa was anxious to set her next plan into action. She didn't expect for Michael and Tamia's problem to be rectified so quickly. God worked in mysterious ways. But she had one more brother who needed help.

Carefully, she stepped onto the temporary stage built by the construction company. Already sitting on stage were Thorne, Michael, and Mikey—her men. God, she loved them so much.

"Welcome, everyone," she began. "My name is Theresa Philips." Applause. "And I would like to welcome you all, and thank you all for coming out. I have to say that this is the most successful company picnic that I can remember. It is my pleasure to also thank the caterers, who also managed the kissing banquette and created such a stir, Misses Tamia and Tamya Davidson. They are also the proprietors of Noah's Ark, a fabulous restaurant/bar located in downtown New Orleans. Thank you, girls. I also need to thank everyone who managed a banquette or game for us today. We had a great day, and you all made it so. Without further ado, I'll let my brother Michael have the floor."

Michael stood and slowly walked to the podium, giving Theresa time to get to her seat. As his brother spoke to the crowd about the yearly performance and estimated figures for the year, Thorne took the opportunity to try to figure out what exactly he would say to his employees. He hadn't prepared a speech because he had been going through some things of his own.

Theresa saw her brother mentally preparing the speech and decided to help him out. "Thorne," she whispered.

He didn't hear her.

"Thorne," she said again.

This time he turned to face her. "What?" he whispered back.

"Just read from the paper."

"What?"

Theresa finally scooted to the seat next to him. "Just read from the paper on the podium. I took the liberty of preparing a speech for you."

"Thanks, Theresa. You're a lifesaver."

"And so, I finish by saying that this year's profits look to be even better than last year's, and it's due to the dedication of employees like yourselves. You all deserve a round of applause." This prompted; the crowd began to applaud loudly. "Now I will turn these proceedings over to my brother Thorne."

Thorne took his turn at the podium. He looked over the crowd at friends and employees whom he had known for almost forever. He had the simple part of the job. It was up to him to recognize employees and departments for service and devotion. And that was his privilege as the eldest CEO of the company.

"Hello, everybody. I'm sure you're ready to get to the races and that table of enticing desserts. I'll make this as brief as possible. First of all, I need Theodore Chambers to come forward, please." When Chambers reached the stage, Thorne shook his hand and continued speaking. "Theodore is our oldest employee out of all our New Orleans-based offices. He has been with the company for forty-two years and plans to stay for three more. He is the company's Employee of the Century because of his many years of dedication to the Connor Corporation. As a show of our gratitude, it is my honor to present to Theodore Chambers on behalf of my brother, sister, and myself a two-week vacation, an all-inclusive seven-day cruise to Aruba for two, and a check for five thousand dollars." Thorne presented Mr. Chambers with an envelope containing the check and his other paperwork, and once again shook hands with the man as he left the stage.

"This next award goes to the company who has shown the most productivity gain over the past year." Thorne continued until he had given out numerous week-long vacations and bonuses ranging from one hundred to one thousand dollars. He was eager for it to be over so that he could get on with the fun of the races himself. When he thought he could take no more, he saw that he had just given out the last award and was reading from the last page of Theresa's well-prepared speech.

"So, in conclusion, I would also like to thank you all for your hard work and your dedication and ask that you continue to help make this company a success. As always, we welcome your suggestions and your advice." Thorne was on a roll. But he was concentrating on finishing his speech and was basically just reading from the paper. "Now, I would like to bring forward to introduce and explain the remaining events the woman I love, Ms. Natalie Davidson."

Thorne paused and looked questioningly at the crowd. He wasn't sure if he had said that. Of course he had. He quickly looked at Theresa. Damn her. Then he did the dumbest thing he could have and tried to correct what he just said.

"Um, I mean . . ." By that time, Natalie was slowly walking onto the stage.

"What did you mean, Thorne?" she asked. "Go ahead and fix it."

"Nat, don't do this in front of all these people." Thorne put a hand over the microphone and bent forward so that only Natalie could hear him.

She just stood there looking up at him. The hurt was so evident on her face it tore at Thorne. This wasn't how he had wanted things to go. He had planned things perfectly for later, but now that was definitely a bust.

"Just move aside, Thorne," Natalie finally said disgustedly, holding her head down and shaking it. "I know that it was a mistake. You didn't mean to say it."

"Nat, you know that's not how—" Thorne started.

"Just move aside, please," she insisted.

"Nat—"

"Move."

Thorne did as he was told and walked to his seat with his head held down.

"I'm sorry, Thorne. I was only trying to help."

"Yeah, it seems everyone is trying to help this situation except me."

He listened quietly as Natalie explained where the contestants for the three-legged race, egg toss, and relay races were to report. The final event for the day would be the dunking banquette.

As the other races began, Thorne went into the house to change into a pair of shorts and T-shirt for the dunking booth. He was determined not to let his little episode with Natalie ruin his whole day. All he had to do was get up the nerve and say the right thing. She still cared for him; he could see it in her eyes. But if he stood a chance now after hurting her the way he just had, he was going to have to do things right.

Thorne stayed in his house as long as he could, trying to figure out exactly how he was going to get Natalie alone with a yard filled with nearly one thousand people. It wasn't going to be easy. And she was probably trying to leave as soon as possible, too.

≈

Eager to get it over with and go after Natalie, Thorne calmly climbed back up the ladder and sat on the ledge. He waited patiently while employee after employee tried to dunk the CEO into the huge tub of water. Thankfully, the water was lukewarm. He found that it wasn't as bad as he thought it might be. Each employee had been given a ticket for only two attempts, and many of them were at the early stages of being drunk, so their aims weren't perfect. He had been dunked only fifty or sixty times so far. More than half of the employees had already been through. Toward the end of the line stood Tamia and Michael, also Tamya and her boyfriend, Roger. He knew that he was almost done and began to taunt his assailants.

"Come on, Bob," he said to the man ahead of his brother. "You can't see two feet in front of you. This is your last shot. Make it good."

Bob wound up his arm and missed the target by a foot.

"Next! I'm starting to dry off," Thorne laughed, as Tamya stepped up to plate.

"Get ready to sink, Thorne," Tamya yelled.

"Oh, I'm scared," Thorne replied, drawing more of a crowd. "It's a girl. I haven't been soaked by a girl yet." At this, the women began to cheer Tamya on.

Her first shot didn't even reach the mark. Thorne's laughing made her so mad her second throw sailed past the mark.

Thorne's laughter grew louder as Tamia's first shot also missed its target. But Tamia didn't play by the rules, anybody's rules. So she threw down her second ball and ran to the target, hitting it with her hand.

To Thorne's surprise, he ended up at the bottom of the tub anyway.

"That's not fair," he yelled, rising to the top of the water. "Michael, she cheated."

"What can I say? My baby doesn't always do things the way everyone else does." Michael bent down and gave Tamia a peck on the lips and a quick slap on her behind. "Good job, baby," he said.

Roger stepped up and dunked Thorne two more times easily. Michael, who also dunked Thorne twice, followed him.

"Are we done yet?" Thorne asked, ready to get out of the water.

"No," Theresa replied, "Mikey and I have to take our turns." She pulled her son forward. "Go ahead, Mikey. Dunk your uncle."

Mikey did as he was told and dunked his uncle easily.

"That's my boy," Michael said, patting his nephew on the back.

"I'm sorry, Uncle Thorne, but Mommy told me to."

"I understand, man. And I forgive you. As a matter of fact, you can make it up to me later by helping me beat up Uncle Michael, okay?"

"Okay," he replied eagerly.

"Theresa, why don't you just put your balls down and save me some time."

"Thorne, you talk too much." Theresa threw her balls and missed both times. She was madder at herself than at him.

"Finally," Thorne said, beginning to ease himself off of the ledge and out of the pool.

"Wait," a voice from the back of the crowd commanded. He knew that voice and slowly sat back down. The crowd parted so that the woman with the voice could come forward.

"Mom?" Thorne said. "Don't tell me you want to dunk me. I'm your son."

"Yes, you are, dear, and I love you very much. And for that reason, I won't dunk you. I have decided to give my two tries to Natalie. I think that she deserves them, don't you?"

Thorne looked over the crowd of people gathered in front of the pool. He didn't like it. Michael's smile told him that he really didn't have a choice. He had got got, too.

"No, I really don't think that she does."

"I think she does," Michael chimed in.

"Who asked you?"

"Well, let's see what everybody else thinks. Who thinks that Natalie deserves two extra throws?"

The crowd went crazy with applause, half of them not even knowing who Natalie was or why she deserved extra throws.

Natalie moved to the front of the group. "I'll take those throws, Amanda. Thank you," she said confidently.

"Now, Natalie, you know this isn't necessary."

"Sure it is, Thorne. I don't like the way you've been treating me lately. This is my chance to get you back."

"Can't we talk about this in private?"

"This is private. There's nobody here but us, Thorne. Me, you, and that bull's-eye."

"Natalie . . ."

"Yes, Thorne?" She picked up the first ball and took aim.

"I'm trying to apologize."

"And you should, but I didn't hear a sorry in that sentence." She threw the first ball and hit her target.

Thorne could hear the yell from the crowd even as he went under the water. When he resurfaced, she was standing there smiling at him. And he thought that she was the most beautiful woman he had ever set eyes on. Slowly, he smiled back at her. *Okay, maybe this was the way things should go.*

"Okay, one lucky shot," he taunted. "That's good. And I do apologize for treating you the way I have over the last few weeks."

"Nice," she said, "but I didn't hear you apologize for making me fall in love with you and then breaking my heart."

The crowd yelled mock boos, aahs, and oohs.

"Natalie . . ."

She threw the second ball and stopped his protest.

Thorne came up again gasping for air. Again, she stood smiling at him innocently.

"I didn't mean to break your heart. And I fell in love with you, too," he yelled, slamming his hand onto the surface of the water, causing a splash.

Nobody laughed. The crowd became quiet as people began to sense the seriousness of what was going on.

Thorne climbed back onto the ledge. "Okay, Natalie, go ahead. Get me back for being a jerk. I was wrong, I made mistakes, and I lost you. I'm sorry. If I could change things, I would, but I can't."

Suddenly, the game wasn't fun for Natalie anymore. She didn't expect Thorne to put everything out there like that, especially in front of everybody. She had forgotten how honest he could be at any given moment.

"Thorne," she said, "you didn't want to change things. You left me out in the cold and shut me out. That's not something you do to the one you claim to love."

"Look," he snapped, "I was going through my own problems."

"Thorne," she yelled back, "I'm the one who helped you find yourself."

"And that's when my problems began," he said, speaking before thinking. But when he looked up at her to fix it, she had already let the ball fly.

"You deserved that one for real," she said as his head bobbled above the waterline.

"I know I did," he agreed. "You've only got one ball left."

"You'll earn it. All I have to do is give you enough time." Natalie slowly walked back and forth in front of the dunking booth.

The crowd was still quiet, waiting to see and hear what Thorne would do or say next.

Thorne stayed quiet and watched Natalie walk back and forth. He loved her. God, he loved her. But what was he going to do with her? That was the question. Here in front of almost a thousand employees, friends, and family members, he had to make a decision. He crossed his arms and thought. She said that he hadn't lost her, but was she going to go for his offer. He didn't think so.

"Cat got your tongue, Thorne?" Natalie asked. She was ready to leave and so were these people, she was sure. But they seemed determined to stick around and see the outcome. She had one ball left, and she was going to use it, but he wouldn't say anything. He was being stubborn. Just as stubborn as she was. Well, she was in it for the long haul. Was he?

"No, the cat doesn't have my tongue," he replied.

"Oh, nothing to say?"

"I have plenty to say," he insisted, but said nothing when she stopped walking and prepared to throw.

"Well . . ."

"Well, what?"

"Say something dumb so that I can use this last ball."

Thorne looked at his mother and winked. He looked at Michael, who smiled at him and put an arm around Tamia. Theresa put a hand to her throat. They knew him all too well.

"Will you marry me?" Thorne asked softly.

There was a collective intake of breath from the crowd. They hadn't expected him to ask her that. He didn't either—at first. But it was the only thing that he wanted at that moment— besides getting out of the pool.

"What did you say?" Natalie yelled.

"I said, 'Will you marry me?'"

Natalie didn't know what to do first. She looked at her sisters, who smiled at her. Then she looked at her friend, who had tears in her eyes. And then she stood there and put her head down. When she looked up, she had tears in her eyes, too.

"Come here," Thorne said to her. He didn't wait for an answer. He didn't need to. If she came to him as he asked, he would have his answer.

Natalie dropped the ball she was carrying and ran to the tank. As if she had on wings, she ran up the ladder so fast to get to him. Once she had the door open, it only took a second to be in his arms again.

The applause and laughter of the crowd finally made them interrupt the passionate kiss. But it didn't hold for long.

"You didn't answer me, Nat. Will you marry me?" Thorne asked. "I need an answer in order for it to be official. Yes or no?"

"Yes, Thorne. You know I will. What took you so long?"

"I'm sorry for everything, Nat. I was just so confused about so many things. But I'm not confused about what I feel for you. You've given me back everything that I thought was stolen from me."

Natalie hugged him again and held on to him tightly. "Oh, I love you so much, Thorne."

Michael stood around the tank with the rest of the family, joyously watching the couple.

"You guys are so corny," he said.

"Shut up, Michael," Thorne replied.

"Are you getting smart, brother?"

"Leave us alone, man," Thorne said, pulling Natalie back to him for another kiss.

"Baby," Michael said to Tamia, "go over there and take care of my light work."

And she did as she was asked and gave the couple a much-needed rinsing off.

But under water they held onto each other, as they planned to do forever.

ABOUT THE AUTHOR

Michele Sudler lives in the small East Coast town of Smyrna, Delaware. Busy raising her three children, Gregory, Takira, and Kanika Lambert, she finds time for her second passion, writing, in the evenings and on weekends. After attending Delaware State College, majoring in Business Administration, she began and continues to work in the corporate banking industry. Recently enrolled back in school, she is currently working hard on time management skills in order to balance family, work, and school.

Stolen Memories is her third novel. Her first, *Intentional Mistakes,* introduced the world to Tia Avery and Jeff Daniels and the lovable Avery Clan. It was released by Genesis Press in April 2005. In her second novel, *One of These Days,* released June 2007, Shelia Daniels and Charles Avery formed a memorable relationship. Michele is currently working on her next novel in the Avery family tree and putting the finishing touches on her novel, *Three Doors Down,* which will be published by Genesis Press in September 2008. Also, look forward to hearing more from Theresa and Michael Philips in the near future.

Besides spending time with her children and writing, Michele enjoys playing and watching basketball, traveling, and reading. She would also love to hear what you think about her novels. Please send any comments to her at: micheleasudler@yahoo.com.

2008 Reprint Mass Market Titles

January

Cautious Heart
Cheris F. Hodges
ISBN-13: 978-1-58571-301-1
ISBN-10: 1-58571-301-5
$6.99

Suddenly You
Crystal Hubbard
ISBN-13: 978-1-58571-302-8
ISBN-10: 1-58571-302-3
$6.99

February

Passion
T. T. Henderson
ISBN-13: 978-1-58571-303-5
ISBN-10: 1-58571-303-1
$6.99

Whispers in the Sand
LaFlorya Gauthier
ISBN-13: 978-1-58571-304-2
ISBN-10: 1-58571-304-x
$6.99

March

Life Is Never As It Seems
J. J. Michael
ISBN-13: 978-1-58571-305-9
ISBN-10: 1-58571-305-8
$6.99

Beyond the Rapture
Beverly Clark
ISBN-13: 978-1-58571-306-6
ISBN-10: 1-58571-306-6
$6.99

April

A Heart's Awakening
Veronica Parker
ISBN-13: 978-1-58571-307-3
ISBN-10: 1-58571-307-4
$6.99

Breeze
Robin Lynette Hampton
ISBN-13: 978-1-58571-308-0
ISBN-10: 1-58571-308-2
$6.99

May

I'll Be Your Shelter
Giselle Carmichael
ISBN-13: 978-1-58571-309-7
ISBN-10: 1-58571-309-0
$6.99

Careless Whispers
Rochelle Alers
ISBN-13: 978-1-58571-310-3
ISBN-10: 1-58571-310-4
$6.99

June

Sin
Crystal Rhodes
ISBN-13: 978-1-58571-311-0
ISBN-10: 1-58571-311-2
$6.99

Dark Storm Rising
Chinelu Moore
ISBN-13: 978-1-58571-312-7
ISBN-10: 1-58571-312-0
$6.99

2008 Reprint Mass Market Titles (continued)

July

Object of His Desire
A.C. Arthur
ISBN-13: 978-1-58571-313-4
ISBN-10: 1-58571-313-9
$6.99

Angel's Paradise
Janice Angelique
ISBN-13: 978-1-58571-314-1
ISBN-10: 1-58571-314-7
$6.99

August

Unbreak My Heart
Dar Tomlinson
ISBN-13: 978-1-58571-315-8
ISBN-10: 1-58571-315-5
$6.99

All I Ask
Barbara Keaton
ISBN-13: 978-1-58571-316-5
ISBN-10: 1-58571-316-3
$6.99

September

Icie
Pamela Leigh Starr
ISBN-13: 978-1-58571-275-5
ISBN-10: 1-58571-275-2
$6.99

At Last
Lisa Riley
ISBN-13: 978-1-58571-276-2
ISBN-10: 1-58571-276-0
$6.99

October

Everlastin' Love
Gay G. Gunn
ISBN-13: 978-1-58571-277-9
ISBN-10: 1-58571-277-9
$6.99

Three Wishes
Seressia Glass
ISBN-13: 978-1-58571-278-6
ISBN-10: 1-58571-278-7
$6.99

November

Yesterday Is Gone
Beverly Clark
ISBN-13: 978-1-58571-279-3
ISBN-10: 1-58571-279-5
$6.99

Again My Love
Kayla Perrin
ISBN-13: 978-1-58571-280-9
ISBN-10: 1-58571-280-9
$6.99

December

Office Policy
A.C. Arthur
ISBN-13: 978-1-58571-281-6
ISBN-10: 1-58571-281-7
$6.99

Rendezvous With Fate
Jeanne Sumerix
ISBN-13: 978-1-58571-283-3
ISBN-10: 1-58571-283-3
$6.99

2008 New Mass Market Titles

January

Where I Want To Be
Maryam Diaab
ISBN-13: 978-1-58571-268-7
ISBN-10: 1-58571-268-X
$6.99

Never Say Never
Michele Cameron
ISBN-13: 978-1-58571-269-4
ISBN-10: 1-58571-269-8
$6.99

February

Stolen Memories
Michele Sudler
ISBN-13: 978-1-58571-270-0
ISBN-10: 1-58571-270-1
$6.99

Dawn's Harbor
Kymberly Hunt
ISBN-13: 978-1-58571-271-7
ISBN-10: 1-58571-271-X
$6.99

March

Undying Love
Renee Alexis
ISBN-13: 978-1-58571-272-4
ISBN-10: 1-58571-272-8
$6.99

Blame It On Paradise
Crystal Hubbard
ISBN-13: 978-1-58571-273-1
ISBN-10: 1-58571-273-6
$6.99

April

When A Man Loves A Woman
La Connie Taylor-Jones
ISBN-13: 978-1-58571-274-8
ISBN-10: 1-58571-274-4
$6.99

Choices
Tammy Williams
ISBN-13: 978-1-58571-300-4
ISBN-10: 1-58571-300-7
$6.99

May

Dream Runner
Gail McFarland
ISBN-13: 978-1-58571-317-2
ISBN-10: 1-58571-317-1
$6.99

Southern Fried Standards
S.R. Maddox
ISBN-13: 978-1-58571-318-9
ISBN-10: 1-58571-318-X
$6.99

June

Looking for Lily
Africa Fine
ISBN-13: 978-1-58571-319-6
ISBN-10: 1-58571-319-8
$6.99

Bliss, Inc.
Chamein Canton
ISBN-13: 978-1-58571-325-7
ISBN-10: 1-58571-325-2
$6.99

2008 New Mass Market Titles (continued)

July

Love's Secrets
Yolanda McVey
ISBN-13: 978-1-58571-321-9
ISBN-10: 1-58571-321-X
$6.99

Things Forbidden
Maryam Diaab
ISBN-13: 978-1-58571-327-1
ISBN-10: 1-58571-327-9
$6.99

August

Storm
Pamela Leigh Starr
ISBN-13: 978-1-58571-323-3
ISBN-10: 1-58571-323-6
$6.99

Passion's Furies
AlTonya Washington
ISBN-13: 978-1-58571-324-0
ISBN-10: 1-58571-324-4
$6.99

September

Three Doors Down
Michele Sudler
ISBN-13: 978-1-58571-332-5
ISBN-10: 1-58571-332-5
$6.99

Mr Fix-It
Crystal Hubbard
ISBN-13: 978-1-58571-326-4
ISBN-10: 1-58571-326-0
$6.99

October

Moments of Clarity
Michele Cameron
ISBN-13: 978-1-58571-330-1
ISBN-10: 1-58571-330-9
$6.99

Lady Preacher
K.T. Richey
ISBN-13: 978-1-58571-333-2
ISBN-10: 1-58571-333-3
$6.99

November

This Life Isn't Perfect Holla
Sandra Foy
ISBN: 978-1-58571-331-8
ISBN-10: 1-58571-331-7
$6.99

Promises Made
Bernice Layton
ISBN-13: 978-1-58571-334-9
ISBN-10: 1-58571-334-1
$6.99

December

A Voice Behind Thunder
Carrie Elizabeth Greene
ISBN-13: 978-1-58571-329-5
ISBN-10: 1-58571-329-5
$6.99

The More Things Change
Chamein Canton
ISBN-13: 978-1-58571-328-8
ISBN-10: 1-58571-328-7
$6.99

Other Genesis Press, Inc. Titles

A Dangerous Deception	J.M. Jeffries	$8.95
A Dangerous Love	J.M. Jeffries	$8.95
A Dangerous Obsession	J.M. Jeffries	$8.95
A Drummer's Beat to Mend	Kei Swanson	$9.95
A Happy Life	Charlotte Harris	$9.95
A Heart's Awakening	Veronica Parker	$9.95
A Lark on the Wing	Phyliss Hamilton	$9.95
A Love of Her Own	Cheris F. Hodges	$9.95
A Love to Cherish	Beverly Clark	$8.95
A Risk of Rain	Dar Tomlinson	$8.95
A Taste of Temptation	Reneé Alexis	$9.95
A Twist of Fate	Beverly Clark	$8.95
A Will to Love	Angie Daniels	$9.95
Acquisitions	Kimberley White	$8.95
Across	Carol Payne	$12.95
After the Vows	Leslie Esdaile	$10.95
(Summer Anthology)	T.T. Henderson	
	Jacqueline Thomas	
Again My Love	Kayla Perrin	$10.95
Against the Wind	Gwynne Forster	$8.95
All I Ask	Barbara Keaton	$8.95
Always You	Crystal Hubbard	$6.99
Ambrosia	T.T. Henderson	$8.95
An Unfinished Love Affair	Barbara Keaton	$8.95
And Then Came You	Dorothy Elizabeth Love	$8.95
Angel's Paradise	Janice Angelique	$9.95
At Last	Lisa G. Riley	$8.95
Best of Friends	Natalie Dunbar	$8.95
Beyond the Rapture	Beverly Clark	$9.95

Other Genesis Press, Inc. Titles (continued)

Other Genesis Press, Inc. Titles (continued)

Daughter of the Wind	Joan Xian	$8.95
Deadly Sacrifice	Jack Kean	$22.95
Designer Passion	Dar Tomlinson	$8.95
	Diana Richeaux	
Do Over	Celya Bowers	$9.95
Dreamtective	Liz Swados	$5.95
Ebony Angel	Deatri King-Bey	$9.95
Ebony Butterfly II	Delilah Dawson	$14.95
Echoes of Yesterday	Beverly Clark	$9.95
Eden's Garden	Elizabeth Rose	$8.95
Eve's Prescription	Edwina Martin Arnold	$8.95
Everlastin' Love	Gay G. Gunn	$8.95
Everlasting Moments	Dorothy Elizabeth Love	$8.95
Everything and More	Sinclair Lebeau	$8.95
Everything but Love	Natalie Dunbar	$8.95
Falling	Natalie Dunbar	$9.95
Fate	Pamela Leigh Starr	$8.95
Finding Isabella	A.J. Garrotto	$8.95
Forbidden Quest	Dar Tomlinson	$10.95
Forever Love	Wanda Y. Thomas	$8.95
From the Ashes	Kathleen Suzanne	$8.95
	Jeanne Sumerix	
Gentle Yearning	Rochelle Alers	$10.95
Glory of Love	Sinclair LeBeau	$10.95
Go Gentle into that Good Night	Malcom Boyd	$12.95
Goldengroove	Mary Beth Craft	$16.95
Groove, Bang, and Jive	Steve Cannon	$8.99
Hand in Glove	Andrea Jackson	$9.95

Other Genesis Press, Inc. Titles (continued)

Hard to Love	Kimberley White	$9.95
Hart & Soul	Angie Daniels	$8.95
Heart of the Phoenix	A.C. Arthur	$9.95
Heartbeat	Stephanie Bedwell-Grime	$8.95
Hearts Remember	M. Loui Quezada	$8.95
Hidden Memories	Robin Allen	$10.95
Higher Ground	Leah Latimer	$19.95
Hitler, the War, and the Pope	Ronald Rychiak	$26.95
How to Write a Romance	Kathryn Falk	$18.95
I Married a Reclining Chair	Lisa M. Fuhs	$8.95
I'll Be Your Shelter	Giselle Carmichael	$8.95
I'll Paint a Sun	A.J. Garrotto	$9.95
Icie	Pamela Leigh Starr	$8.95
Illusions	Pamela Leigh Starr	$8.95
Indigo After Dark Vol. I	Nia Dixon/Angelique	$10.95
Indigo After Dark Vol. II	Dolores Bundy/ Cole Riley	$10.95
Indigo After Dark Vol. III	Montana Blue/ Coco Morena	$10.95
Indigo After Dark Vol. IV	Cassandra Colt/	$14.95
Indigo After Dark Vol. V	Delilah Dawson	$14.95
Indiscretions	Donna Hill	$8.95
Intentional Mistakes	Michele Sudler	$9.95
Interlude	Donna Hill	$8.95
Intimate Intentions	Angie Daniels	$8.95
It's Not Over Yet	J.J. Michael	$9.95
Jolie's Surrender	Edwina Martin-Arnold	$8.95
Kiss or Keep	Debra Phillips	$8.95
Lace	Giselle Carmichael	$9.95

Other Genesis Press, Inc. Titles (continued)

Last Train to Memphis	Elsa Cook	$12.95
Lasting Valor	Ken Olsen	$24.95
Let Us Prey	Hunter Lundy	$25.95
Lies Too Long	Pamela Ridley	$13.95
Life Is Never As It Seems	J.J. Michael	$12.95
Lighter Shade of Brown	Vicki Andrews	$8.95
Love Always	Mildred E. Riley	$10.95
Love Doesn't Come Easy	Charlyne Dickerson	$8.95
Love Unveiled	Gloria Greene	$10.95
Love's Deception	Charlene Berry	$10.95
Love's Destiny	M. Loui Quezada	$8.95
Mae's Promise	Melody Walcott	$8.95
Magnolia Sunset	Giselle Carmichael	$8.95
Many Shades of Gray	Dyanne Davis	$6.99
Matters of Life and Death	Lesego Malepe, Ph.D.	$15.95
Meant to Be	Jeanne Sumerix	$8.95
Midnight Clear	Leslie Esdaile	$10.95
(Anthology)	Gwynne Forster	
	Carmen Green	
	Monica Jackson	
Midnight Magic	Gwynne Forster	$8.95
Midnight Peril	Vicki Andrews	$10.95
Misconceptions	Pamela Leigh Starr	$9.95
Montgomery's Children	Richard Perry	$14.95
My Buffalo Soldier	Barbara B. K. Reeves	$8.95
Naked Soul	Gwynne Forster	$8.95
Next to Last Chance	Louisa Dixon	$24.95
No Apologies	Seressia Glass	$8.95
No Commitment Required	Seressia Glass	$8.95

Other Genesis Press, Inc. Titles (continued)

No Regrets	Mildred E. Riley	$8.95
Not His Type	Chamein Canton	$6.99
Nowhere to Run	Gay G. Gunn	$10.95
O Bed! O Breakfast!	Rob Kuehnle	$14.95
Object of His Desire	A. C. Arthur	$8.95
Office Policy	A. C. Arthur	$9.95
Once in a Blue Moon	Dorianne Cole	$9.95
One Day at a Time	Bella McFarland	$8.95
One in A Million	Barbara Keaton	$6.99
One of These Days	Michele Sudler	$9.95
Outside Chance	Louisa Dixon	$24.95
Passion	T.T. Henderson	$10.95
Passion's Blood	Cherif Fortin	$22.95
Passion's Journey	Wanda Y. Thomas	$8.95
Past Promises	Jahmel West	$8.95
Path of Fire	T.T. Henderson	$8.95
Path of Thorns	Annetta P. Lee	$9.95
Peace Be Still	Colette Haywood	$12.95
Picture Perfect	Reon Carter	$8.95
Playing for Keeps	Stephanie Salinas	$8.95
Pride & Joi	Gay G. Gunn	$15.95
Pride & Joi	Gay G. Gunn	$8.95
Promises to Keep	Alicia Wiggins	$8.95
Quiet Storm	Donna Hill	$10.95
Reckless Surrender	Rochelle Alers	$6.95
Red Polka Dot in a World of Plaid	Varian Johnson	$12.95
Reluctant Captive	Joyce Jackson	$8.95
Rendezvous with Fate	Jeanne Sumerix	$8.95

Other Genesis Press, Inc. Titles (continued)

Other Genesis Press, Inc. Titles (continued)

Sweet Tomorrows	Kimberly White	$8.95
Taken by You	Dorothy Elizabeth Love	$9.95
Tattooed Tears	T. T. Henderson	$8.95
The Color Line	Lizzette Grayson Carter	$9.95
The Color of Trouble	Dyanne Davis	$8.95
The Disappearance of Allison Jones	Kayla Perrin	$5.95
The Fires Within	Beverly Clark	$9.95
The Foursome	Celya Bowers	$6.99
The Honey Dipper's Legacy	Pannell-Allen	$14.95
The Joker's Love Tune	Sidney Rickman	$15.95
The Little Pretender	Barbara Cartland	$10.95
The Love We Had	Natalie Dunbar	$8.95
The Man Who Could Fly	Bob & Milana Beamon	$18.95
The Missing Link	Charlyne Dickerson	$8.95
The Mission	Pamela Leigh Starr	$6.99
The Perfect Frame	Beverly Clark	$9.95
The Price of Love	Sinclair LeBeau	$8.95
The Smoking Life	Ilene Barth	$29.95
The Words of the Pitcher	Kei Swanson	$8.95
Three Wishes	Seressia Glass	$8.95
Ties That Bind	Kathleen Suzanne	$8.95
Tiger Woods	Libby Hughes	$5.95
Time is of the Essence	Angie Daniels	$9.95
Timeless Devotion	Bella McFarland	$9.95
Tomorrow's Promise	Leslie Esdaile	$8.95
Truly Inseparable	Wanda Y. Thomas	$8.95
Two Sides to Every Story	Dyanne Davis	$9.95
Unbreak My Heart	Dar Tomlinson	$8.95

Other Genesis Press, Inc. Titles (continued)

Uncommon Prayer	Kenneth Swanson	$9.95
Unconditional Love	Alicia Wiggins	$8.95
Unconditional	A.C. Arthur	$9.95
Until Death Do Us Part	Susan Paul	$8.95
Vows of Passion	Bella McFarland	$9.95
Wedding Gown	Dyanne Davis	$8.95
What's Under Benjamin's Bed	Sandra Schaffer	$8.95
When Dreams Float	Dorothy Elizabeth Love	$8.95
When I'm With You	LaConnie Taylor-Jones	$6.99
Whispers in the Night	Dorothy Elizabeth Love	$8.95
Whispers in the Sand	LaFlorya Gauthier	$10.95
Who's That Lady?	Andrea Jackson	$9.95
Wild Ravens	Altonya Washington	$9.95
Yesterday Is Gone	Beverly Clark	$10.95
Yesterday's Dreams, Tomorrow's Promises	Reon Laudat	$8.95
Your Precious Love	Sinclair LeBeau	$8.95

ESCAPE WITH INDIGO !!!!

Join Indigo Book Club©
It's simple, easy and secure.

Sign up and receive the new
releases
every month + Free shipping
and
20% off the cover price.

Go online to www.genesis-
press.com and click on Bookclub
or
call 1-888-INDIGO-1

Order Form

Mail to: Genesis Press, Inc.
P.O. Box 101
Columbus, MS 39703

Name _____

Address _____

City/State _____ Zip _____

Telephone _____

Ship to (if different from above)

Name _____

Address _____

City/State _____ Zip _____

Telephone _____

Credit Card Information

Credit Card # _____ ☐ Visa ☐ Mastercard

Expiration Date (mm/yy) _____ ☐ AmEx ☐ Discover

Qty.	Author	Title	Price	Total

Use this order form, or call 1-888-INDIGO-1	
Total for books	_____
Shipping and handling: $5 first two books, $1 each additional book	_____
Total S & H	_____
Total amount enclosed	_____
Mississippi residents add 7% sales tax	

GADSDEN COUNTY
PUBLIC
LIBRARY